Haller, born South African, was educated at the Grey Schools in Port Elizabeth. This was followed by a six-year sojourn in the British South Africa Police in the then Rhodesia, during which he served for some time as a public prosecutor. He bicycled throughout all of the countries of the British Isles before settling down to business back in South Africa. He became a passionate motorcyclist, undertaking several long-distance tours throughout Southern Africa. He recently retired, having been involved in the earthmoving equipment business for many years.

He has fulfilled a long-held desire to write during the lengthy Covid lockdowns and this is his first publication. He has already written a further three books, all in line for publication.

I would like to dedicate my first publication to my ever smiling, always forgiving wife, Fiona. Thank you for your patience and unwavering support of my quest to become a writer.

In tandem, I also wish to dedicate this book to my son, Sean, daughter-in-law, Zulfa, and their dear Mia for your family's support of my venture, particularly your provision of a laptop and unlimited pipeline to the internet!

Alan Haller

FLY AWAY – A SOPWITH JONES ADVENTURE

AUSTIN MACAULEY PUBLISHERS™

LONDON * CAMBRIDGE * NEW YORK * SHARJAH

A CIP catalogue record for this title is available from the British Library.

ISBN 9781398472839 (Paperback)
ISBN 9781398472846 (ePub e-book)

www.austinmacauley.com

First Published 2022
Austin Macauley Publishers Ltd®
1 Canada Square
Canary Wharf
London
E14 5AA

To the educators at the Grey Schools who afforded me a fine education, not appreciated by me at the time, but thank you.

To the training staff of the British South Africa Police, who turned a schoolboy into a man with life skills and some common senses, in particular Mike Lambourne, thank you.

To Terry Miller and Stan Jankowski, my Australian friends, who convinced me to join them on an extended bicycle ride around the British Isles, thank you. That wonderful, physically challenging trip, experiencing the Home Country's ambiance and meeting their peoples was a game changer in my life.

To Pierre Gonneau, navigator in chief of innumerable and extended motorcycle tours around Southern Africa, thank you. Those rides taught me more about my own country and its people than anything else.

To my erstwhile business partners, Griff Hawkins and Steve Roberts, who taught me many things, good and bad, thank you both.

For it is experiences like these in life which, combined, add to the reservoir of information I draw from to be able to write.

To my old friend, Arthur Lightfoot, upon whose real character I modelled the First Sea Lord, thank you for your encouragement and support.

To the spectacular Royal Navy Website, www.royalnavy.mod.co.uk , this enlightened me, along with the rest of the world, about their magnificent equipment and capabilities.

To my friend and editor, Erith Harris. Erith has kindly spent many long hours painstakingly pouring over my books with his correction pen. He tells me he enjoys it, but even so, he deserves a medal, thank you.

Author Biography

I have not had any of my work published other than in junior and high school magazines, social newsletters, and business publications.

An early retiree at the age of sixty after a very full and varied life which saw me starting my working life as a policeman for six years in the then Rhodesia after my education at Grey Junior School and Grey High School in Port Elizabeth (Gqeberha) South Africa. I subsequently built swimming pools, then tennis courts in the heyday of their popularity in Johannesburg. Later I built large swimming pools for educational and municipal institutions throughout South Africa. I progressed from that into the earthmoving equipment business for the rest of my working life, working for and owning companies in that field.

The fact that I enjoyed writing led me to try and occupy myself during the Covid lockdowns, so I wrote a hundred-and-fifteen-thousand-word personal memoir of all amusing, unusual and deeply painful things that I have experienced in life. Having derived great enjoyment and a refreshingly cathartic experience from that task, I decided, upon its completion, to try my hand at a fictional novel and this is the result! I have recently completed a sequel to this novel.

Synopsis

A manuscript of Fictional Action Adventure, based on Topical Facts.

The manuscript is a work of fiction approximately seventy-one thousand words long. There is reference to factual things, places, and events; information about which is in the public domain or based upon personal knowledge.

A central character, Sopwith Jones, holds the story together by continuing to surprise both himself and those around him in the way he handles the hurdles he is forced to face.

Using his outstanding abilities as an aeronautical engineer, he has privately developed a solar powered aircraft, the design of which he unwittingly exposes to a corrupt Minister in the South African Government, who tries to manipulate this ground-breaking technology for his personal gain. Sopwith reacts by fleeing to the United Kingdom whose government realises his potential. He is assisted by the Royal Navy. During his flight from South Africa an attempt is made to stop him by an Air Force jet, but he eventually lands on the Royal Navy aircraft carrier, HMS Queen Elizabeth which conveys him and his aeroplane to England.

Once there he decides to flee yet again after hearing a false rumour that he will be extradited back to South Africa. He marries a vivacious Royal Navy Fleet Air Arm pilot who accompanies him on his second flight, this time unaided and through the continent of Africa. His aircraft is shot down by Boko Haram jihadists in central Africa, but he and his wife survive the attack and move on, eventually finding themselves landing at Palma in Mozambique. All the while during their flight both the British Government and the corrupt South African Minister attempt to track them down. At Palma they are captured by jihadists and held hostage along with another pilot. This pilot is beheaded, a video of which is sent to British Government to demand a ransom. The video, along with other advanced surveillance technologies, allows them to be tracked and their location discovered. They are rescued, but not before Sopwith has killed the leader of the jihadists.

Once back in England and finally hearing that he would not be extradited because the South African request had been exposed as false, Sopwith agrees to partner with the British Government to continue the development of his solar powered aircraft. Before much can be done about this, MI6, who had a small hand in his rescue from Mozambique, detect that a hit man has been sent to England to kill Sopwith in retribution for the death of the jihadist leader in Mozambique. Despite being very close to preventing the hit man from capturing Sopwith, MI6 fail to do so, and the hit man takes he and his wife hostage and forces them to flee yet again. This flight is much shorter, with Sopwith managing to shoot the hit man while they are airborne over the English Channel and disposing the body into the sea. Sopwith and his wife return to England where Sopwith changes his mind about his future and sells his innovative solar-powered flight technology, resulting in him becoming wealthy and thus being able to disappear from the limelight. Maybe he will surface once more in another Sopwith Jones novel? In fact, I have now completed a sequel.

The novel has many interesting supporting characters, and the current topical subjects, settings and locations make it a great read for any reader, whether enjoying the satirical look at corruption in South Africa, or just enjoying the love story then the drama, all of which is written in an inoffensive style.

Chapter One

Aled Jones was born and grew up in Wales at the time of the development of manned flight. He started out his working life as a lowly coal-mining labourer. However, being a keenly intelligent man he worked his way into a minor management position on the mine where he worked. Aled became absolutely fascinated with the concept of flight and aircraft when the Wright Brothers flew for the first time at Kitty Hawk in 1903; an event which fired his imagination with enthusiasm, dreaming of a better life than working on the mine. Over time he eventually realised, however, that he would not manage to do anything about this for himself, but instead pinned his hopes on a better future for his newly born son. He named his only son Sopwith, after the dashing and wealthy English sportsman Thomas Sopwith, who, in 1912, had founded the Sopwith Aviation company where he had built the famous Sopwith Camel; the most successful English aerial combat aircraft of the First World War.

So young Sopwith grew up in a home environment where he was encouraged at every opportunity to follow a career in the field of aviation, by a visionary father who could see the wonderful future possibilities aviation might present. Aled saved every spare penny to help his son achieve his own dreams, and through great sacrifice was able to afford to enrol Sopwith at Cranfield University, the first in the United Kingdom to offer a degree in aeronautical engineering, from where he graduated with a BSc Eng. Aeronautical.

The mighty British aviation industry was however in a steep decline when Sopwith first started looking for employment, and he could not find work, even with his prestigious degree. Any hope for the future of the industry in the United Kingdom disappeared with the complete failure of the world's first passenger jet, the De Havilland Comet; its production being terminated in 1964. Luck sided with Sopwith however, because in 1965, the South African Government established the Atlas Aircraft Corporation, and actively searched worldwide for trained aeronautical engineers to staff the new company. Encouraged by his determined father, Sopwith applied for a position with Atlas, was accepted, and was soon on his way to South Africa. He slotted easily into his position with the new company, soon becoming a well-respected engineer. As well as settling into his job, he likewise enthusiastically took on the South African lifestyle, loving every minute of the sunny climate so far removed from the wet dankness of Wales. It was not long before he found a girlfriend, also an expatriate from Wales, whom he married. As with Sopwith's parents, they too had only one son, who they could not resist also naming Sopwith. They maintained many of their Welsh traditions and paid particular importance to ensuring the next Sopwith Jones generation was fully aware of his heritage. Sopwith grew up in a very similar way to his father; in a home environment which was encouraging and supportive, but very biased towards his father's ideals, which revolved mainly around the future of aviation. He soon established a strong desire to follow in his father's footsteps. He was a handsome, well-spoken young man, who had achieved excellent school results, and was a keen sportsman. His father enrolled him at the University of the Witwatersrand (Wits) where he obtained an MSc in Aeronautical Engineering; in his final year achieving the distinction of being the university's top academic student, and simultaneously obtaining his Private Pilot's Licence; a first for the Jones family. On graduating he was snapped up by Atlas Aircraft Corporation because their production had increased proportionately along with the increasing severity of anti-apartheid sanctions being imposed by the international community against South Africa, which had, in turn, made it virtually impossible to procure parts and equipment for the manufacture of aircraft.

Sopwith junior was extremely fortunate to have his skills stretched to the limit by the requirements of his first job, where he was forced to be extremely innovative in the face of the international embargo. He revelled in the challenge and was soon renowned within the company as one of their leading engineers by enabling the seemingly impossible to be achieved. He became a workaholic, and although he very much liked the idea of having a girlfriend, he just did not seem to have time for one. One thing he did have time for, though, was exercise, knowing that physical fitness had a direct beneficial impact on mental fitness. He religiously spent two hours daily in a gym, working on cardiovascular exercises and delighting in martial arts training. He was a very fit, agile, good-looking man, with dark brown hair and grey-blue eyes; his formerly pale Welsh complexion being tanned by the African sun. Over time he had also become extremely interested in trying to find a practical way in which to use solar energy to power aircraft and completed a doctorate with that subject as his thesis. The winds of change were blowing in South Africa though, and as the advent of democracy dawned in South Africa, with the release of Nelson Mandela from prison, so did the requirement wane for a stand-alone aviation company; Atlas Aircraft being eventually absorbed by state-owned arms manufacturer, Denel.

Sopwith was not comfortable with this, as he had found, when interacting with Denel management previously, they were more deviously – than intellectually minded, so decided to rather resign than take up a new position at Denel. He had no other opportunities in his field in South Africa and did not want to go back to Europe or America to look for a position, so made the decision to work on his own, following his passion for aircraft powered by solar energy. He had built up a small pension, and his father and mother, both of whom passing away some years before, had left him a tidy nest egg. He made the decision to look for a new base, wanting to get away from the overpopulated metropolitan area of Johannesburg and Pretoria where he had been working. He believed that for practical research in his new field he needed a coastal area which had more varied sunshine hours than inland and decided on a small coastal town called Port Alfred where he had found a working airfield; originally a training field during the Second World War, but where a flying school was now situated. He rented a house in the town and relocated there together with his few worldly possessions.

After arriving in Port Alfred and settling into his rented house, Sopwith paid a visit to the flying school and met the manager, Rob Pretorius, thinking it odd that this chap introduced himself as 'Major', but then thought nothing more of it. Despite the seemingly odd title of Major, Sopwith found that he liked Rob, explaining to him that he needed to hire a hangar on a long lease, should there be one available, as he was working on an experimental aircraft in his private capacity. He did not elaborate on the solar energy aspect of the project, preferring to keep that information low key at that early stage of the venture. As it happened there was a hangar available at the very farthest end of the parking apron, which suited Sopwith perfectly, not wanting visibility to the public at that stage, so a deal was struck. He found a handyman in the town who had soon built him office space within the hangar, along with some practical work benches, and with electrical outlets being installed to both office and benches. Once he had established a good Wi-Fi internet connection, he felt that he was ready to get his project in motion, so next started out looking on the internet for a used Cessna 172 aircraft. He found one close at hand, in nearby Port Elizabeth, where he inspected and bought it, then flew it to Port Alfred. He had chosen the 172 for several reasons, the most important being that it had a high wing configuration which he would be using for his new photovoltaic collection system, but also that it is reputed to be the single most successful aircraft manufactured in the history of light aircraft. He had found a 1975 vintage 172M model, which had drooped leading edges to the wing to improve low speed handling. He had a great deal of work to do, involving stripping the aircraft, developing his energy collection system, and simultaneously building a new electric motor. He worked like a robot, methodically and seemingly endlessly. However, he remembered to eat properly, continued his gym time at the small gym in town, and slept enough hours, but certainly had no time for any social activities. 'Major' Rob Pretorius initially tried to get Sopwith to join him, and other staff, for a beer after work, but gave up after Sopwith continually declined the invitations. Ever so slowly the 172 was stripped of its Lycoming four-cylinder petrol engine, along with fuel tanks and any additional weight superfluous to Sopwith's design needs. Solar energy is traditionally collected by photovoltaic cells which capture photons and convert them to electric potential, and although Sopwith was using this basic concept, it was to be highly modified. Instead of these cells being arranged, as was normally done, in panels, he was using micro-engineering to create miniscule cells which would be contained in an electrically conductive skin that he had developed, and which would be applied to the wing surfaces and spine of the whole aircraft. He had determined the collection needs to feed the most modern, lightweight lithium batteries to enable them to continuously power his newly-designed 100 kW electric motor, able to achieve a cruise speed of 200 km/h indefinitely, if there was light in the sky. He gradually started to assemble the completely new motor, built of composite and innovative materials, thus making it fifty percent lighter than any motor of its size on the market.

Eventually, with all the old analogue flight instrumentation replaced by the most modern Garmin digital instrument panels and a fine Satnav system, his '172 Solar' (as he had named it) was ready to fly. Having registered his craft with the Experimental Aircraft Association of Southern Africa he received his ZU register number and flew it for the first time one gusty spring morning. He flew for some five hours, putting the machine through its paces, recording voice notes about issues that needed adjustment or correction. He was ecstatically happy with its performance, being particularly pleased about the near silent operation of the electric motor, making the aircraft magnificently quiet in flight. He landed only after he had tested every possible flight function and manoeuvre, and taxied into his hangar, where he stayed seated in his aeroplane for a long time. He clearly reflected on what he had achieved, slowly absorbing the fact that he had just made history. This had been the first flight on the planet of a standard aircraft type powered entirely by solar energy. He was convinced that his design innovations could be similarly adapted to much larger aircraft of diverse configurations, whether for passenger or cargo use; possibly changing the future of powered flight forever.

Chapter Two

With his 172 Solar now literally 'off the ground', Sopwith needed to test fly it for as many hours as possible to identify and eliminate any issues that may have arisen, so came up with an excellent idea which would require Rob's help. Deciding to confide in 'Major' Rob, he phoned him.

"Hello Rob, Sopwith here. How about we go for a beer and a meal this evening?"

Rob, doubtless very surprised by this invitation, accepted immediately, agreeing to meet at the 'Ocean Basket'.

At the restaurant, after some light banter, mainly to do with Sopwith's seclusion, he explained to Rob that he had developed a solar energy power system for the 172.

"My God, man," Rob reacted, "that is totally amazing, and you have done this right under my nose without me even realising what you were doing! Well done, I'll drink to that!" and clinking Sopwith's glass with his, took a deep draught of beer.

"Well, I do need your assistance now though." said Sopwith. "I would like to put flying hours on the aircraft to help iron out any bugs, and the best way to do it would be to include it in your training fleet. Do you think you could do that for me? At no cost to you of course."

"I am sure that will be possible, but I will have to first get authority from head office, though, as well as sort out some sort of indemnity for both parties. But leave that to me, and I will let you know once I have wrapped it up."

"Good man" said Sopwith, and they finished their meal over conversation about the performance of the 172 Solar.

It was only while he was driving home that Sopwith thought about the fact he knew absolutely nothing about the ownership of the flying school but accepted that it had little to do with him anyway; then, losing that train of thought, moved onto other matters.

About ten days later, 'Major' Rob called him.

"We are good to go." he said. "I have the authority I need as well as the purpose-drafted indemnities. Let's meet this afternoon and get those signed, and discuss check lists for the 172 Solar; the pilots are going to need them."

Indemnities were duly signed; check lists and detailed instruction given to the flight instructors, and the 172 Solar took its place in the training fleet of aircraft. Sopwith digitally monitored the aircraft's functions and performance, collated the information, then carefully stored all data for reference. Sopwith was delighted with the progress of these test flights; his development still well below public radar, just as he had wanted it to be at that stage. The indemnities had included a confidentiality clause which forbade the instructors and students who flew the Solar to publicly disclose any information about it. Sopwith knew very well that if he prematurely made his development public knowledge, any yet unseen problems could arise and possibly shatter his dreams.

It was with great surprise that, about a month after the test flights began, he received an unannounced visitor. He was busy in his office in the hangar when a black BMW SUV, with a flashing blue light behind the front grill, drove into the hangar. It pulled to a stop, and a black man climbed out of the vehicle. This chap was certainly dressed to kill, wearing an extremely expensive-looking suit, diamond-studded cufflinks, and the sharpest pointed crocodile skin shoes that Sopwith had ever seen. The driver, wearing mirror sunglasses, remained seated while his passenger walked into Sopwith's office.

"Mr Sopwith Jones?" he questioned, "How are you?"

"I am Sopwith, yes, and I am fine thanking you."

"Ah, good. I am Barnabas Masondo, Minister of Trade, and Industry in our country's government. I am very pleased to meet you because I have heard nothing but good things about you. I apologise for arriving without making an appointment, but I am a very busy man, and had to fit this visit into my schedule at the last minute, you understand? Let us have a cup of tea."

Sopwith's mind was reeling. What on earth was going on, he thought to himself as he prepared a cup of tea for his guest and coffee for himself in his tiny kitchenette. Handing the Minister his tea, Sopwith said:

"I am very pleased to meet you too Mr Minister but am very curious about the nature of your visit."

"Oh! Mr Sopwith, that is so easy to answer. It is all about the electric aeroplane. I must congratulate you on the work you have done for us so far. This is a very pleasing invention for us and will go a very long way in promoting the efficiency of our government departments to our own population, as well as to the Americans and even our old colonisers."

Only Minister Masondo knew what his real intentions were, and that was to hi-jack Sopwith's achievements. He would then create a State-Owned Enterprise and loot it to the extreme; something that had happened to several South African SOE's already, and which the Minister had had a hand in.

"I am not quite sure I understand your train of thought Mr Minister," a bewildered Sopwith replied.

"That, too, is easy to explain Mr Sopwith. You have invented something on government property and used government-owned facilities, so we, the democratic government must take ownership of the invention."

"Government property and facilities?" questioned the now stunned Sopwith.

"Yes, Mr Sopwith. This airfield is owned by our government and the flying school is a State-Owned Enterprise, especially created for black empowerment of our country's pilots. Major Pretorius is an officer in the South African Air Force, seconded here to run the school. Did you not know this?" The Minister now had a gleaming grin stretched across his face.

Sopwith was silent, his intelligent brain working at warp speed. He wanted to scream at this man that he was a manipulative knob-head, then throw him out of his office, but he knew he could not do that. He rationalised the situation and determined that there would be no way to argue the matter, other than trying litigation, and that would be a very last option. He would just have to outsmart the Minister.

"Well Mr Minister, that is all very interesting. However, the 'invention' that you refer to is nothing more than a very old Cessna aircraft to which I have made some modest changes. Before it amounts to anything worthwhile to anyone, there are many months of testing to be done to try and get those changes to work properly, and there is no guarantee that they will work correctly at all."

"Ah, Mr Sopwith, your white people will never understand the ways of Africa. Time is never an issue, so please take as long as you need, and I will make sure that Major Pretorius is instructed to continue assisting you for whatever period you might need such help. I must inform you, of course, that you are now bound by the Official Secrets Act, and must not divulge any information regarding your invention, or our democratic government's interest therein, to any one at all. To that end, be aware that I have instructed the State

Security Agency to maintain a close and protective watch over yourself and the ongoing project. Ah, and that being for the security of the project, of course." His gleaming grin had now become impossibly wide. "Hamba kahle, Mr Sopwith, I have a luncheon appointment with our mayor of the town." Barnabas Masondo bade farewell in isiXhosa, meaning, 'Go well, but carefully'.

Sopwith Jones was in a rage, and he stormed across the apron and made his way to 'Major' Rob's office, and barged straight in.

"You bloody bulging asshole; you are full of shit!" he shouted in anger, "Why didn't you tell me that this school of yours was a government facility?"

"You never asked," replied Rob, "and I don't understand your anger in the slightest. What the hell is this all about?"

"You deny knowing that I have just been visited by a government minister?"

"I have no idea what you are talking about. Please calm down and just tell me what is going on."

Sopwith's anger slowly ebbed with his comprehension that Rob seemed totally naïve about what had taken place. He sat down and breathed a heavy sigh of relief, accepting that Rob was probably not in the enemy camp; even beginning to think of him as a real Major, not just some trumped-up title. He recounted what had taken place and ended by asking Rob if he could be relied on as a friend.

"Sopwith, I never thought it would be of any interest to you that this place is an SOE, and that it being so might have caused what has happened. My hierarchy have obviously picked up on your development from my seeking permission to use the Solar in the training fleet. The fact that they have gone with it to a senior government minister, and their trying to do what they are, is untenable. Yes, you can rely on me as a friend."

"I am grateful for that Rob, thank you. I really need to consider what I should do next."

"I will help you as much as I can, given the circumstances that I have a few years to go before I can go on pension, and so cannot afford to endanger my position."

"I understand Rob. Any thoughts on how I should handle things though?"

"Well, off the top of my head, all I can think of is that you should get out of Dodge, with Dodge being South Africa. If the SSA goes after you, there will be no place to hide, simple."

Sopwith drove home with a heavy heart and the constant questions of what to do and where to go ricocheting around in his brain. A very sweaty gym workout helped his mood somewhat, a fillet steak and fried eggs helped some more, and then he decided to give Rob a call, just to perhaps start bouncing around a few thoughts on his next move. Rob answered his cell call immediately, and very breezily said, "Hi Sopwith, I cannot talk now. I am about to sit down to dinner. We will catch up tomorrow at the airfield, bye," then terminated the call. Rob had never been that abrupt before, so Sopwith started worrying again, about what might be happening behind the scenes. The following morning, on arrival at the airfield, Sopwith walked to his aircraft, as he did every morning, to conduct a visual inspection. He became aware of Rob walking alongside him; a very unusual occurrence for Rob who was normally pretty much office bound.

"Bad news, Sopwith! After you left my office yesterday two SSA agents called on me. They explained that they had been tasked with watching you and I have had to falsely place one of them, who will be keeping an eye on you, on site in the Pilot Training programme. I will point him out to you when I get the chance. Keep walking man. The other has got digs in town and will no doubt be following you around. The real bad news though is that they have put a tap on your cell phone, so be bloody careful what you say on it. Better still, try and get a new prepaid one as a secure line. O.K., that's my news. Be careful and I will try and keep you updated as I hear things. Cheers," then off he walked, back towards his office.

'This is getting interesting,' mulled Sopwith. Rather than being angry about this development he took it as a challenge. They had thrown down their gauntlet, so all he had to do was outwit them. That evening he went to the ski boat club on the banks of the Kowie River in Port Alfred on the pretext of wanting a beer. What he really wanted was information, and over a beer started chatting to some locals there. As benignly as possible he asked if they knew who the oldest lawyer in the town was. With much hilarity and verbal sparring about why one would need an old lawyer, he got his answer. Ben Dougmore, an old timer, was still practising in town out of sheer boredom.

So as not to spoil his routine to his watchers, he went out to the airfield the following morning and inspected the Solar. He then drove back into town, very aware of a Toyota car following him. He parked in the centre of the town, then quickly started walking in and out of various shops until he was sure that his follower was not behind him, even if he had attempted to follow. Sopwith assumed, hopefully, that his watcher would be prepared to wait for Sopwith to return to his car rather than follow him around. Sopwith found Dougmore's tiny office above one of the local shops, its entry access being from within the shop. This well suited his newfound stealth mode. Knocking, then entering the office, Sopwith found, seated within, an old man with clear blue intelligent eyes, and a delightful face full of character.

"Good day sir," he said, offering his hand. "I am Sopwith Jones and am terribly sorry to barge into your office without an appointment."

Old man Ben stood up a little creakily, and shook his hand, wearing a mischievous smile. "Ben Dougmore. Sit down please, you are welcome. I am delighted to have a visitor. Business is not as brisk as it was when I was younger, but that suits me anyway."

Sopwith liked the man immediately. He was calm, intelligent, and bored; just what he wanted.

"So, Sopwith; what a very unusual name. You must be from English stock?"

"No, Welsh in fact. My grandfather started the family tradition of using the English Christian name after an aircraft manufacturer he admired."

"Oh yes, I recall the Sopwith Camel; wonderful old aeroplane it was. So, Welsh then? Yours is the only nation on earth that can perhaps sing better than a traditional African choir. And I suppose you are still building aeroplanes in the family tradition, are you?" he said chuckling at his jocular poke about the Jones family's heritage involving aeroplanes.

"In fact I have actually modified an existing aircraft," Sopwith began. "I have developed a unique aircraft," and he continued with the story of his development, and the government minister who wanted to take ownership of the project.

"Well, this is a pretty unique situation, no doubt," replied Ben, "but nothing I would not be able to tackle for you, starting with registering your intellectual property rights...."

"Wait up," Sopwith interrupted, "I do not want you to litigate. I need to get out of South Africa together with my aircraft. I have left out the fact that the SSA is watching me and that they have tapped my phone."

"How extraordinary!" Ben exclaimed.

"Yes, indeed! So what I need from you is to be my proxy, as I cannot communicate with anyone at all without being spied on. I would like you to make direct contact with the British Government, not just through the local embassy. Ideally, I need you to communicate with someone in the highest position possible in their government and seek asylum on my behalf. The fact that both my grandfather and father were born in Wales should be of some assistance."

"Indeed," Ben added.

"By means of the most secure way possible, I would like you to let them know exactly what is going on here, leaving nothing out. May I assume you're online, and know how to use a PC?"

"Hey, Sopwith, I may be a fossil," Ben chuckled, "but I have kept up with technology," he said, pointing at a newish-looking laptop on a side desk, "and I am just about as good on that thing as my grandson is!"

"Great!" replied Sopwith. "Here is an external hard drive showing videos of my aircraft in flight, as well as mountains of data recording test flights, which will prove the capabilities of the Solar to any reasonably intelligent aviation engineer. I would like you to go at this like a dog after a bone; fearlessly, and with passion and determination. I am going to leave this corrupt country, aboard my aircraft, come hell or high water!"

"Just up my street," beamed the old lawyer. "I really need a challenge; been sitting around rotting recently. I am your 'go to' man from this moment."

"Payment?" asked Sopwith.

"Oh, don't worry unduly about that; I have made enough money in my life. I will keep you abreast of any expenses along the way and you can pay those, but no fees will be required at all."

Sopwith was delighted at Ben's response, not only because it was saving him money, which he did have available anyway, but that there was passion in the old man to help solve the problem.

"How do I get in touch with you?" asked Ben.

"For the time being by phoning a fellow named Rob at the flying school. Tell him only that you have news for me. I will then contact you somehow once I hear from him," said Sopwith, giving Rob's number to Ben. Immensely pleased with how well the meeting with old Ben had gone, Sopwith left his office and walked back to his car.

He had guessed correctly that the follower had just sat waiting for him to return to his car, so he was presumably unaware of the meeting just held with Ben.

Sopwith resumed life as normally as possible, completely ignoring his followers. Rob had eventually pointed out the chap stationed at the flying school, but Sopwith had no need to worry about him at all, as he continued to monitor the daily test flights of his baby. He had also managed a brief secluded moment with Rob and told him he had met with Ben Dougmore, who would be contacting him at some point.

After ten days, and having heard nothing from Ben, Sopwith again visited Ben's office, curious to know what progress the old man had made, if any. He was surprised, but totally delighted, to see a note taped to the office door, which read: 'CLOSED for a while. I have taken an overseas holiday'. He correctly assumed that Ben had really taken his mission to heart and had physically travelled to the UK to accomplish it.

Ben Dougmore awoke to the sounds of traffic, got out of bed and, switching on a kettle, reflected on how happy he was. Firstly, he was in London, a city that he loved dearly, even during winter as it was now. Secondly, he was embroiled in an exciting challenge, which, if he could pull off, would make him a very proud senior citizen, and today's meeting might just prove to be the clincher to his success. He had been in London for two weeks, enjoying the city and West End shows, which broke the monotony and frustration of trying to get a productive line of communication going with the British Government. After initial, fruitless meetings with government information offices, he at least got a sense of the various British Government departments, and had identified, as his target, the Department for Business, Energy, and Industrial Strategy. They were situated at 1 Victoria Street, so by moving into the Victor Hotel within walking distance of the Department, he had started persistently visiting them until he had eventually got himself an appointment with the Permanent Secretary, one Priti Patel. The meeting had been a success, and the very intelligent lady seemed not only to take a liking to Ben but was completely taken with Ben's proposal to not only save a man of British heritage from criminal abuse, but also to bring his new technology to their country. The meeting had ended with Priti assuring Ben that she would take the matter up with the Home Office, to obtain their approval to let Sopwith into the UK.

He had since been called by the Department asking him to meet with Priti today, and once breakfasted he walked to their offices with a spring in his step. Once in her office, she proudly announced to Ben that she had had all the necessary approval from the Home Office, so it was 'all systems go'. The old man could not stop himself hugging this lovely lady, and then, calming himself, told her that this was just the beginning, as he now needed the Royal Navy on board, to get Sopwith and his aircraft from South Africa to Britain. He explained his reasons for this to her and left with her assurances that she would set up a meeting for him with the Royal Navy. He had to wait a further week, but this did not bother him at all, as he continued to enjoy the attractions of London, taking in more West End shows. He had made no contact with Sopwith, if by now he must have seen the note on his office door, and so had put two and two together.

He was called to a meeting at the Office of the First Sea Lord in the Ministry of Defence premises in Whitehall; the First Sea Lord being the Chief of Staff of the Royal Navy.

Ben took the London Underground (which he disliked as it felt as if he was travelling in a crowded cattle truck) to Westminster Station, and after walking another three hundred metres he stood at the entrance to the Main Building of the Ministry of Defence on Horse Guards' Avenue.

"Ben Dougmore to see the First Sea Lord," he gaily announced to the security personnel there.

"This way sir," was the immediate response, after a brief frisking of his person, and he gained the strong impression that they had been briefed to expect him. He was shown into a very grand office which looked more like a small ballroom. The first person he saw was the same Priti Patel he had been dealing with thus far, and she walked across to him.

"Good morning, Ben, thank you for joining us," she said, shaking his hand briefly, and turning towards the other occupants of the room, announced, "Gentlemen, this is Mr Ben Dougmore; Ben, this is the First Sea Lord and Rear Admiral Ron Hubbard, head of the Navy's Fleet Air Arm. Along with them is the Navy Director of our Carrier Strike Force, Rear Admiral Geoff Briggs." Ben's hand was shaken by all three, then all sat down with glasses of cooled water close at hand. He realised that he was with the absolute hierarchy of the Royal Navy, but rather than being intimidated, he glowed proudly within, having got to this level in his mission.

"We know why you are here Mr Dougmore," said the First Sea Lord, a man almost as old as himself, impeccably dressed in his crisp white uniform and supremely confident in himself, "but we would like to hear your proposal first-hand, so please go ahead."

After taking a sip of water Ben began: "Gentlemen, we have a man who has been betrayed by his family's adopted country. Consequently, he has looked to his native heritage for assistance, and has been given that, thanks to the Permanent Secretary here," he said, looking at Priti, receiving an appreciative smile of thanks in return. "However, there is one remaining problem, and that is getting him, and his unique aircraft, to your country. The only reason I am here talking on his behalf is that he is being closely watched by the country's security agents, and I assure you that the minute they hear that he might be trying to evade their plans, he will be arrested. I can only imagine that various operatives of your government might be able to spirit him out of the country, to yours, but that cannot be done along with his aeroplane, which must be brought here as well; it is an integral part of Mr Jones' plan." Ben looked around whilst taking another sip of water and saw that he had a rapt and attentive audience.

"There is only one way out for him, and for your country to benefit from his designs, and that is for him to fly. He can fly all day, not having a need for fuel, but he can only cover about two and a half thousand kilometres in a day. So what I propose, gentlemen, is that he flies onto one of your aircraft carriers, and you bring him home. I should think that would be quite easy, don't you?" he ended.

"Thank you, Mr Dougmore," said the First Sea Lord. "It is as I understood it to be," and looking at the Director of Carriers he asked, "Can this be done Geoff?"

"Most definitely," the Director replied, "but I first need to assess any possibility of intervention by the South Africans...."

"You have answered my question Geoff," interrupted the First Sea Lord. "Have a proposed operational plan on my desk in forty-eight hours. Also, please include all risk assessments and cost. I will get the PM's approval. My apologies, but I need to move on everyone; a luncheon appointment awaits me." At this he bade goodbye and left the ballroom.

'Goodness', Ben thought; 'do all important people live by their stomachs only?' Ben leapt up and gave his favourite lady of the moment a high five, which hurt his arthritic shoulder a bit, but was surprised when the two other officers present joined in, after which his shoulder was the worse for wear.

The Director of Carriers spoke first. "I am delighted; we need a good challenge such as this. Ben, you had better give me your contact details so that I can inform you about detailed plans of the operation once approved." Ben promptly obliged, after which he left the magnificent building, as proud as he had ever been in his life, and the next day was on a flight back home.

Once home and in his office, he phoned Rob and told him that he had news for Sopwith. Sopwith arrived at Ben's office within the hour and Ben told him the good news.

"Hey old man, you have performed a miracle!" Sopwith told him before giving him a bear hug. Old Ben laughed out loud and pulled out a bottle of fine single malt whisky with two tumblers.

"This is deserving of a toast!" he said, and pouring two measures, then passing a glass to Sopwith, clinked his glass and announced, "To your future young man; may it be wonderfully successful," then drank. "And you need a successful future, to be able to afford to pay for my costs in London. I was there for three weeks, and you know how expensive it is over there!"

Sopwith replied with a hearty laugh and told the old man to give him his costs. Ben explained that all they now awaited was news from the Director of Carriers, and assured Sopwith that the second he heard anything, he would call Rob.

Sopwith resumed his 'normal' life, but immediately changed one thing, and that was to take the 172 Solar out of service with the flying school. He told Rob publicly that he had picked up some problems that needed attention, but when he caught Rob alone, explained that he was getting the aircraft ready to leave. He could not give Rob any further detail as he was only alone with him for a short period but did manage to pass him the new cell phone number for the prepaid one he had surreptitiously bought that day. He had also phoned in to Ben and given him the number, and after Ben had thanked him, told him that there had been no word yet from the Royal Navy. Sopwith set about preparing his aircraft to leave. He had not previously removed the two passenger seats in the rear of the plane, so now did just that, turning it into cargo space. He installed a one hundred litre tank, equipped with a tap, to hold drinking water, and made a secure space for two pee buckets, ensuring they could not fall over and spill! After only a few days of working on the 172 in the hangar, the SSA man pretending to be a student, came into the hangar.

"Hello suh," he greeted, adding the 'sir', Sopwith supposed, to enhance his 'student cover', but responded, greeting him politely.

"Why you hide it away now?" he asked Sopwith.

"It is not hidden at all, chap; just parked in my hangar for repairs. Why are you interested anyway?"

"O.K. I just want to fly it," came his reply.

"I did not know you were flying yet; I thought you were still attending ground school?"

"Oh ah! You see the other one pilots like it and asked me to check it." If his complexion would have allowed it, he would have been glowing red at the lies he was trying to worm out of.

"No problem lad, just tell them that it will be back in the air soon. Goodbye now," and he turned his attention away from the spook. 'Hell, they don't teach them very well these days,' he thought to himself.

Rob, in the meantime, was starting to have difficulty with the spooks of the SSA as well. The one stationed in town seemed to be the senior of the two and had taken to regularly coming into Rob's office during the day while Sopwith was in his hangar and asking him about Sopwith. Recently it had come to a bit of a head.

"Lesedi, stop bugging me please. I have work to do. I have told you repeatedly that I have no idea about what Mr Jones does in his own time."

"But you are a whitey, you must connect to him and find out for us," Lesedi tried to say with authority.

"Stuff this race card issue of yours Lesedi. Just because I happen to be as white as Mr Jones, does not make me automatically capable of being his friend or confidant. He is a brilliant engineer, with a doctorate in engineering, in fact; he talks a different language to me."

"I thought he spoke English?" Lesedi said with concern.

"You bloody dork, of course he speaks English! What I mean is that he is exceptionally clever, and we cannot discuss things on the same level. And by the way, please remember that I am a commissioned officer in the same armed forces as you my brother, so don't bloody try and order me around to try and do your dirty work for you. I have had enough of you bloody pestering me. Now bugger off out of my office!" Rob knew that he might have pushed the man too far, but this exchange amazingly produced unexpected results, for Lesedi replied, divulging a mine of information.

"I will arrest you too, Major Pretorius, if you are not more careful! Yes, I said, 'arrest you too', because that is what is going to happen to your doctor; he will be locked up. The government is tired of waiting for him to finish his electric plane. They will lock him up and finish it themselves, you understand? So you be careful and don't swear at me ever again," Lesedi said, glaring at Rob with red eyes.

"O.K., O.K! I am sorry Lesedi. It is just that I am so busy, and I really don't know how I could get any information from the man even if I had the time. I do not have your specialised training either," he conceded, trying to butter him up, then continued, "When are you going to arrest him?"

"That is not decided yet. I think my boss is checking with his own boss and then I think they also gotta get permission from the prime minister. I think, but I dunno."

"Fine, but please let me know when, because I have someone else wanting to hire the hangar that Jones is using."

"Alright, I will. Just remember to tell me if you see anything strange with the man." 'Phew!' Rob thought when Lesedi left his office; the last thing he needed was to fall foul of the SSA, which did not have a good reputation for how it treated prisoners. He phoned Sopwith immediately.

"Sopwith, I hope you are getting your ducks in a row. These clowns look like they are planning to arrest you. All we can hope for is that they do tell me when that is going to happen, then I can let you know. That is as much as I can do for you now."

"Thanks mate. I expect no more, and please do not get yourself into trouble over me."

Sopwith continued getting ready for his trip. He loaded all his computer equipment, some special tools that he needed some food (in the form of rusks and dried fruit) and filled his water tank with purified water. He checked his aeroplane thoroughly every morning to ensure it was not being tampered with, even though he was keeping the hangar securely locked and there had been no sign of forced entry.

On the 5th of January, his cell phone rang, and he answered, "Sopwith here."

"Hello Sopwith, Barnabas here. How are you?"

"Fine thank you, Mr Minister."

"How is your electric aeroplane?"

"The plane is good sir. I do have some serious electronic issues that have caused me to ground it for a while until I resolve them."

"That is why I phoned you Sopwith, because I have heard such stories. Now, not because we are in any hurry you see, but do you not think our government engineers may be able to assist you?"

"Definitely not, Mr Minister. I do know what the problem is, but it will take time to put right."

"This is a pity that you are refusing my help," said the Minister, in a much less friendly tone than he had ever used before. "You see, you must understand, our government has always worked as a collective, and so not one of us is non-expendable. This must be something you should pay attention to. So, my advice Mr Sopwith is to remedy your problems as soon as possible so that you can hand the completed projected over."

"I understand Mr Minister."

"I certain hope you do," he stated, terminating the call.

'This is starting to get tense,' thought Sopwith, and dialled Ben's number. Ben answered immediately.

"You beat me to it Sopwith; I was just busy printing off details from the Royal Navy before I phoned you. I have everything you need from them, so come over and collect the details as soon as you can."

Later that morning Sopwith collected the file from a beaming Ben, then returned to his office to study it. Going over the pages, each of which was boldly labelled 'CONFIDENTIAL INFORMATION' he found the details of the operation extremely simple. HMS Queen Elizabeth, the Royal Navy's newest and largest aircraft carrier, would be sailing westwards on a voyage from the Tasman Sea, where she had been conducting exercises with the ANZAC navies. She would set course to pass just north of Prince Edward Island in the Southern Ocean, then alter course towards the northwest to bypass the Cape of Good Hope. The rendezvous point for Sopwith to meet the ship would be slightly northwest of Prince Edward Island, about two thousand kilometres due south of Port Alfred; well within the 172 Solar's flight range. He would be intercepted by air support and guided to the carrier. His call sign, and that of the carrier's aircraft, was specified, along with which dedicated radio channel to be used. It all seemed so terribly easy on paper, but one issue that bothered Sopwith was the date on which the ship would be at the rendezvous: 10th of January, still five days hence. He had a sick feeling of foreboding that his impending arrest was going to be attempted before that.

Full of nervous energy he continued loading essential items into the 172 Solar until he was done; leaving only his laptop and clothes bags to be taken on the day he was to leave. He then went carefully over his office, with the proverbial fine-toothed comb; burning every piece of paper there, leaving no written evidence of his presence; abandoning everything else in his office. He went through his small house in similar fashion, and by the 8th, he had completed all preparations necessary to leave the country. Even though he had heard nothing from the Minister or the SSA spooks, his nerves were nevertheless jangling. Having finished a simple supper that evening, he wondered whether he was going to be able to sleep that night. He was, in fact, going to get hardly any sleep at all.

There was a loud noise from the front door of his house, and it burst open to show the SSA operative from town (who Rob had told him was named Lesedi) pointing a pistol at him, and shouting, "You are under arrest Mr Sopwith, you are under arrest!"

Sopwith, with controlled calmness, just stood in the small entrance hall.

"Hell Lesedi! Calm down man; what is all this fuss about?"

"I am arresting you!" shouted Lesedi.

"I can see that, but why the dramatics? You could have knocked, rather than busting the door down." 'Calm him down and get him talking,' Sopwith thought, 'and try to get him into the house.'

"Lesedi, I am not quite sure why you are arresting me, but I am not going to fight about it. I am a doctor of science, not a criminal, so come in, have a drink, and tell me what this is all about please." And then, standing back, showed Lesedi into the house. Lesedi seemed to be calming down, and the bait of the drink was doing its trick.

"O.K. man. Have you got brandy?"

"Sorry Lesedi, I only have a little bit of whisky, but if I put some coke in for you it will taste the same. Is that alright?"

"Yes, that is good!" As he walked into the lounge, his pistol was still in hand, but now hanging by his side. Sopwith went to pour the drink and asked him to explain why he was being arrested.

"It's the boss' orders. They said I must tell you that you have broken the Official Secrets Act by, um, withholding the information."

Sopwith stretched out his arm to give Lesedi the glass, and as Lesedi took it in hand, Sopwith kicked him in his groin with all his substantial might. As Lesedi started to double up in pain, he chopped at his wrist, and the pistol fell to the floor.

"Sorry chap. But I really do not want to be arrested right now," he said to the man writhing on the floor in agony. "Please do not take this personally, but I will have to tie you up for a bit. I will let someone know you are here so you will be alright."

Picking up the pistol, Sopwith kept a loose aim on the man just in case he should try anything to retaliate and pulled a roll of duct tape out of a drawer......no one should ever be without duct tape, ever, was one of Sopwith's principles. He hoped that Lesedi didn't try anything stupid because he knew nothing about guns and did not know whether the safety catch was on or off, let alone where on the weapon it was located. He did a good job of binding Lesedi's ankles together with no resistance being offered by Lesedi who still had tears pouring from his eyes. He sat him up against a chair and forced him to drink some coke, 'for the shock', and then bound his arms and hands firmly together. Lastly, after apologising again, he taped Lesedi's mouth closed, and dropped the pistol on the floor.

Gathering his clothes and computer bags, he picked up his car keys and left the house, failing in his attempt to properly close the broken front door. He stowed his cases, got into the driver's seat, started the car, and as he switched the headlights on, the front door of his house swung open, and there was Lesedi, doing little bunny hops and moving slowly forward. His arms stretched out in front of him, and somehow or other, had his pistol stuck between his bound hands. Sopwith slung the car into gear, not wanting to test if Lesedi had any actual control of the pistol wedged between his hands. Sopwith gunned the motor and as his car started responding, there was a loud bang, and the rear window shattered into millions of tiny pieces. Instinctively he ducked, but kept going, and there was another loud bang, and he heard a 'twang' noise, but did not see anything. By this time he was well on his way and heard and saw nothing further from Lesedi.

My word, what a fool he had been, Sopwith thought to himself as he sped away. He had tied Lesedi up so well, but he had left his arms and hands in front of his body so that he still had limited use from his shoulders. 'I am certainly not very good at this type of thing,' his thoughts continued, 'and I did not even consider taking his gun or cell phone away.' There was no doubt that Lesedi would free himself, certainly not too easily, and it would take time, but he would do it. Then it will be an easy phone call for him to ask for backup and join the hunt for Sopwith. He decided to drive to the airfield, but thought twice about driving in, and decided, rather, to carry on along the road towards Bathurst. Before he passed the end of the perimeter fencing, he drove off the road and into some bushes, hoping he was out of sight to passing traffic. Trying to get his mind thinking logically and rationally, he knew who his first call would be to. He phoned Ben, waking him up, apologised and explained what had taken place.

"Ben, please immediately send a message to the Royal Navy. Let them know I must leave a day early, which I will do tomorrow at first light. Let them know that I will plot a course slightly to the east to try and compensate for this. I will phone you again tomorrow when I am in the air." Ben confirmed that he would send a message immediately.

Sopwith's next call was to Rob, who was fortunately not yet asleep. Once more Sopwith explained what had transpired that evening.

"Rob, I intend to fly out at first light tomorrow. I assume the SSA will be looking for my car, so may not go to the airfield first thing, but I cannot take the chance of going in blind. Are you with me on this?"

"Of course. You must come to your hangar on foot, from the south. I will mosey around the place on some pretext or other, and if all is clear, I will be standing by the back door that you never use. I have a key and can let you in there. If I am not there, stay put unseen somewhere, and we will see what develops. I will be there just before sunrise which tomorrow will be..." and pausing to think, said, "...at 0513."

"Thanks Rob, I really appreciate this, and please do not get caught up in any trouble. I would rather go down than see you in trouble."

"No worries about that mate; I will keep my nose clean. See you in the morning."

Sopwith tried to make himself comfortable enough in his car to get some sleep, but his mind was much too active for that. Worrying about what tomorrow would bring; trying to calculate how far east he should change his course to intercept the carrier a day early; making sure he let Ben know he had got off the ground, and many other thoughts kept him awake, until he finally dozed off. Thankfully he managed three hours of sleep, before his alarm woke him at 04h30.

He had three quarters of an hour to get to his hangar. It was a very dark pre-dawn, and he made his way, with difficulty, through the bush to the perimeter fence. Once there, he unclipped the ever-present Leatherman from his belt and snipped a hole in the lightweight fencing. Re-tracing his steps, he retrieved his two bags, and started on his walk. With a slight lightening of the sky, and by limiting his path to the mown grass within the perimeter, it became an easy, albeit long walk, which made him appreciative of having maintained his high level of fitness. Constantly checking his watch, he measured his pace, and at exactly 05h13 crouched down in some light shrubbery overlooking the door that Rob had referred to. Rob was there! He walked over to Rob, who turned without a word, unlocked, and opened the door, and ushered Sopwith into the hangar.

As Sopwith walked in, the lights in the hangar came on, and he heard a shout, "Keep walking straight ahead! Stop when I tell you then put your bags down! You are under arrest!" The voice had come from his left-hand side, and he had looked in that direction, but saw no one. He knew however that the voice belonged to the SSA agent stationed at the school. He did what he was ordered to do and stopped immediately when told and placed his bags on the floor.

"What now?" Sopwith asked.

"Put your hands behind your back and keep them there. I am approaching you from behind and have a 9mm pistol aimed at your back. Do not turn around or I will shoot you, and I will not miss. I am then going to place handcuffs on your wrists, and if you try and resist, I will shoot you. I am not Lesedi; I know what I am doing! Do you understand?"

"I do," was all that Sopwith could say, thinking to himself that although this youngster was junior to ball-aching Lesedi, he certain seemed to be more intelligent, or was he just better-trained?

Sopwith felt the man's presence before he heard him come up behind him, then take hold of one of his hands. As Sopwith felt the cold steel of the handcuff being positioned, a loud 'clunk' rang out, with Rob calling, "Go Sopwith, go!" He bent to pick up his bags and looked over his shoulder. There was the SSA agent comatose on the floor, and behind him stood Rob, grinning idiotically, holding a long steel aircraft tow bar in his hands! Rob had chosen to stay on guard at the door rather than enter the hangar behind Sopwith. When the lights came on, he kept back, heard the instructions, picked up the tow bar, and had given the agent a mighty whack over the head when he was trying to cuff Sopwith.

"Hell's teeth, Rob; you have saved my hide, thank you! Wipe your fingerprints off that bar and leave it on the floor next to him. They have to think that I hit him, not you." Rob quickly carried out Sopwith's instruction. "O.K., that's done. Now Rob, get the hell out of here; you have done more than enough. Go, please, I am fine now!"

Rob came up to him, and giving him a big bear hug, said, "Bon Voyage my friend. Send me a postcard from somewhere please," then smiled and walked out of the door. Sopwith, taking no risks, used the handcuffs to secure the agent's wrists behind his back, then kicked his gun away from his hand. He had to hurry as he had one final job to do. After placing his last bags in the plane, he quickly pulled off the relatively new vinyl ZU registration letters from the side of the plane. These would be replaced with others later.

He then rolled the hangar doors open and pushed the 172 Solar out into the early morning sunlight, completed his external checks, then climbed aboard. Once seated and belted in, and having completed all his pre-start checks, he turned the motor on, and silently taxied to the closest runway.

As with all electric motors there was no torque curve, such as that found in internal combustion power plants, so when he wound the actuator wide open, all the aircraft's 100 kW of power was instantly available. He sped along the runway, lifting off the ground at a mere 90 km/h, and he was airborne. He stayed low to be less visible and made the promised phone call to Ben.

"Ben, I am in the air, and could never have managed this without your help. A very deep thank you, old man; I admire you so much and hope we will meet again. Don't forget to confirm with Navy that I am on my way; departure time was 05h42. Did the Navy acknowledge my change of plan?"

"Yes, young man, they did, but said nothing further, so your instructions must remain the same. Fly away my friend and fly safe!" he ended. Sopwith had no way of knowing, of course, that there were tears running down the old man's cheeks.

Chapter Three

Sopwith maintained the southerly heading that he had chosen to prematurely intercept HMS Queen Elizabeth's westward course across the Southern Ocean, and slowly gained altitude the further he flew into the wide-open space of the Indian Ocean, until he reached his chosen flight level of three thousand metres above sea level. There was full sunshine with no wind or clouds, and he marvelled at the spectacle of the never-ending shiny carpet of water that stretched out before him.

Back at the air school, things were nowhere near as serene as in Sopwith's cockpit. On Lesedi's discovery that Sopwith had taken off, leaving his compatriot unconscious on the hangar floor, he phoned his superior in panic and reported on what had taken place. His superior immediately contacted the Minister of Trade and Industry, from whom he had received his instructions for the SSA operation in Port Alfred. Barnabas Masondo, ignoring protocol, and without going through the Minister of Defence, immediately got hold of the Brigadier General of the South African Air Force.

"Brigadier, an activist has stolen a government aircraft from our flying school in Port Alfred. I need you to order action to stop this aircraft immediately. It is critical, and I will immediately clear this with the Minister of Defence, but in the meantime, I order you to do this for our country!"

"Yes sir, I understand, but the best I can do is scramble a Gripen from Air Force Base Overberg at Bredasdorp, which is about seven hundred kilometres away, and it will have to refuel at Port Elizabeth before continuing the chase."

"Do it; I order so!" said Barnabas, ending the call.

(As part of a massively corrupt arms deal at the dawn of the new democracy, the South African Air Force had taken delivery of 27 SAAB-BAE Systems Gripen fighter jets during the programme to rearm the country's defence forces. The Gripen is a mighty fine aircraft, and with a top speed of over two thousand kilometres per hour, it is a champion, except for the significant factor of its limited operational range of only eight hundred kilometres).

The Gripen did land in Port Elizabeth to refuel (by which time Sopwith was only four hundred kilometres out to sea) and immediately afterwards started the chase to intercept the 172 Solar. The Gripen is equipped with very high-performance long-range radar, and in no time at all its pilot picked up Sopwith trundling along at two hundred kilometres per hour.

Sopwith, totally oblivious of the chase going on, continued his heading, when suddenly a grey flash flew past the front of the 172 Solar. He tracked the aircraft as it slowed down, recognising it as a Gripen. He had only one thought when he realised what it was, and that was 'Oh my God, I am in very deep shit!' Sopwith's VHF radio was tuned to the international open communication channel, and the very next thing was that his headset came alive with a clear voice of authority.

"Unmarked Cessna 172, this is Gripen zero seven, do you read me?"

"Gripen zero seven, this is Cessna 172; I read you strength five."

"Cessna 172, you are to change course immediately onto a heading to return to Port Alfred."

Sopwith's mind raced and the first thing he decided to do was slow down dramatically, making it difficult for this attack fighter to stay in proximity, because one thing he knew was that the Gripen could not fly anywhere close to the slow speed of the Cessna. He was approaching his very slow stall speed of only 70 km/h when his headset burst into life once more.

"Cessna 172, I repeat, change course. If you do not, I am authorised to attack. Please confirm and comply, Cessna 172."

Sopwith's racing mind assumed that the Gripen must have refuelled at Port Elizabeth, and knowing where they were now, he reckoned that the Gripen must be coming up to the edge of its range before having to turn back to reach land before it ran out of fuel. So, he decided to try and play for time.

"Gripen zero seven, I have heard your instruction and am trying to comply, but it seems like I have a flight systems failure, so I am having difficulty changing course."

"Cessna 172, what is the nature of your systems failure?" enquired the Gripen pilot.

"Gripen zero seven, I seem to be losing all power and am having difficulty keeping above stall speed. I believe I am on the threshold of having to put out a Mayday call."

There was silence from the Gripen, and Sopwith could imagine the pilot asking someone for new instructions under the changed circumstances. He watched the Gripen circle his 172, seemingly endlessly; feeling as though time had stopped completely. Suddenly, the Gripen changed course and headed directly towards the 172, and when Sopwith saw the flash from the single 27mm cannon mounted on one side of the Gripen's belly, he knew that the Gripen had fired at him, and there was nothing to do but wait out the nanosecond before he was hit by the cannon round and blown to pieces. The was a slight 'smack' sound and Sopwith saw a small piece of the aluminium skin of the motor's cowling in front of him flip up, and that was all. The Gripen flew above him, and disappeared, with no further communication. 'Luck rides with me again,' thought Sopwith. Not only did the Gripen's shot substantially miss him, but it was low on fuel and had to head home, and there were no other South African Air Force aircraft available that had the range to now attack him from land.

The report of the failed attempt to get Sopwith and his aircraft back to Port Alfred filtered back via all the people who were involved. Minister Barnabas Masondo was delirious with anger, and the two SSA agents on the ground in Port Alfred feared for their futures. Major Rob Pretorius, on the other hand, said a silent prayer of thanks, and then passed the news on to Ben Dougmore too, who was delighted to hear of Sopwith's narrow escape.

Sopwith had regained altitude, confident in the knowledge the 'flesh wound' that his baby had sustained was no impediment to his continued journey, so he flew on above the vast, empty, and shining Indian Ocean and slowly crossed into the Southern Ocean. He ate some of his stored food, drank water and relieved himself, and although tired, knew that he would be able to carry on flying for as long as was necessary.

Without knowing the exact position of the HMS Queen Elizabeth, he had estimated that he had about two thousand three hundred kilometres to fly, and at just after 16h00 hours that afternoon, he had covered two thousand kilometres.

Sopwith could not have known, but he was only one hundred kilometres adrift in his calculations, and at about that same time, the 400 km range of the radar aboard HMS Queen Elizabeth Air Traffic Control Island picked up the 172 Solar, heading in her general direction. Lieutenant Commander Karl Brighill, in command of Fleet Air Arm 809 Squadron, consisting of twelve Lockheed Martin F-35s aboard R08 (Queen Elizabeth's pennant number) was informed by the Air Traffic Control of the incoming aircraft. Brighill called Lieutenant Alison Murray, the PFW (Pilot Fixed Wing) he had selected to carry out the escort of the 172.

"Ali, your pickup is 400 km out, so get yourself ready," he told her, "We have agreed that you should meet him at 200 km, giving you an hour to prepare and orientate him. Good luck, and please bring him in in one piece," he smiled at his F-35 Pilot. Fleet Air Arm Rear Admiral Ron Hubbard in charge of the operation had chosen 809 Squadron for the pickup because of the F-35's capacity for low speed, enabling it to escort the 172 Solar in at its own speed. The F-35 is the most modern jet fighter in the world, capable of vertical take-off and landing, and of course flying at very low speeds when necessary. Brighill, the Squadron Commander, had chosen Alison, mainly because she was his most competent pilot, but also because she was very calm and well-spoken, and who, he believed, would be ideal to talk the 172 pilot into his first ever landing on an aircraft carrier. Ali was thrilled at the challenge and could not wait to get into the air.

Carefully doing all her visual pre-flight checks, she climbed aboard her aircraft, and with an engineer helping her, strapped herself into the sophisticated ejection seat. She donned her helmet which incorporated a heads-up display of major functions, and in addition was faced by a panel with large touch-screen display of all the aircraft's avionics. She went through her pre-start check list, and giving the engineer a 'thumbs up', after which he left her side, and removed the mounting ladder. Ali closed her canopy, and with another 'thumbs up', together with a voice command to the ground engineers, they started the massive jet engine mounted behind her.

"Tower, this is Foxtrot zero three. Romeo zero eight, do you read? Over."

"Foxtrot zero three, strength five, go ahead, over."

"Tower, permission to take off please. Retrieval mission flight plan submitted to ATC, over."

"Foxtrot zero three, wind straight on bow, 20 knots. Proceed in your own time. Good luck, out."

Ali pushed the throttle lever forward and her F-35 rolled forward, towards the rear of the carrier's deck. She performed a one hundred and eighty degree turn on a marker, using her right wheel brake to assist, lined up the F-38's nose towards the bow, and stopped. Here she stood on her brakes and fully opened the throttle. The plane shivered in tune with the awesome sound, straining at its imaginary leash. Having checked all functions, and opened the top jet intake, she released the brakes and thundered towards the ski jump at the bow. In seconds the F-35 was in the air, flying as sweetly as a bird. At the right altitude she closed the top intake, and then settled on a course to intercept the 172, as it was already visible on her radar.

Sopwith was shaken out of a little reverie by his headset coming alive with a pleasant female voice.

"Solar, this is Foxtrot zero three; do you read?" There was a deliciously crisp Scottish lilt to her speaking voice.

"Foxtrot zero three, this is Solar. Reading you strength five, go ahead."

"Solar, change your radio to channel twelve please, I will call you on there." And Sopwith changed channel.

"Solar this is Lieutenant Alison Murray from Fleet Air Arm Squadron 809 aboard HMS Queen Elizabeth, pleased to meet you. We have this channel to ourselves so speak freely." Sopwith was in awe of the sound of her voice.

"Good afternoon, Alison, Sopwith Jones here, but please call me Sopwith. Wonderful to hear your voice; it has been a bit lonely up here for the past twelve hours."

"I can imagine. Please call me Ali. I should be visible to you soon. I will be guiding you in to your first carrier landing. I hope you are as excited about it as I am."

"Oh hell yes, and rather nervous too……I do not have too many flying hours under my belt."

"The fact that you have got this far is enough for me. How are you physically, alright?"

"I am in showroom condition, I promise," replied Sopwith without adding that he had fallen in love with her voice. 'Keep talking baby,' he said to himself.

"Good. O.K., there you are, do you see me?"

"Yes, I have you visual. That is certainly a beautiful machine you are in."

"Indeed, a Lockheed Martin F-35 to be precise, my only girlfriend," she teased.

"Well as long as she allows you a boyfriend, that is great," responded our dyed in the wool bachelor, suddenly becoming a flirt.

"O.K., here is the deal. Keep on this heading, and when I tell you, you must please turn ninety degrees to starboard. That will have you on a direct heading to the runway."

"You mean ship, don't you?"

"Sopwith, don't think ship, think runway. It is seventy metres wide and two hundred and eighty long, more than enough to land your little lady on. Forget about being on the water, you will be landing on a runway just as you always do, O.K.?"

"O.K., I get your drift."

"I will fly alongside you throughout your entire approach to guide you in. I am the only one talking to the ATC, so you just have me to communicate with. O.K. make your ninety degrees turn here please."

Sopwith took his plane through a gentle turn until he saw two vessels on the water far ahead of him, one rather slim and the other much bigger and broader.

"I hope it is not the thin ship I have to land on?" he said.

"Sopwith cut that out! You are going to land on a runway. In any event the 'thin' one is an escort destroyer, and that does not even have room for your little toy." 'Mmm she is getting a little flirty too, nice!' mused Sopwith.

"O.K. Sopwith, let's see ten degrees of flap and reduce speed please." And Sopwith set the flaps at ten degrees while turning the actuator down. He could see the, uh, 'runway' clearly now, and if he did not look at the other ship or surrounding sea, he could be easily have been landing anywhere on terra firma.

"View your threshold as the first white line on the runway. There is a 20-knot wind direct from your front. Any motion of the runway will not be visible to you until you are almost down, and if you see a rise or fall, ignore it, just put your plane down regardless, are you with me?"

"Yes, yes, I think I want more flap now."

"Not yet Sopwith, I will tell you when to pull twenty degrees; keep calm. Remember forget any motion; you may have a hard landing, or you may float a bit, but put her down, and unless you forget where your brake pedal is, you have more than enough room to stop…You O.K. still?" Alison asked the silent Sopwith after a couple of minutes.

Sopwith was concentrating hard on the threshold, making sure his approach angle was perfect, and wishing he could apply extra flaps when he heard Ali tell him:

"Twenty degrees of flap now," and then after a short while, "O.K., flare out now."

Sopwith gently pulled back on the control column, bringing the attitude of his aircraft parallel to the runway just above the threshold mark, and as he was about to touch down, the runway, or deck rather, rose to him on a big sea swell. Disregarding Ali's instruction instinctively, he held the plane up, and only when the deck subsided below him, did he put his 172 smoothly down on the surface, and started braking. He was totally surprised by how much runway was left in front of him as he finally came to a stop.

"Well done, Sopwith," Ali spoke, "You didn't listen to me, but regardless, executed a perfect landing. Shut down completely, do not get out, and wait for the engineers to tow you in. I will be landing shortly."

A little tow tractor approached and attached a tow bar to the 172 and started pulling the craft. Now Sopwith could see Ali's F-35 coming into land. The top jet intake was wide open, and the rear exhaust nozzle was pointing straight down, enabling the jet to come down vertically and very noisily. It settled on the deck with a slight rocking motion, and the very loud jet was shut down. The 172 was brought to a stop, and the engineers started lashing the wheels to the deck, and indicated to Sopwith that he should get out, which he did, and walked in the direction that was indicated. Within a minute his baby was sinking into the hold of the carrier on a lift and disappeared before his eyes.

He looked back and saw Ali climbing out of the F-35, and when she was on the deck, removed her helmet and shook her wavy dark hair, while flashing a very pretty smile at him.

She was not tall, probably about 1.7 metres, and shapeless in her flying suit as she walked towards him. Upon reaching him she gave him a spontaneous hug, saying, "You are a star Sopwith!" Sopwith felt the softness of her breasts press into him briefly and he felt totally energised. 'You don't need Red Bull to give you wings,' he thought, 'Home grown adrenalin does the job just fine!'

She motioned for him to follow, and they entered a lift in the side of the ATC Island, and once Ali pressed the button, they too subsided into the hold. They got out and his 172 was parked in front of them, small by comparison to the other military might parked close by.

"Grab your clothes and laptop. Don't worry about anything else, there is no such thing as theft aboard, believe me," as Sopwith retrieved those two bags.

"Follow me; I will talk as we walk," she said. "As a guest aboard, you are not allowed anywhere without a chaperon, and I, luckily, am your chaperon."

"What makes me so lucky?"

"I am sure you would prefer hanging around with a lady rather than Mr Beef over there," she remarked, having a good chuckle as she pointed out a rather dangerous-looking bulky sailor. "Seriously, it releases me from all the mundane, everyday tasks for a while."

They were walking along narrow corridors; continually making random turns, with the result that Sopwith was completely disoriented within minutes, which Ali detected with a smile.

"The other reason is that you will get totally lost in here. There is a phone app available for directions, but I may not give it to you. There are seven decks below the flight deck, and believe me, it's like a warren." They entered another lift and descended, until they emerged on deck five.

"This is your cabin deck, and you will find navigation a little easier here, the main corridors being named after famous London streets." They walked a long way further, twisting and turning down 'London Streets' and finally came to a cabin door.

"This is your cabin, Sopwith," Ali said as she opened the unlocked door. "You must have impressed someone greatly because you have a single berth with your own shower and toilet; a rare commodity around here; reserved for heads of department only. Oh….and luckily for we few female officers as well. Cabin doors cannot be locked but must be closed to constantly ensure an airtight seal, but don't worry, the air-conditioning is really good."

Sopwith placed both bags on his bunk and turning to Ali asked her what came next on the agenda.

"Your call. The time is now 18h00, and the Officers' Mess is open until 20h00. If you want a shower and rest before dinner, that will be fine, or an early dinner and early night. You must be pretty whacked."

Sopwith replied that an early dinner sounded like the best option, so closing the cabin door securely, they headed off for the mess. Sopwith was pleasantly surprised with the good quality of the food served, and they ate while Ali described some of the facilities aboard, which included a few gyms, so suggested they have a workout some time the following day. On arrival back at Sopwith's cabin after dinner, he was really feeling very tired, but not too tired to try a little flirting.

"Are you coming in for a nightcap?" he asked, wearing his best smile.

"Watch your step, Casanova," Ali replied with a lovely smile, "and anyway I am not allowed to, sorry. I will let you sleep in a bit tomorrow, so will collect you at 07h00; O.K.?" Sopwith showered and climbed into his bunk, falling asleep as his head hit the pillow.

He was dressed and ready at 07h00 the next morning when his cabin door opened, revealing the much-changed form of Ali. Gone was the flying suit, to be replaced by a figure-fitting white cotton shirt, which did complete justice to her shapely breasts. Above her officer's epaulettes, her creamy complexion glowed, and she wore just a touch of lipstick. Her wavy, lustrous dark hair had been well-brushed and tied in a very short ponytail. She wore black slacks which showed off her very good hips and derriere. He stared; she gave him a small smile, and said, "I do try to look feminine occasionally!"

While walking to the mess for breakfast, she told him that he had been summoned to attend a debriefing of his trip to R08 from South Africa. She had been tasked to get him to the Rear Admiral's quarters by 09h00. So a leisurely, substantial breakfast was eaten, while making plans for future activities aboard. Ali informed him that there was a Tesco-type shop where he would be able to buy some gym clothes, as he had not brought any with him. She walked him to the Rear Admiral's quarters, where he insisted that she accompany him into the debriefing, as she had been part of the journey. Introductions to the officers were made by Ali, and the meeting began with the Rear Admiral asking Sopwith to describe his flight in detail, to which he readily complied.

"This is outrageous!" exclaimed the RA, when Sopwith told of the shot being fired at him. "And must immediately be reported as a crime to the International Criminal Court at the Hague. Attempting to shoot down an unarmed civilian aeroplane is downright terrorism."

"I agree that it ought to be sir, but I think it would be circumspect not to. If we do, it is going to publicise the whole mission, giving credence to their lies that I have stolen government property. I am also certain that there will be at least some people who will object to the R08 being used for what is essentially a civilian matter."

"Hmm, I don't like it one little bit," he grumbled, "but I dare say you have the right idea Jones."

"And I survived without a scratch. All I will need is for your engineers to apply a small patch to my aircraft, and I won't tell a soul," said Sopwith trying some humour, which did not seem to be appreciated. After Sopwith had completed his entire version of events, the RA announced.

"Well done sir. We have planned a little ceremony in the Officers' Club for you this evening, so Lieutenant Murray, ensure your charge is there by no later than 18h00."

After a fascinating day touring the R08 guided by Ali, Sopwith showered and dressed in his best for the evening's event. His best was not much, a smart white dress shirt with a new pair of Levi denim jeans and moleskin loafers, but he reckoned he looked reasonably presentable.

"Hmm, Sopwith, you certainly clean up nicely," she commented on collecting him, and guided him to the Officers' Club, which was a perfect re-creation of an old English pub, with faux oak beams, horse brasses and other memorabilia on the walls. Ali made introductions, and offered Sopwith a beer, asking what brand he desired.

Looking at the barman, Sopwith asked, "Do you perhaps have Old Speckled Hen?" his favourite English beer.

"Absolutely sir, coming up!" he retorted, and drew a pint of perfectly frothed beer. As Ali joined him with a beer shandy, he noticed Lt. Commander Karl Brighill setting himself up to make an announcement. Tapping a glass with a spoon, he quietened the room.

"Ladies and gentlemen, I present to you Mr Sopwith Jones. Please come up here Sopwith." "Good evening, all," Sopwith greeted, as he moved up and stood by Brighill's side.

Brighill continued to speak: "Not only has this man developed a unique aircraft, and broken records whilst flying it to us in the Southern Ocean, but yesterday made his first ever carrier landing on our deck. He had received no prior training, yet pulled off such a perfect touch down, that it puts a few of us here to shame." This remark caused a ripple of laughter around the pub. "As you all know, we record every take-off and landing, and always rate everyone's first landing for their certificate. I am pleased to announce that Sopwith achieved the perfect score of ten out of ten!"

There was applause from around the pub, and Brighill presented Sopwith with a neat, little gilded certificate to commemorate his first carrier landing.

"Here is also a cloth 809 Squadron badge for you to wear with pride, as we have also decided to make you an honorary member of 809 Squadron," and to further applause, Sopwith received his badge, while there were calls of 'Down,

down!', and he had to chug back his beer. Ali and Sopwith stayed for one more beer, the maximum allowable in one night, and walked to the mess for dinner.

Over the next week at sea, Sopwith and Ali spent a lot of time in a gym together, ran circuits around the flight deck when allowed, and explored every corner of the vast vessel. Sopwith was beyond impressed; in fact, was in awe of the 'four acres of sovereign territory' as it is described by the Royal Navy; fully equipped to provide every need for the seven-hundred-strong crew complement. Sopwith and Ali also came to know each other ever more personally, sharing stories about their respective youths and career paths.

One evening, Ali told him that there was something she wanted to show him, and they walked to the very rear of the ship on deck two, whose corridors are named after Edinburgh streets. Once at the stern, and under the canopy of the flight deck, Sopwith saw the huge amount of effervescence in the turbulent wake of the ship. The low sun of the impending sunset lit up the miniscule bubbles like bouncing, sparkling diamonds. They were very isolated here and it felt terribly romantic. Sopwith dared to put his arm around Ali. She leaned into him, and instantly they were locked in a deep and passionate kiss, unlike anything that Sopwith had ever before experienced. He was feeling giddy with it all, but just as quickly as the kiss started, Ali pulled away saying, "We cannot carry on."

"Oh dear," Sopwith moaned, "I was really enjoying that."

"So was I, don't worry, but relationships on board just cannot happen; it's a respected rule. It's really very difficult for a woman aboard when you stop to think about it. There are only sixty or seventy of us here, and generally we are treated in one of three ways. Either as female Royal Game, admired but untouchable, or treated as men, which also is not so cool, or there is a small group of men who make it a mission to try and get in our pants, or at least make us know that that is really what they want."

"I am beginning to understand," said Sopwith softly into her hair.

"I have really grown to like you, Sopwith, very much, and if we ever got the opportunity on dry land, I would like to go out with you. Deal?" she said pecking him on the cheek with her lips, then turned to walk back.

Neither Sopwith nor Ali knew what plans the Royal Navy had for him, going forward, so it was a pleasant surprise when they were called into a meeting with the RA on the following day, where he explained the Navy's planning.

"Thanks for coming in Lieutenant Murray and Mr Jones; take a seat. The HMS Queen Elizabeth is headed into the Atlantic for exercises with the

Americans. We will therefore be sailing to within one thousand kilometres of the English coast for you to fly to England, Mr Jones. Your destination is Royal Naval Air Station Yeovilton, in Somerset. Lt. Murray, you are to accompany Mr Jones as PFW in command, and to get Mr Jones and his aircraft safely into Yeovilton. You are to depart the day after tomorrow, so please prepare yourselves and the aircraft. Any questions?" Sopwith had none, but Ali immediately asked:

"How will I return to R08, sir?"

"Ah, there's the thing Lieutenant; there is no way that is possible at this time, so we are granting you a spot of gratuitous leave. I am sure you and Mr Jones might enjoy that?" And he gave her a wink. 'The cheeky bloody sod!' she thought, as she blushed.

"New orders will be conveyed to you at Yeovilton in due course. Now, I have a lunch appointment with my Staff Officers, so will you please excuse me?" Sopwith nearly gagged as he immediately thought of all these highly important people and their stomachs; or perhaps it was just an easy way to bring a meeting to a close? he wondered.

Walking away from the meeting Sopwith told Ali how happy he was that she would be accompanying him, and she too said she was happy, but a little perplexed about how and when she would be returning to her squadron.

They spent the rest of the day, and that following, in preparation. Sopwith supervised the minor repair needed to the nose cowling of the 172, as well as the fitment of a GPS transponder, which he had not considered in the initial build. They also fitted an IFF (Identification Friend of Foe) transponder, being as how they were to fly into densely populated airspace. He also repacked his gear to make sure there was enough room for Ali's kit too. He stuck the new vinyl aircraft registration to the side of the plane. This false registration had been provided by the Fleet Air Arm to cater to the innumerable 'plane spotters' that there are scattered around Britain, because if they had spotted an unregistered aircraft, they would have got their knickers in a knot and their blogs lit up with queries and speculation.

On the morning of 21st January, with their last items of kit ready to pack into the 172 Solar, Sopwith and Ali were disappointed to hear from ATC that it would not be possible to leave the ship, as the weather closer to England was showing heavy rain and deep cloud cover. However, the R08 was to be refuelled and provisioned at sea that day as well, so would sail in a large circle whilst undertaking this task, thus maintaining their approximate distance from the coast at one thousand kilometres. Watching the intricacies of placing the fuel lines between the tanker and carrier in the rough sea conditions, and the transfer of provisions, was entertainment enough for Sopwith to pass the time on what seemed like a wasted day. At least his 'holiday cruise' had been extended by two days, as he had arrived on board a day early and was now leaving a day later than scheduled.

On the following morning, the weather had cleared and the forecast en route to Yeovilton was clear for the rest of the day, so Sopwith and Ali loaded their kit into the Solar. While saying goodbye to those that he had got to know aboard, he noticed that the farewells between Lt. Commander Brighill and Ali seemed particularly sad, with Brighill looking downright uncomfortable.

With Ali occupying the pilot's seat, they had an easy take-off from the HMS Queen Elizabeth, and climbed to three thousand metres, on course to Somerset in the southwest of England.

"This plane is such a pleasure to fly," Ali commented, "It's so responsive and light on the controls. You've certainly made a magnificent flying machine out of an old Cessna, Sopwith. Where to next with your developments?" she asked.

"That will depend entirely on completing full flight trials and then obtaining certification from the UK Civil Aviation Authority. Once that is done, I will need some major financial backing to build more experimental models and take the developmental phase further to larger aircraft. Time will tell, and I can only take it one step at a time. And I will of course need a test pilot," he added, but received no response from Ali.

To make more conversation, Sopwith commented that he did not know that Fleet Air Arm aircrew were armed, having noticed a pistol on her hip.

"We are all issued with 9mm Browning pistols and are trained to use them. It depends on where we're operating as to whether we carry them while flying. But this is my issue weapon, so I must take it with me, and the best place to carry it is on my person."

Their flight was without incident, finally leaving the Atlantic Ocean behind at Land's End and flying north of Plymouth, over Dartmoor and then on to Exeter. Eventually, after only five hours in the air, they spotted the town of Yeovil, and then close by, the Royal Navy Air Station Yeovilton.

"Yeovil Tower, this is Solar," Ali reported in.

"Solar, Yeovil Tower, we have you on radar."

"Yeovil Tower, Solar, permission requested to come straight in from the west onto runway zero nine."

"Solar, Yeovil Tower that is affirmative."

"Yeovil Tower we would like to come in steep to try and avoid the happy snappers if there are any about today?"

"Solar there are a few, so…uh…O.K, try and avoid them."

Ali had the 172 Solar lined up on a direct heading to runway zero nine and flew in a steep and fast descent at full power, then pulled up and rotated into a very fast landing in the centre of the two-thousand-metre-long runway. Sopwith's stomach felt as if it was leaving his body via the seat of his pants, and he exclaimed, "Whoa cowboy, don't bend my plane!"

Ali laughed aloud as they taxied under direction to an apron in front of hangars to the south-east of the airfield, where they were directed to taxi straight into a large, empty hangar. As they came to a halt, so the doors were rolled closed behind them.

They were met and welcomed by the Station Commander, Lt Commander Godlonton-Shaw, who walked them to the Officers' Quarters on site. He explained along the way that he had been instructed to secure the 172 Solar and extend his full courtesy and hospitality to the two of them until further notice, then added: "It seems you are quite an important man, Sopwith." They were each shown to very comfortable rooms with en suite bathrooms and invited for a drink in the Officers' Mess at 17h00.

After showering and changing, Sopwith set up his laptop and mailed a short message to Ben Dougmore to let him know that they were safely in England and asked him to discretely pass the news on to Major Rob Pretorius.

They enjoyed a pleasant drink and chat with the commander and a few other officers. The chat was somewhat one-sided with, with innumerable 'where?', 'when?' and 'how?' questions being fired at them. Dinner was wholesome and tasty; Exmoor lamb cutlets served with mashed potatoes and peas.

Both Sopwith and Ali were keen on an early night, and Ali pecked him on the cheek and left for her accommodation. Some while after Sopwith had gone to bed and fallen asleep, he awoke to sense someone moving at the side of his bed, and on trying to sit up, Ali put a hand on his chest and pushed him gently back, saying, "It's only me." He watched her taking her pyjamas off in the dim light, enjoying the view of her beautiful, very dark-nippled breasts, as she slid into the bed next to him. He knew he was not dreaming, but it felt like a dream; her silky-soft smooth body pressing up against him. She slipped one of her legs over his hip, bringing her already moist sex hard up against his leg. He turned and taking her into his arms, she said softly, "I did make a promise, and here we are on dry land, so...."

He started kissing her and in no time, she was on top of him, urging him on. They made love, slowly at first, but then with more intensity, until they were both sated. Sopwith was no virgin, but had not had sex in a very long time, so it turned into a really a heavenly experience, and as tired and as sated as he had been a short time before, he rose to the occasion yet again. After what eventually felt like hours of delicious lovemaking, Sopwith lay looking at Ali, and said, "You know, I love you; will you marry me?"

"Slow down Sopwith," she said, slapping his bare bum, "you are such a gentleman, which is one of the many things I love about you, but just because you have made love to me does not mean you have to ask to marry me. We live in the 21st Century my darling."

"I know, I...uh...well, I do love you," he stammered.

"Thank you but let us get a bit settled before we think too big, O.K?"

Sopwith and Ali's arrival at Yeovilton had, in fact, been spotted and even photographed by two 'plane spotters' and both of whom would post pictures and questions on Internet spotting sites, corroborating the arrival of an unusual aircraft at Yeovilton.

Chapter Four

The South African Air Force pilot of the Gripen fighter aircraft which had taken a shot at Sopwith was at peace with himself. When he had been ordered to shoot the 172 Solar, he had decided to purposely miss the plane, knowing that he would not have been able to live with himself if he had killed a defenceless civilian. He had to make the missed shot a close call though, knowing the on-board camera footage would be analysed as to why the shot had missed. It turned out to be almost too close for comfort, but at the end of the day he decided that there had been no harm done, so no foul. He was, however, unwittingly about to cause much more damage than the missed shot.

During his spare time he was an ardent follower of plane-spotting sites on the Internet. He enjoyed keeping up with which new aircraft, both military and civilian, were taking to the skies. The spotting was most prolific in the UK, with several sites and blogs on the Internet to choose from. He was browsing through the 'Plane Spotting UK' Facebook page, when a post caught his attention, because the picture on it looked distinctly like the 172 Solar.

He read the post: '*I spotted something strange yesterday at RNAS Yeovilton, one of my favourite airfields. This plane looks much like an early model Cessna 172, but certainly does not seem to fly like one. I nearly missed it because it was eerily quiet, coming in from altitude in a steep-powered dive, but not making a sound. It was under full power and flared out with power and landed just out of my sight in the centre of runway 09. It appears to have a military registration, but I cannot properly make it out. See picture. Anyone else seen the aircraft or know anything about it?*'

He looked at the picture again. Although when he had seen it above the ocean, it had borne no registration, this plane was the same colour, specifically the shiny dark top surface of the wings and top of the fuselage. He scrolled down, to where there was another picture, and this time he was sure it was the 172 Solar. In this picture it was evident that there had been some repair work done on the motor cowling, where his shot had clipped the plane, as shown by an unpainted, bare aluminium strip in the white cowling. The picture was blurred by the speed of the plane and so he also unable to make out the registration letters on the fuselage but was sure it was the same plane. The post below it further served to confirm what he thought: *'I photographed it from the east, and likewise nearly missed the picture because I was not aware of its approach until the last second because it was so quiet. I agree that is came in under full power, but silently. Very unusual indeed. Comments anyone?'* There were a few jocular comments about it possibly being a UFO, but there were many more from genuinely interested parties.

At least he knew that the pilot of the 172 Solar was still alive, and he also knew where the plane had now turned up and could not resist telling his Commanding Officer this news.

His CO, eager to score some brownie points, sent an email to the Brigadier General of the Air Force with the same news, detailing the Facebook page. This, in turn, was passed on to Minister Barnabas Masondo.

Sopwith and Ali meanwhile were marking time in the cold, wintry Somerset days. Sopwith had been asked to be patient, and to await a meeting which was being set up with important government role-players, and Ali was awaiting new orders from the Fleet Air Arm. Apart from enjoying their new-found love for each other, there was little else to do. They had toured the Fleet Air Arm Museum situated at the airfield, both fascinated by the variety of aircraft that had served over the years. They had been given a tour of the whole base and viewed the many helicopters that are stationed there. It was while on this tour that Ali came across an indoor shooting range at the airfield.

"Sopwith, I have to keep my eye in, so let's go to the range, and while I'm at it you might as well learn something about handguns," she suggested. She drew a 9mm Browning from the Air Arm's armoury on the pretence of needing it for herself, but it was for Sopwith to use. Equipped with this additional firearm they started spending time in the range. Ali was very competent with her 9mm and enjoyed honing her skills. Sopwith slowly learnt which way was up on the Browning he was using, over time becoming quite good; surprising himself, as shooting had never held any interest for him. They started challenging each other to see who best shot was, and although Ali mostly outshone him, Sopwith's skills became nearly as good as hers. On fair-weather days, they went to the combat range, diving and rolling around, to shoot at pop-up targets. Sopwith thoroughly enjoyed these sessions because of their physicality; becoming very proficient in the skills involved.

Two weeks later (with their 'honeymoon' pretty much over, Sopwith, now a competent marksman, was starting to become quite frustrated with the lack of progress in going forward since his arrival in England) the long-awaiting meeting was announced. It was to take place in the hangar where the 172 Solar was parked, no doubt so that it could be shown off.

Some of the airfield staff busied themselves setting up tables and chairs, with an urn for hot drinks, a large LCD TV screen for video presentations, and the rest of the paraphernalia required for a high-powered meeting. Royal Navy and Fleet Air Arm flags, alongside the Union Jack were hung up in the hangar, and some potted plants were dragged in to brighten the atmosphere. Ali had volunteered to act as a hostess to help seat the attendees, pour teas, and generally ensure things went smoothly.

On the morning of the meeting the invited delegates turned up, mostly by car, but two arrived in separate helicopters. Sopwith thought of it as a government Oscar Awards Ceremony, with all the key actors being paraded into the hangar, as if they were terribly famous and popular. He had to rein in these thoughts, because this fuss was all about him and his aeroplane; he should have been grateful for the attention he and his craft were getting.

He was warmly greeted by the Permanent Secretary of the Department of Business, Energy, and Industrial Strategy, Priti Patel; Ben Dougmore's most helpful contact. The First Sea Lord, who had given the nod to the 'rescue mission', made a point of welcoming Sopwith. There was also a Director General from HM Treasury, the Permanent Secretary of the Home Office, and an observer from the Prime Minister's Office, along with several their deputies. Priti chaired the meeting and began with a precise account of events since her first meeting with Ben Dougmore, then with Home Affairs and finally with the Navy, whose representatives there present she thanked profusely.

The First Sea Lord gave a detailed account of picking Sopwith up in the Southern Ocean, and thanked RNAS Yeovilton for hosting Sopwith and his plane. Sopwith was then called on to give a presentation on the 172 Solar and its development.

He showed video footage of the aircraft's performance, and a summary of recorded data, thus substantiating its capabilities. He ended up by explaining that although certification was still needed, he was confident that it could evolve into a production aircraft and hoped he would be able to move on to developing larger, similarly powered aircraft. Thus far that the meeting had been all rhetoric and back-slapping, but Sopwith knew the real importance of the meeting would now be broached.

The Permanent Secretary of the Home Office announced that Sopwith's British citizenship had been approved, based on his Welsh heritage; this news being met with a round of applause. He further added that Sopwith's new passport was in the making and would be presented to him as soon as it was ready.

Priti then cut to the chase. "Mr Jones, as you have seen, we are all very proud and happy with the efforts that have been made to remove you from the untenable situation in which you found yourself in South Africa, and we welcome you 'home' with enthusiasm. What we would like to explore next is the possibility of supporting your further development of solar-powered aircraft. On my department's behalf, I wish to extend our invitation to partner with you, ensuring the right strategy to take you forward to becoming a major employer in Britain. I believe that we have the support of HM Treasury?" she said looking at their Director General.

"That is correct, Ms Patel. After lengthy consultations with the PM, we are glad to announce that in the best interests of our economy, we are prepared to underwrite expenses for this development. Such funding is subject, of course, to the submission of full business plans, models and budgets, to be submitted by your Department, Ms Patel." This statement drew loud applause as well.

Sopwith was especially pleased that he had been granted citizenship, and although not surprised that the British Government was showing an interest in supporting his endeavours, he needed to think long and hard about whose financial support he should finally accept.

"Ladies and gentlemen," he began, "I am most humbled and grateful for all of the efforts you; your various departments and staff have made to get me here today, along with your offers of continued support. I am carefully considering my future in industry, and will revert to you in due course," Sopwith concluded graciously, and, having learnt a trick about ending meetings, said, "I am told that the staff of Yeovilton Officers' Mess have prepared a special lunch for you all, so please accompany me there and let's enjoy it."

On leaving the hangar, the First Sea Lord sought out Ali. Walking with her, he said, "Good day, Lieutenant Murray. I have been asked, seeing that I was coming down here, to let you know that there are new orders awaiting you at our offices in Whitehall, so will you please report there tomorrow when convenient?" Ali smiled inwardly as she had taken many orders in her time, but never directly from the First Sea Lord himself.

Meanwhile in South Africa, during this period that Sopwith had been waiting for the meeting at Yeovilton to be called, Barnabas Masondo had taken to the Minister of Police the nugget of information he had received about the whereabouts of Sopwith Jones. There he had laid an entirely spurious charge of theft of government property, namely, 'one electric aeroplane', against Mr Sopwith Jones. He sent the details of the charge to the South African High Commission in London and instructed the High Commissioner to engage the British Government in extraditing Sopwith Jones back to South Africa to face the charge. Using the necessary pedantic protocol, the High Commissioner eventually met up with his British counterpart on the same day as Sopwith was attending the meeting in Yeovilton. The British Commissioner received the written submission, saying that it would be studied by his government. By the time that the First Sea Lord arrived back at his office in Whitehall the next day, there was a memo waiting to inform him of the extradition request submitted by South Africa, as the Navy information systems had picked up the name Sopwith Jones, a person of interest.

"Now this is certainly bloody codswallop!" he mumbled to no-one there and thought of the problems that the extradition request might cause Sopwith Jones. He knew that the charge against him must have been trumped-up, but the extradition request was now in the system, and red tape is most often extremely difficult to untangle.

The message, on its way to the First Sea Lord's desk, had also crossed the desks of only two other people, but already there was a rumour about it making the rounds of the offices, mainly because their 'rescue' of Sopwith Jones had become a popular topical subject.

When Ali arrived at the Main Building in Whitehall from Yeovilton that afternoon, she had been directed to see a Lieutenant Commander Anthony Baxter, who she was told had her new orders. Ali did not know the man, and her first impression on meeting him was that he seemed a bit of a pompous prig but kept her thoughts to herself.

"Ah, Lieutenant Murray, welcome, welcome; do sit down. Would you care for a cup of tea?" he asked. 'All I care about is getting out of here', she thought, politely declining the tea.

"Your fame precedes you Lieutenant, through your service records, of course. My, my, you have flown substantial hours in an F-35, haven't you? That must be so much fun."

'Fun,' she thought, 'you would not know what fun is, even if I stood on my head and farted.'

"Ah well, there has to be an end to all that flying stuff eventually. So I'll tell you what…you have been transferred from Fleet Air Arm 809 Squadron to my office, Logistical Support Planning. Now what do you say to that, old girl?"

Ali jumped out of her chair and almost screamed at him, "What? What did you say?"

"Well, sorry I didn't mean to offend or be sexist; I take back what I said."

"I couldn't care if you call me an old girl or a young whore. What did you say about me being transferred? To this office you say?"

"Yes indeed, direct orders from somewhere above, I believe."

"From how far above?"

"The very top, I have heard."

Ali stormed out of his office and made her way to the First Sea Lord's suite and forced her way into his office past a very timid secretary. She may not really have been timid at all, but the swirling cloud of black-haired anger that came towards her certainly intimidated her at that moment.

"Lt Murray, I am busy," the First Sea Lord said, as she came bursting into his office.

"So am I sir, very busy sorting out some horrible mistake."

"Oh," he said, "I see you have already seen Lt Commander Baxter. I rather did expect you to make an appointment after seeing him. Sit down please."

"So what is this all about?" she fumed.

"Alison, uh, may I call you Alison?"

"Certainly, sir."

"Alison, our next order of F-35s has been cancelled indefinitely. Treasury tells us that there is simply not enough money to go ahead with it. As you well know, we have twelve pilots finishing their specialised F-35 training, and of course you know how much that all costs. We cannot side-line those chaps after such an expense, but we have had our money's worth out of you, so amongst others, your head was on the block."

"Sir, is this the way one gets to the top of the pile, by being so brutally blunt?"

"Probably."

"Clearly there has been no consideration given to my skills; no consultation with me. I am being side-lined into a stinky bloody office in stinky bloody London to perform…uh…logistics, which for all I know is some kinky sexual activity."

"Alison, please calm down. I accept that this has not been well thought out. Please report to Lt Cdr Baxter's office tomorrow so at least I know where to find you, and in the meantime let me see if I can do some damage control. Please."

"You need to do more than damage control sir; you need to get a brain!" and she stormed out.

Lugging her bag from reception, she walked across the Thames on Westminster Bridge, hardly even noticing the London Eye, and on to the Union Jack Club, just across the road from Waterloo Station, where she had booked a room for the night. She sat down on her bed in the room and burst into tears, an extremely rare event in her life. She couldn't imagine not being able to fly any longer, but above all, she felt so aggrieved by how quickly and brutally this had all happened. It dawned on her that Lt Cdr Brighill aboard the HMS Queen Elizabeth had already known of her fate, and that was the reason he had looked so depressed upon her departure. After much navel-gazing when she eventually stopped crying, and with the help of two whiskies, each of which she had downed in one gulp, she believed she had made up her mind how to handle things in the morning. She should have phoned Sopwith, but did not try, rather going to the restaurant to have dinner, feeling much better about herself having decided. She met a pilot there whom she had flown with many years ago, and reminiscing with him, enjoyed a wonderful meal of freshly battered cod and chips with garden peas and tartare sauce; soul food for her. After a good night's sleep, she enjoyed her walk back to the Main Building, this time, in the early morning light along the route, she admired the magnificent London Eye and Big Ben.

She went straight to Baxter's office, who chirped, "Reporting for duty is you, Lieutenant?"

"Not likely! I am waiting on the First Sea Lord," and she busied herself on her phone sending Sopwith a message to say that she was fine, would be having another meeting later in the day, and would chat to him later. She was not kept waiting very long before the call came that she could go through to the First Sea Lord.

"Good morning, Alison, I trust you are in a better frame of mind this morning?" he greeted her.

"Yes sir, very much so. May I please apologise for my extremely bad behaviour yesterday?"

"No need at all, and under the circumstances I should be the one apologising, but let us move on, I have had consultations with......"

"I have found a solution sir!" Ali interrupted him. "I propose, seeing that there is a distinct possibility that Mr Jones is going to partner with the government, (she had absolutely no idea what Sopwith actually had in mind) that I am seconded to whatever form that organisation may take, as a test pilot."

The First Sea Lord remained silent for a long while, pondering his options, and eventually said, "I like the idea a lot. In fact, it's a perfect solution, even given that it is going to take a little ingenuity to work out the practicalities of such a move. Yes indeed! Right then, Alison, report for duty back at Yeovilton," and he gave her a grand smile.

'If you can't beat them, join them in shifting costs around,' she thought to herself.

She strode back to Baxter's office and he, sensing her good mood, asked, "So has the boss convinced you that this is the right move?"

"On the contrary, sir, I convinced him of the right move. I have been seconded to become Sopwith Jones' test pilot for his new developments."

"Jones, eh? Well, I have some news for you on that score. Jones is being extradited to South Africa," said Baxter, having been a recipient of the now vastly exaggerated rumour of the extradition request.

"You don't say," Ali chuckled, "So will they extradite me along with him?" she continued, as if the man had actually made a joke.

"No, you don't understand. There was a memo to the boss yesterday informing him of the extradition; I am definitely not having you on."

Ali stood dead still, holding her tongue. There was no way she could try and impose on the First Sea Lord yet again to determine if this was true. Lt Cdr Baxter was in a senior enough position to know what was going on and certainly would not have told a blatant lie about Sopwith. Then, with no emotion showing, she realised that possibly she had been duped by the First Sea Lord, who had so readily acceded to her request, knowing full well Sopwith's impending fate, and that she would have to come back with her tail between her legs. She decided that she had to switch to plan B, which she had seriously considered the previous evening, and that was to resign her commission.

"Sir, may I use your computer for a short while?" she asked Baxter.

"Certainly, help yourself. I was about to go to the canteen for a cuppa anyway," and he left the office. Ali typed a clear letter of resignation, addressing it to Lt Cdr Baxter, who was officially the Commander of her last ordered posting, other than this morning's agreement by the Sea Lord to her request, which she had by now decided was false. After printing and signing it, she awaited his return from his 'cuppa'.

"Sir, I have had a change of heart, and have firmly decided to resign my commission, so please accept my letter of resignation," she said, handing him the letter.

Totally nonplussed, he took the letter saying, "I will see to it that it is processed."

She left the office, hyperventilating in angst over what she had just done, along with a terrible fear about Sopwith's fate. After collecting her kit from the Union Jack, she boarded the 09h50 train at Waterloo, reaching Yeovil at 13h00, and then took a taxi to the airfield.

She found Sopwith working on his laptop in his room and having given him a hug and a passionate kiss, she immediately started a verbal barrage.

"Sopwith, we have to get out of here."

"We? Get out of where? Why?"

"We have to go. They are going to capture you!"

"Slow down darling. What is this all about? Firstly, the 'we'; what about your new posting? Secondly, who on earth is going to try and 'capture' me?"

"Alright. Honey, my answer is yes."

"Yes what, darling?"

"Yes, I accept your proposal, I want to marry you."

Sopwith, floored by all of this, and not being able to make head or tail of anything, said, "Please darling, just give it to me one step at a time. OK, so you want to marry me; why now?"

"Well, I love you, but I also want to come with you. And I have resigned from the Fleet Air Arm."

"Come with me where?"

"You are to be extradited to South Africa, so we have to get out of here before they can do that."

"That's impossible. Three days ago we both heard that the Home Office has made me a Citizen, and a country cannot extradite its own citizens."

"I know, but have you got your passport yet? No, you haven't, so they can."

"I can't believe this is happening. How on earth did you hear this news?"

"From Lt Cdr Baxter at HQ. He saw the memo that was sent to the First Sea Lord about it."

"Are you absolutely sure about this."

"One hundred percent sure."

"And you have definitely resigned?"

"Yes, I gave Baxter my letter of resignation."

Sopwith slowly absorbed what she had said. Her story sounded insane, but she certainly was not, and was so sure about the validity of her information, coming from one of the highest government offices in the land.

"So, we leave. How and where to?" he asked her.

"Well, we leave in the Solar of course. The 'where to' bit is a bit trickier; we'll still have to figure that out."

"OK, so we figure that out, fine. But are you saying that we can just get in the Solar and fly away without being spotted in a country blanketed by radar?"

"No, no. I will file a flight plan with ATC here. They do not know that I have resigned. I have at least a week before my resignation surfaces on the desk of someone who knows what my involvement with you is. Lt Cdr Baxter's head is so far up his arse he will follow the pedantic step-by-step procedure of processing my resignation before he tells anyone in the know. He is well-pleased not to have to put up with me in his office, which was the intention. And in any event, I remain a commissioned officer until such time as my resignation has been formally accepted."

Sopwith surrendered himself to her ideas, and said, "Right then, we have some planning to do, let's get on with it."

They immediately agreed that they could never avoid detection over either Europe or the North American countries, so only one option remained, and that was over Africa. Where in Africa their first stop was to be became the debate, so they studied Google Maps. They talked loosely about their destination, with some thought even being given to Australia. They quit that idea after a short discussion, as it would be impossible to get there in the Solar, and it was a

Commonwealth country anyway, which would afford them no diplomatic protection anyway.

The best they could think of was to find some sort of haven in Africa, and by working through Ben Dougmore in Port Alfred, Sopwith would have to fight the South African Government, proving their dishonesty. Armed with calculators, they started figuring out how and where to go in Africa.

Their calculations showed that they should be able to avoid all radar coverage by flying over the Atlantic and skirting Portugal. They could then track eastwards of Madeira and the Canary Isles to make landfall in Morocco, south of the major centre of Agadir. This plan would require every second of daylight available at that time of the year and would doubtless be a risky flight. Short of trying to hide under a bush at Yeovilton, this clearly was their only option, so they agreed on it, and started their preparations.

They frenetically repacked the Solar, carefully analysing what they needed. Apart from Sopwith's data storage devices and their personal kit, the critical items would mostly be food and water. By late that evening they had assessed what additional items they still had to procure. On the following morning Ali caught a taxi into the village of Yeovil and shopped for extra provisions. Sopwith busied himself with disconnecting the electrical power feed to both the IFF and GPS transponders that had been fitted to the Solar aboard HMS Queen Elizabeth. Upon Ali's return, Sopwith packed while she went to the Quartermaster's Stores.

"We are going on a test flight over the Atlantic," she explained, "so I need two ten-day survival packs please," making no mention of the fact that there was no room for a life raft aboard the little aircraft. Receiving them, she added, "And two cartons of water sachets, just in case." Those extra two hundred litres would supplement the one hundred litre tank that had remained in the aircraft.

After that, she sought out the base chaplain, and explained to him their decision to get married, making an appointment with him to perform the marriage late that afternoon. With that done, and while Sopwith completed the packing, Ali went off to finalise their preparations to leave by filing a flight plan with Air Traffic Control. This was a critical part of their planning. Her filing would be totally fictitious, but she had to make it totally believable somehow. She climbed the steps into the tower, and offering a gay hello to the staff there, she chose the only lady on duty.

"Hi luv, we met the other evening in the mess, you remember?" This was partly true, as Ali had only seen her in passing, but backfooted as she was, the controller could only say, "Yeah, how are you?"

"Could be better. Been enjoying some ground time but must get into the air again. You know the strange plane in the hangar down there?"

"I heard about it; haven't seen it though."

"Yeah, well it is some new design thing, and I have to take it and the civilian on a test flight tomorrow."

"He is yummy!" she said, "Wish I could trade places with you."

"He does look quite hot; I'll give you that. I'll let you know what I think of him, alright." Ali grinned inwardly, 'If only this girl knew that I'll be marrying him later'.

"We will be leaving at first light tomorrow," and when the controller started entering the information into her computer, Ali gave her the false registration details.

"We'll be flying westward over the Atlantic to nowhere, and returning on the same course, only arriving YEO by last light."

"Uh…long flight hey?"

"Yeah, some sort of endurance stuff, I think. You got that all in your computer, luv?"

"Yeah, have fun for me tomorrow; boring as hell up here at the moment."

A relieved Ali was delighted, and as she walked back, she knew that they would have at least a twelve hour, and more than two-thousand-kilometre head start tomorrow, before anyone decided that something had gone wrong. Under the circumstances, she and Sopwith could not have asked for more.

"Wedding time!" she called to Sopwith when she got back, and they walked hand in hand to the small inter-denominational chapel. The chaplain was there to meet them, and they started by filling in all their details on the required Home Office marriage document. This done, the chaplain performed a very short wedding ceremony. Sopwith had secretly spent time carefully weaving a ring out of fine copper electrical wiring, and now placed it on the delighted Ali's finger, giving her a kiss, which she returned with passion. They both signed the marriage form. The chaplain witnessed it, giving them a copy for themselves.

"Well, Mrs Jones, I declare that you are stuck with me now!"

"Mr Jones, there is nothing that can unstick me, not even a flight into darkest Africa."

They had an early dinner that night, made love briefly but eagerly, and were asleep early. Before first light they were up, showered and dressed. They both wore their 9mm Browning's in holsters on their hips, with Ali having convinced Sopwith that he should take the borrowed one along, 'just in case', as she put it. Having done one final check of the Solar in the hangar, they pushed it out, and were parked on the threshold of runway 27 precisely as the sun rose, with Ali in the pilot's seat.

"Yeovil Tower, Solar, do you copy."

"Solar, Yeovil Tower, strength five."

"Yeovil Tower permission to take off on runway 27, heading due west on flight plan submitted to ATC."

"Roger, Solar, in your own time, please go ahead. Enjoy it, Lieutenant." It was the lady who had received the flight plan.

The Solar took up much more runway than usual to get into the air because of the extra weight aboard, and when they finally took to the air Sopwith was grateful that they had not overloaded excessively. Now they could fly away.

Late that afternoon, the First Sea Lord asked his secretary to get Lt Murray on the phone as he needed to talk to her about certain decisions that had been made regarding her posting onto Sopwith Jones' development project. The secretary told him in due course that Murray was not available as she and Jones had gone on a test flight. The First Sea Lord was distinctly troubled by this news, as with no agreements yet in place regarding Jones, there had been no calls or authorisation from a Fleet Air Arm facility for test flights in the Solar.

"Martha," he instructed his secretary, "get back to Yeovilton, please, and tell them that I have to speak to Murray the minute she lands." He knew that it should not be long before that happened because sunset was not far off, and the Solar needed light for sustained flight. He had a further thought, then picking up his phone; he looked up the extension number for Lt Cdr Anthony Baxter, then, calling him, asked him to come by to see him. By the time Baxter arrived in his office, the First Sea Lord could see that it was quite dark outside now. Telling Baxter to take a seat, he once more looked up a number, and dialling it, got through to the administrative offices at RNAS Yeovilton himself.

"Your commanding officer please, First Sea Lord here!" he barked into the phone. A short while later he heard, "Godlonton-Shaw here, sir."

"Are you aware that the civilian aircraft you are housing temporarily has gone on a test flight?"

"No sir, I am not. I have been in Portsmouth all day."

"Right, then establish as quickly as possible if a flight plan was filed, and regardless, tell me if that aircraft is on the ground at your airfield or not. Phone me back as urgently as possible."

"Will do sir, goodbye."

He looked across the desk and became aware once more that Lt Cdr Baxter was seated there, and said, "Thank you for coming, Baxter. Now tell me, did Lt Murray return to your office the other day after meeting with me?"

"She did sir."

"And tell me, did she say anything to you about her orders at all? Did she perhaps chat or discuss anything with you?"

"Yes sir, she looked well pleased with herself, and told me that she would be working with that criminal Jones."

"Criminal, what do you mean 'criminal'?" boomed the First Sea Lord.

His face reddening, Baxter replied, "Well sir it is just...uh...that I was told Jones was to be extradited to South Africa to face criminal charges."

"And who the bloody hell told you that?"

"Well sir...uh...I really can't say. It was just scuttlebutt."

"So, let me get this straight. Based on some 'scuttlebutt', as you call it, you told Lt Murray that she would be working with a criminal?"

"I did sir," his face now a deep red colour.

"Do you mind telling me how Lt Murray reacted to this information you so generously shared with her?"

"She resigned her commission sir," Baxter replied, looking now like he was on the verge of tears.

"What do you mean 'she resigned her commission'? Why do I not know about this?"

"Sir, she typed a letter of resignation and submitted it to me. I accepted it and I have correctly sent it to personnel for them to start processing."

"Are you bloody stark raving mad?" The First Sea Lord shouted and got up from his chair and stalked around his desk towards the seated officer with a murderous look in his eyes. He started saying, "I am going to......" when the ringing of his telephone saved them both from what was no doubt about to become a very ugly incident. He glared at Baxter, and then walked back behind his desk, and sitting down, answered his phone.

"Godlonton-Shaw here sir. Lt Murray yesterday filed a flight plan for a test flight over the Atlantic today commencing at first light and ending at last light. She and Sopwith Jones did take off according to the plan at first light this morning, but they have not yet returned. It is now twenty minutes past last light here sir."

"Oh my God!" moaned the First Sea Lord. "Thank you for coming back to me. There is absolutely nothing more you can do other than informing me immediately should they, by some miracle, reappear. Prepare statements from everyone involved and await further orders regarding this matter. Thank you once again. Good night."

He stared at Baxter for a long time, not saying a single word. He eventually spoke evenly and calmly.

"Lt Murray and Mr Sopwith Jones are gone. They have disappeared. They have run away. They have flown away. They have gone into hiding," and then he bellowed at the top of voice, "They have fucked off, because of you, you little dipshit, whose mouth does the impossible by actually functioning without a single brain cell to operate it! They have fucked off because of you Baxter, and I am going to have your guts for garters!"

He stared again at Baxter, who was shaking like a leaf. "You are suspended from duty pending a full court martial. Now get out of here! No, wait. Your last duty before your suspension begins is to get Lt Murray's letter of resignation out of 'processing' as you call it. Undo whatever has been done so far to 'process' it and have it on my desk before I leave this office tonight. Now get out!"

The First Sea Lord sat at his desk, considering what action he would need to take, and who he needed to inform in the morning. Tomorrow was going to be a very long day.

Chapter Five

Mr and Mrs Jones' (Sopwith liked the sound of that) flight in the 172 Solar had gone very well. The sky had remained sufficiently sunny between puffy clouds after they left England, and the further south they flew, the clouds disappeared completely. They had flown very low the whole way, ensuring that they stayed below any possible radar coverage, and although this was tiring, they shared the flying, while alternatively taking turns to have a rest. They had seen no other aircraft, only occasional ships in the far distance, and were happy that they had remained undetected.

The most excitement they had was a period of complete hilarity when Ali needed to have a pee. There was no room anywhere for her to squat over a pee bucket, so that had to be placed on her seat, and she squeezed herself above it against the cockpit roof like a contortionist, with her bare bum in the air. Sopwith mockingly tried to unsettle her by tickling her butt cheeks, but despite much laughter, she had managed to complete the task successfully.

Their Satnav guided them silently past Las Palmas and the Grand Canary Islands, well out of radar range, and they made landfall over Morocco in the Tan-Tan Province, just north of the Western Sahara area of Morocco. Staying well south of the town of Tan-Tan and flying as far inland as the fading sunlight allowed them, they started searching for a place to land. The landscape here was still quite hilly, even so far south of the Atlas Mountains, so they continued further southwards.

They eventually saw what seemed to be an isolated enough area of level ground, perhaps an ancient flood plain, and Ali brought the Solar down very slowly and carefully, touching down like a butterfly with sore feet, in complete contrast to her landing at Yeovilton.

The first thing Sopwith did was hammer three steel pegs into the ground to tie down the aircraft, in case a big wind blew up. He had just completed tying the last rope, when he saw what he first took to be an apparition in the fading light but realised soon enough that it was a real person walking towards them. He speedily drew his 9mm and pointed it at the approaching, turbaned Moroccan, who was wearing a battered old AK47 slung across his chest.

"Don't move fellow. I can actually use this," he said, waving the 9mm around a little.

The stranger placed his hands together as if in prayer in front of him, then unslung the AK47 and placed it carefully on the ground beside him. Sopwith then saw that the stranger looked very old, certainly older than the beaten-up old AK he was carrying, making him feel a little foolish about pointing his 9mm at him.

"I am looking after the goats, only," he said in heavily accented English.

Sopwith's heart rate slowly returned to normal and all he could say was, "Ah, good for you!" and he replaced the 9mm in its holster. He hadn't noticed, but Ali had witnessed the whole event, and said to Sopwith, "Great reactions, soldier," and gave a little chuckle. She then took a cup of water to the visitor and introduced herself to him.

It turned out that he was a local Berber tribesman by the name of Amastan, tending to his Draa goats further south than his normal grazing grounds, and the AK47 was to shoot any jackal which might try to prey on them.

"To be very much cold in the night," Amastan said, wrapping his arms around himself and shivering to demonstrate his point, then said, "I get the fire." He wandered off, returning regularly, to place small sticks and dried camel dung onto a growing heap of fuel for the night's fire.

The three of them ate around the fire, keeping warm in the rapidly cooling evening. Amastan shared some of his khobz bread with them, and they in turn offered him some tinned Spam, which he was totally enthralled by, never having eaten such spiced meat in his life before.

He spoke to them with pride about his goats that he was herding, explaining that he had to come further south to look for grazing as it had been terribly dry, telling them also that he could round them all up with one whistle in the morning. He chatted to them a little about his youth, many years before, when he had fought in numerous skirmishes that the Berbers had been involved in those days.

The area was very sparsely populated, he told them, and he had wandered over to where they had landed out of sheer curiosity when he saw strangers in the area. He did not once ask where they had come from, or where they were going; such things were of no interest to this man who lived such a simple and uncluttered life.

The three of them settled down to sleep around the smouldering fire, Amastan using a goat hair mat-cum-blanket that he carried like a bandolier draped over one shoulder; Sopwith and Ali in their sleeping bags, which had been part of their essential packing.

They were all awake at first light. Ali brewed a billy can of tea; a cup of which Amastan accepted as another special treat. He then whistled for his goats, which appeared, seemingly miraculously from nowhere, then trekked off with them trailing after him.

"Good fellow," Sopwith said to Ali, "but I think you took his arrival, while bearing an AK47 a little lightly, don't you?"

"Not at all," she replied, giving him a quick kiss, "I saw him a moment after you had, and had my weapon out just as quickly as yours, watching your back. I chuckled out of relief that he seemed too old and decrepit to have caused any damage, and to try and show him there was no tension. I am very aware that Africa is wild in more ways than one."

Sopwith had spent much of the previous day, while flying, contemplating their next destination after Morocco, and had not yet come up with any ideas. Although they had a detailed map of Africa, as well as the Satnav which would guide them anywhere, they had no access to the internet to research what was happening on the ground. They could, unwittingly, fly into any one of the apparently ever-present hotspots of political turmoil, or terrorism that seemed to be plaguing parts of Africa. Earlier that morning, while staring up at the crystal-clear sky full of stars, he had, however, come up with the seed of an idea, which was now beginning to germinate, of where next to head for.

In London, that same morning, the First Sea Lord was in action from a very early hour. The first thing he did was to phone the Permanent Secretary of the Home Office and inform him of Sopwith's disappearance.

"I would like you to organise, as quickly as possible, the gathering of the necessary evidence that the charges laid by the South Africans against Jones are a sham, which I do not doubt they are for one minute. The thing is, mounting an international search for a missing British naval officer is one thing, but if you throw in a South African citizen who is the subject of an extradition request, that's quite another; things can get messy. Perhaps expedite the issue of Jones' British passport, if that has not yet been done, and please forward it to my office."

The Permanent Secretary, fully aware of the background, immediately ordered his embassy in Cape Town to obtain affidavits from Major Rob Pretorius in Port Alfred, where Sopwith had test-flown his aircraft, as well as from Ben Dougmore, the lawyer who had full knowledge of the background to the South African Government's attempt to claim Sopwith's personal research and development work as their own. He also organised for Sopwith's passport to be sent to the First Sea Lord's offices.

The First Sea Lord then called an emergency meeting of all his senior staff and aides. He began the meeting: "I do not know how, but we have to find Lt Murray and Mr Jones. They may have taken off on their own accord, but their departure was directly caused by one of our own officers, who is, in due course, to be court-martialled for his grave error.

All we know about their travel capabilities is that they have a range of some two thousand five hundred kilometres per day in sunshine weather. We have absolutely no idea in what direction they first flew, as they have disabled both their IFF and GPS transponders. The only minute positive in this whole affair is that Godlonton-Shaw at Yeovilton informs me that Lt Murray drew a Browning 9mm pistol from their armoury and has not returned it, meaning that they are at least minimally armed in the event of their falling into danger. I have yet to discuss this matter with the PM but assure you that I will undertake to get his authority to utilise all our resources and take all necessary action possible. Now go away, put on your thinking caps, and find a way to do this. We'll meet again at…uh…14h00."

Meanwhile, that same morning, but in Pretoria, South Africa, Minister Barnabas Masondo was informed about the disappearance of Sopwith Jones. He too believed Jones must be found, not by the British, but by himself. The 'rewards' he had planned to be personally siphoned-off after a successful SOE under his direction had built unique, sought-after electric aeroplanes were just too great to be ignored. As he was only the Minister of Trade and Industry he would have to rely on help, even if it meant having to make cuts to his dreamed-of riches.

He requested a meeting with the Minister of Defence and explained the situation to him. He, however, told Masondo there was not much he could do to help, and advised him to rather seek out one of the many 'security companies' (modern speak for mercenaries, which seemed to serve many governments around the world to undertake their dirty undercover work) and gave Masondo some names and contact details.

Sopwith discussed his newly formed idea with Ali; his thoughts being that the only way they would find some type of temporary refuge was to be involved with a multinational construction operation, such as the building of a large, new infrastructural project, or the establishment of a new mine or mineral exploration hub. He was clear in his mind that they should avoid contact with any forms of government. Possibly they could work their way into a civilian operation posing as news reporters, or simply lost travellers.

The most he knew about any such projects was awareness that various road and mining projects in the Democratic Republic of Congo (DRC) had some South African contractors working on them. However, he was ignorant about any details, such as where exactly such projects might be located, but suggested to Ali that they should be able to spot such large construction operations from the air.

They both agreed this seemed about their only option at that point, so plotted a course in the direction of the DRC. They estimated the furthest they could go in one day, by overflying northern Mauritania and the northern parts of Mali and would be able to get as far as Niger.

In the fine, early morning sunlight they packed the 172 Solar, and took off on their south-easterly heading. They flew without any interruption for about ten hours over the vast empty and arid spaces of Mauritania and Mali before they crossed the border into Niger, well north of any major towns. They were flying at an altitude of about five hundred metres above ground, over scrubby bush and combretum thickets, when their tranquillity was suddenly interrupted. Ali was at the controls, and Sopwith was gazing around at the scenery, when he spotted several small flashes spark from the ground a little in front, and to the right of their aircraft. As he began wondering what had caused them, there were two 'thwack' sounds as if something had hit the Solar, followed by a third 'thwack', and their electric motor stopped instantaneously. He studied the instrument panel and saw that the master electrical power switch had tripped. He immediately reset it, but it immediately tripped again.

"We have lost all power, love; look for a place to put us down in one piece!" he called to Ali. Ali had very little room to manoeuvre at this low altitude but managed to line up with an area of grassland ahead that looked to be free of trees and shrubs. She brought the Solar down calmly, and somehow kept it in the air just above the ground, at well below stall speed, then landed as gently as possible at about forty kilometres per hour. Ali knew she had to fly as slowly as possible before they touched down, not having any idea of the ground surface underfoot. This approach ensured that the little plane handled the rough, bumpy ground without any damage before it came to a quick halt.

"We have taken some shots from the ground. Ali, take a brief look around the plane and see if you can see any damage, and then watch my back please. I am going to look in the motor compartment to try and find the cause of our power loss."

"Just two small holes in the rear fuselage," Ali called out, as Sopwith opened the cowling. He spotted the problem instantly. The main earth cable was hanging loose, having been shot through.

"Found the problem!" he called, moving back to the cabin to fetch tools, "Just keep your eyes peeled. We have a few 'clicks' on them, but those rotten rats might be on their way here, knowing we have gone down."

Sopwith found the necessary tools, and reattached the earth cable, which luckily had enough slack to enable him to do so. Bending over, he had just finished tightening the locating nut, when he heard a branch snap behind him. Without turning he looked back under his armpit, and 'Bloody hell!' there was an AK47-wielding fellow sneaking up behind him. Fear-fired adrenalin pumped into his system as he dropped to the ground, drawing his Browning at the same time, grateful for their workouts on the combat range. The sound of a burst of automatic rifle fire rang out as he rolled, and drawing a bead on the nasty fellow, squeezed the trigger of his 9mm. It emitted a loud blast, and the insurgent dropped to the ground. Sopwith knew he had hit the man; exactly where he did not know, but the man lay prostrate.

At that moment Ali screamed out, "They are coming! I can see them back there; are you alright? Hurry!"

"I am fine!" Sopwith called back at the same moment reaching down to relieve the motionless man of his AK47, and two spare magazines which had been tucked into his belt.

"Get in Ali. The motor should be fine; let's get out of here. I will watch our back until you are ready to roll."

As Sopwith heard the Solar's motor starting to turn, he could see a small group of men, still a few hundred metres distant, working their way towards them through the combretum thickets. Once it had reached full revs, Ali called out,

"Let's fly!" Just then some shots rang out, and Sopwith amazed himself by standing his ground and putting the AK47 to his shoulder. He fired a burst of automatic fire back at them and saw them all drop to take cover. He waited a further thirty seconds or so, then fired another burst of .762mm rounds in their direction, then leapt into the plane.

Ali released the brakes and they rumbled off over the uneven ground, taking to the air amongst puffs of dust as bullets hit the ground around them, but they were heartily relieved to hear there were no further 'thwacks. They gained altitude in silence until Sopwith ventured, "Well, I never!"

"Understated in the extreme, as always, my dear Mr Jones! You behaved like a professional soldier back there; out of context from your usual profession, mind you!"

"You know, I don't even know where the safety catch is on an AK. I just pulled the trigger in the hope that it was not set in the 'safety on' position. It gives me the shivers to think that the nasty fellow was creeping up on me with his rifle set on automatic!"

They both naturally assumed their attackers had been members of Boko Haram, the violently anti-Western terrorist group that had been plaguing north-east Nigeria for many years; sometimes also operating in neighbouring countries.

With daylight fading fast they headed due north for as long as the light would allow. Their northerly track led them away from Nigeria, hopefully far from their attackers' area of operation. As they searched the landscape below with anxious eyes, they were relieved to happen across a very arid piece of open, level land, upon which Ali brought the Solar down to a gentle, bumping stop. Immediately they prepared for the night.

While they quenched their thirst, Sopwith, using his ever-present duct tape, taped over the bullet holes in the fuselage and cowling, following this up by eating a basic meal from one of their emergency rations packs, then settled down for the night, after first deciding to post guard on a shift basis, with one of them staying awake, duly armed with the AK47. At least it was a warm evening, this location being much farther south than they had been the previous night.

At 14h00 that same afternoon, the First Sea Lord's staff had met as arranged, to consider the first report being presented to speculate upon the possible flight paths of Murray and Jones.

"There are only two possible choices of route," the speaker started the report. "First, they could have flown into Europe, and, unlikely as this is, we have checked every coastal Air Traffic Control from Portugal to Norway, with no result, as was expected. If it had been summer, they may have been able to reach Iceland or even Greenland, so those destinations have been ignored as possibilities. That leaves only Africa as a destination. We have ruled out the likelihood of them managing to pass undetected through the Strait of Gibraltar to fly into North Africa, so that leaves only Western Africa. By our calculations they certainly could not have made landfall before sunset, any further south than Morocco, or very far inland, so we believe their first destination would have been somewhere in Morocco. We have checked with all Moroccan ATCs, but they report no sightings or communication."

"So this highly academic guess leaves us where?" the First Sea Lord queried sarcastically.

"Nowhere other than knowing on which continent they are, sir."

"Right, let us then accept that they are in Africa. Any bright ideas on how we are going to find them on that vast continent, gentlemen?"

"We can ask Home Office to contact all their embassies and......."

"Oh bollocks man!" interrupted the First Sea Lord, "We live in the information age, and you want to suggest that our bloody embassies 'keep an ear to the ground'? We do not have any drones in the Fleet Air Arm fleet yet, but as a start, please ask the Royal Air Force if they have any surveillance drones available with which they may be required to assist."

The First Sea Lord then turned to Rear Admiral Ron Hubbard, the commanding officer of the Fleet Air Arm.

"Ron, I want to task you to look into the possibility of using Project Oberon, so please get hold of Joint Forces Command. For those of you not in the know, the Ministry of Defence has stopped using the European Union's Galileo space project for information-gathering; all in the name of Brexit, of course. I knew that the MOD had, some time ago, tasked the defence laboratory at Porton Down to develop our own satellite surveillance system, code-named Project Oberon. I know too, that the first of these synthetic aperture radar satellites, called SAR, has been launched into space, and is named NovaSAR. The big questions you need to ask Joint Forces Command is what sort of information we can get from it. I leave that in your capable hands; please revert directly to me when you have some Intel."

"One more area needs attention if no one has yet thought of it. Will someone please get onto the intelligence services at GCHQ and get them to key in 'Cessna

172', 'silent aircraft', 'Sopwith Jones', 'Lt Murray' and 'Africa' into their Tempora internet monitoring project. Those keywords may just sniff something out of the internet."

"Lastly gentlemen, I need orders to go out to HMS Queen Elizabeth. On her return from her playtime with the Yankees, she is no longer to go back to Portsmouth, but must be provisioned at sea once more. At the same time, I would like her to take on board a company of Royal Marines please – I will get the authorisation for that. I have this very uneasy feeling in my creaky old bones that tells me this whole thing might end up a little messy. Have her hold station off Gibraltar which will allow her to either go southwards along the African west coast, or east to go through the Suez.

Thank you, gentlemen that will be all."

In South Africa, Minister Barnabas Masondo was still waiting for a call from a 'security specialist' to whom he had sent word to contact him as a matter of priority.

At sunrise the following day, and after a totally uneventful night, both Sopwith and Ali knew they had not had enough sleep, and their love life was temporarily in tatters, but that was a small sacrifice to pay for feeling secure. They ate rusks and drank tea and then, as soon as possible got airborne again, once more in very good weather. Their heading to the DRC would take them across the north-east of Nigeria and a sliver of Cameroon, then over the Central African Republic, so they decided to fly higher than they had been, for fear of becoming a target once again for the hotheads who had already tried once to take them out. While flying over the Central African Republic they would proceed at a lower altitude. When, after an uneventful flight, they crossed into the DRC, they saw a huge thunderstorm building up in the south and had to skirt the massive cumulo-nimbus build-up. Keeping a careful eye on the huge storm, they found they had to travel much farther eastwards than planned, until eventually, when they we able to head more towards the south again, found themselves over the north-east of the DRC, having managed to avoid the storm completely.

In the far distance Sopwith thought he could see a scar in the lush green, bushy vegetation, and asked Ali to head towards it.

They soon came across a large river, which their Satnav informed them, was the Kibali River, and the scar was alongside the river. As they got closer Sopwith could make out what seemed to be a canal being dug to bypass a bend in the river. Ali carefully lost altitude and they flew a wide circle around the huge construction site. Sopwith could see a large fleet of earthmoving equipment engaged at digging away at the canal, which appeared to be nearing completion. At one end of the canal, where it re-joined the Kibali River, there were large concrete structures in the process of being built. Numerous temporary-looking structures were built on a site alongside the project, including a large collection of mobile-home type housing units and office facilities, in the otherwise unpopulated area. More importantly, from Sopwith and Ali's point of view, an unsurfaced airstrip ran along the one side of the compound: the windsock hanging listlessly in the still air.

"A large project like this has to be undertaken by an international company," Sopwith said, "The DRC, on its own, does not have the capacity to build something like this. I reckon we take a chance and put down. What do you say, love?"

"I'm all for it; I'll approach from the south, away from the construction."

Ali brought the 172 Solar down to earth smoothly, landing perfectly, as only she seemed to be able to do with consistency. The small strip was totally deserted, but not far away from the offices. A few people looked their way, but otherwise totally ignored them.

They removed their holsters, hiding the pistols in their waistbands covered by their shirts, not wanting to be seen walking around with guns. They locked the cabin doors and walked towards the buildings, asking for directions to the 'management' offices. They were shown a mobile office building, and after Sopwith had knocked, he opened the door and walked in. It was air-conditioned inside and very comfortable compared to the humid heat without.

"May we see someone in charge?" asked Sopwith.

"That will be me," answered a very friendly-looking man, dressed in shorts and T-shirt emblazoned with 'Building Africa' across his chest.

He stood up from a desk, his hand extended, "Alan Vosloo, consulting engineer of this project."

Sopwith offered his own hand in turn, and said, "Sopwith Jones," then turning towards Ali said, "Alison Jones, my wife."

Ali shook his hand too and they were offered a seat and something to drink. They both nearly yelled, "A cold coke, if you have!" and Alan walked to a fridge and pulled out three ice cold Coca-Colas.

"Sopwith; that is a very uncommon name. I remember reading about an aircraft in the First World War with that name; any connection?" asked Alan.

"Right in one guess, Alan. My grandfather was an absolute aircraft nut right from the dawn of manned aviation and named my father after that aeroplane's designer. My dad passed the name on to me."

"What a great story. So what brings you folk here?"

"We are flying through Africa," Sopwith replied, quite truthfully, "and we had to deviate from our heading to avoid a massive storm earlier, I wonder if you saw it?"

"Yeah, it certainly was a big one, and fortunately passed to the north of us."

"Well, being a bit off track, we decided to put down when we saw your strip with nothing else in sight, to check out our plane and hopefully have a bit of a break."

"That'll be absolutely no problem at all. We have a couple of guest houses that are not in use now, so you're welcome to make yourselves at home. No longer than two nights, unfortunately, as we are expecting a big government delegation wanting to tour the site the day after tomorrow. Quite honestly, they are more interested in the food and drink that we can provide for them, than looking at the progress of the job."

"That is wonderfully kind of you, Alan. Do you perhaps have access to the internet so that we can contact our friends to let them know where we are?"

"Yes, we have; the whole site is covered by Wi-Fi. Here is the password," he offered, and wrote it down, passing it over to Sopwith. "Please join us for dinner tonight. It will be great talking to different people for a change. We do not have many visitors here." He then called someone to show them the way to a guesthouse.

They walked back to the plane, unloaded a few bags and were taken to a very comfortable mobile home. They raced to see who could get into the shower first, but it resulted in a tie, so they both ended up in the shower together and, of course, finally ended up by making love. This was enormously satisfying to them, made even sweeter by the sense of safety and comfort of being where they were.

They walked to Alan's mobile home later, to be joined also by two of Alan's senior engineers. They were all South Africans, employed by the South African company that was engaged in the project. Alan described, with pride, the nature of the undertaking, which he called the 'Azambi Hydro-electric Project'. Part of the Kibali River's flow would be diverted into the one-kilometre-long canal currently under construction. At the far end of the canal, the point at which the river was re-joined, the water's discharge would drive two hydro-electric turbines, creating power for the Kibali Gold Mine further to the south. He further explained that this type of generation system, known as 'run-of-river', was a relatively recent innovation; far cheaper than building a dam on the river.

Their hosts were curious about Sopwith and Ali's 'flying safari', as they had termed it; their questions being fielded and answered ad lib. They stuck close to the truth by saying that Sopwith was an aeronautical engineer taking some time out, and Ali was a recently retired air force pilot, but made no mention of the unusual aircraft they were flying. Sopwith very pointedly quizzed Alan on other large construction projects ongoing in Africa and was excited to hear of a massive international infrastructural project underway in northern Mozambique.

After a tasty meal of braaied rump steak and fresh salads, along with good conversation and a glass of Merlot from the Western Cape winelands, Sopwith and Ali went back to their guest house with its lovely comfortable bed, after two nights of sleeping rough on bare earth.

The day had passed in England with no progress being made in trying to find the two flyers, and in South Africa, Minister Masondo was still trying to contact security specialists.

During the next morning and with a full day still available to plan and get themselves organised, Sopwith and Ali set about doing just that. The first thing Sopwith did was to send a detailed email to Ben Dougmore explaining exactly what had taken place, including when and why they had left England. He told Ben they were at the construction site at Azambi but that it was their intention was to try and find a place further to the south to hole-up while they entrusted him to fight the South African Government's false charges. They then checked-over the 172 Solar very carefully and re-stocked their water supply. They still had plenty of food available, so that presented no problem.

Alan invited them on a tour of his project, and although it was extremely interesting, Sopwith spent as much time as he could trying to subtly get details from him about the big project in Mozambique. He learned, as they walked and talked, that there were huge natural gas deposits under the sea floor off the northern Mozambique coast. The construction, centred on the Afungi Peninsula, included tapping into the gas deposits and laying undersea pipelines to bring the gas ashore. Massive pre-treatment facilities and gigantic storage tanks were being built, as well as a quay to enable ships to collect the processed, liquefied natural gas (LNG) for export. Alan pointed out, too, oddly enough, that South

African engineers and contractors had been slow to react to the emergence of the project, and so had hardly any representation on site, with most entities involved being French, Australian, Dutch, and Korean. That sort of multinational make-up suited Sopwith's thoughts of doing a disappearing act for a while and made up his mind that the Afungi Peninsular project would be their planned destination the following day.

Sopwith and Ali enjoyed a pot-roast dinner, as well as some more good wine, once again with Alan and his associates, and at the end of their evening together bade them farewell, explaining they intended leaving at very first light. Sopwith had been nervously anticipating that Alan might offer them fuel for their aircraft, but this did not happen. Sopwith presumed that because they had not asked for any, none had been offered.

Before settling down, Sopwith checked his email inbox and was disappointed that there was not yet any reply from Ben Dougmore. For the second night in a row, they were about to enjoy each other and their lovely bed to the maximum.

At that day's progress briefing to the First Sea Lord at Whitehall, Rear Admiral Ron Hubbard reported on the NovaSAR satellite. He informed the meeting that the satellite was being successfully used to monitor ocean traffic. Only with the help of the PM's office had he received agreement from Joint Forces Command to help on this mission, but they required precise and workable co-ordinates on where to begin looking.

"Thanks Ron," said the First Sea Lord. "That is of no virtual use to us, as we cannot point at the map of Africa and say, 'there'. What about Royal Air Force drones?"

"The very same problem, sir," replied the officer who had been tasked to find out. "They also need far more defined reference points than simply 'Africa'."

"Thank you. Has there been no feedback of any kind? Not even from our spooks at GCHQ who sniff the internet?"

There was silence in the room.

"What is the present position of HMS Queen Elizabeth?" he asked.

"Just off Gibraltar. She will be re-fuelled and provisioned en route to-morrow."

"Right then, gentlemen that's all we can do for the moment. If anything of interest breaks, I want to be the first to hear about it."

Minister Masondo finally had a meeting set up for the following day with an organisation calling itself 'Security Without Borders'.

That same evening, at the Azambi Hydro-electric Project, Jules Demet, a young Canadian trainee engineer, was returning to camp from the construction site, and upon passing the airstrip for the first time since Sopwith and Ali landed, saw the Cessna 172 parked there. He had not been aware of its arrival at all, nor did he know what it was doing there, but none of that interested him. He was an enthusiastic plane-spotter, and just like any keen birder would do on seeing an uncommon species of bird, he took a good look at it. He was pretty certain he knew what type of aircraft it was and took good clear pictures of it to post online. Back in Canada he had forever been hanging around airports in his spare time, but this would be his first online post from Africa, and he was terribly excited about that. Returning to the camp he first had dinner, as he had been on site all day, and was very hungry. He then showered, but before going to bed he set up his laptop and downloaded the pictures he had taken with his cell phone. He first compared the plane to pictures of Cessna aircraft on their homepage, and decided that it was a 172, albeit quite an old model. He posted the pictures on his favourite site, the Facebook page 'Plane Spotters of Canada', and posted: *'Hi everyone. You all know I am in Africa for the year, but I have to show off that there are actually planes in the region! This is an old Cessna 172 I saw parked on our little dirt runway today. Miss Ya all, keep spotting and posting.'*

It did not take long after Jules had pressed the 'enter' key on his laptop before a silent alarm notification went off in the inner workings of the Government Communication HQ in Cheltenham, England; the home of the Tempora internet monitoring system. The alarm was in response to the system picking up the trigger words 'Cessna 172' and 'Africa' in Jules Demet's Facebook post. After spotting the high alert status, the operator who had detected the alarm called his superior. All details of the post were gathered and forwarded, by email, to the First Sea Lord's office, and marked 'Urgent' as well as 'Highly Confidential'. Those words ensured that the duty office read the email immediately and he picked up the phone to Rear Admiral Hubbard.

"I am terribly sorry to bother you in the middle of the night sir, but I have had word from GCHQ regarding their internet monitoring. I think we have found Lt Murray sir," and told him about the Facebook post that had been detected. Hubbard instructed that the Facebook post be read aloud to him, and having listened to it, asked, "So where in Africa is the little dirt runway then?" The duty officer remained silent.

"Are you on Facebook? Do you know anything about Facebook?"

"I am sir. A little sir."

"Well log onto Facebook now, go into that page, like the post, or whatever you are meant to do on there, and ask the guy who posted it to be your friend. If you get that right, ask him where he is. This is the easy way, and if you don't get that right, it is going to take time to find out who the poster is, and his location, so I will very much appreciate your best efforts here, officer."

Having posted his pictures, Jules Demet decided to send an email to his family, updating them on his experiences in the DRC. It had been a while since he had last sent them an email, so he had a lot to write about. After an hour of writing, he pressed the send button and was just about to shut down when he received a notification from 'Spotters of Canada'; someone had liked his post already! He was not going to miss this opportunity, so opened the Facebook page. He was only a little sad when he saw that it was not one of his regular friends on the site, but a person unknown to him. This person had liked the post and asked to be a friend. 'Why not,' he thought, 'they must be like-minded if the post has been seen and liked.' He accepted the new friend and saw that he was an officer in the Royal Navy Fleet Air Arm, so it made sense that he liked aviation posts. Once he had 'befriended' this person, he was asked where in Africa the little dirt runway was situated. Although cautious on Facebook, Jules did not see why he couldn't tell this new friend where he was, so explained by return:

'I am on field study, working with engineers building the Azambi Hydro-electric Project on the Kibali River in the Democratic Republic of the Congo. The dirt strip serves the construction site, and this is the first plane I have seen since I have been here.'

'Thank you,' came the reply, and then Jules noticed that his new 'friend' had logged out of Facebook immediately after replying. 'Hmm,' he thought, 'oddball, that guy.'

The duty officer telephoned the Rear Admiral once again and passed on the detail he had obtained.

"Hallelujah! Well done, my man! Keep a lid on all of this for the time being and leave the rest up to me. Thank you once again."

Hubbard was not yet ready to wake up the First Sea Lord with the news; he had work to do. He struggled for a while to get hold of someone at Joint Forces

Command who could action the use of the NovaSAR, but finally did, and asked that the construction site at Azambi be photographed by the satellite as soon as possible. He could not go back to sleep, so remained seated in his small home office doing some paperwork, awaiting news of the satellite search.

Joint Forces Command had set the task in motion through an operator; a civilian IT professional, who sat at a console littered with monitor screens and keyboards. He had begun the task by doing an internet search on the Azambi Project and found a rough location online. He then refined this using Google Earth, and once he had pretty accurate coordinates, he started his control of the NovaSAR satellite, which orbited the planet every ninety-seven minutes, and could photograph swathes of the earth varying in width, dependant on the resolution required, in daylight or darkness, even though cloud cover. He initially set the resolution very low to first try and find the airstrip as the satellite closed in on the coordinates he had entered. On the first pass nearing the exact coordinates, in total darkness, the operator saw the airstrip quite clearly and the aircraft parked there in low resolution. He saved a still picture of it, then spent the next ninety-odd minutes revising the resolution and camera angles. When the satellite next passed over, dawn was just breaking, and he received very good, clear pictures of the aircraft, partially side on, then directly overhead and then from the other side, as the satellite moved on. He saved these pictures, and while awaiting the next orbit to take a final round of pictures, studied the ones he had last taken. There were two people walking towards the aircraft, each carrying bags. The operator became concerned for what the next pass would reveal. On the last pass over the airstrip, now in broad daylight, the images revealed his concern to have been correctly founded. There was no longer an aircraft on the strip. He attached the pictures that he had saved to an email report which he then transmitted to the Joint Forces Command duty officer.

The intrepid flyers could never have known that high resolution pictures had been taken of the two of them just before boarding the 172 Solar in preparation to leave Azambi airstrip. They took off as the sun rose, on a heading which would overfly Rwanda, Burundi, and Tanzania and onward to the most north-easterly corner of Mozambique. They had more than enough daylight to get to their destination, as they estimated that they only had a little over two thousand kilometres to travel.

In Port Alfred, Ben Dougmore, upon arriving in his office after a two-day break to spend some time with his grandchildren in Port Elizabeth, was thrilled to receive Sopwith's email. Ben had already been visited by an envoy from the British Embassy in Cape Town and had provided a sworn affidavit that Sopwith's aircraft development had been all his own work, with no input from the Government. The envoy had informed Ben that Sopwith had fled the UK for fear that the South African extradition request would be carried out but could provide no information as to where Sopwith had fled. So, the news Sopwith had provided in his email was no news at all to Ben, other than him now knowing that they had been briefly staying at Azambi. Ben fired off a quickly worded mail to Sopwith to tell him, firstly, that he was running from nothing, as the British Government certainly had no intention of extraditing him, and secondly, that his British citizenship was assured. He set up the mail so that he received a 'read' notification. Ben forwarded the email he had received from Sopwith to the embassy, in the hope that it might be of some assistance to the British Government in their efforts to find Sopwith.

In Pretoria, Minister Masondo had his first meeting with one Kenneth Le Grange, the purported owner of 'Security Without Borders' (SWB). Masondo explained his quest to find the missing Sopwith Jones who was apparently accompanied by a British military pilot, Alison Murray, and that it was understood that they had left England for Morocco. This information had been gleaned by the South African High Commission in London and been passed on to Masondo.

"Minister, please let me first explain that our services are not cheap. We pay excellent salaries to our highly trained staff. The cost of logistics and travelling throughout Africa is extremely expensive, and that of obtaining information is just as dear. Above all, we offer a solution-driven service without your having to know how we achieve our outcomes."

"This I understand," said Masondo, knowing how easy it was for him to authorise expenditure on an 'emergency tender' basis. "I definitely want you to locate this man and bring him to me."

"OK, I will draw up an agreement, which, once signed, and a five hundred thousand Rand deposit received, we can begin. I will in the meantime start making enquiries around the continent."

Le Grange knew, that as powerful as the internet was to the western world, the colloquially-termed 'bush telegraph' in Africa is almost as effective as the internet.

The Joint Forces Command duty office emailed the results of the NovaSAR satellite's achievements to Rear Admiral Hubbard, who received them without having slept at all since receiving the call about the whereabouts of Sopwith and Alison. He read the email with disdain, thinking that they were so close, but still far from bringing them in. He studied the photographs which were so clear that he could recognise both Jones and Murray when he zoomed in on them. He phoned the duty officer back, imploring him to continue the search using the satellite.

"We cannot help, sir. NovaSAR cannot be used in that sort of application. Even if by some pure fluke the satellite picked up an image of the aircraft in flight, by the next orbit that plane will be over ninety minutes, or hundreds of kilometres, away. The best we can do for you is to react as quickly as possible once you have a possible firm static location again."

Hubbard phoned the First Sea Lord at home with an update. Whilst not being too pleased that he had not been told about it at the outset, and disappointed with the outcome, he was still upbeat.

"We are at least getting warmer. We know that by the end of the day they can be no further than about two thousand kilometres away from that airstrip, which narrows down our search area distinctly. I will immediately be commanding the HMS Queen Elizabeth to sail through the Suez and southwards, parallel to the east coast of Africa. Do you know if the Royal Marines have boarded yet?"

"They have sir, together with the refuelling and provisioning completed yesterday."

The First Sea Lord then made the satellite call to the aircraft carrier and ordered them to make way, full speed ahead for station in the Indian Ocean off the coast of Dar es Salaam.

He had no sooner ended that call when his email alerted him to an incoming message. The message which had originated at the British Embassy in Cape Town, and arrived on his desk the long way round, was a copy of Sopwith's mail to Ben Dougmore, with the vital clue that they were '*to try and find a place to hole-up further south.*' So they now knew, at least, that Sopwith and Murray were heading south from Azambi which was situated in the north-east of the DRC.

The First Sea Lord, with a large map of Africa on his desk in front of him, put his deep-thinking cap on and pondered their next move.

Kenneth Le Grange had spent hours on both cell phone and satellite phone contacting his sources of information across the continent, promising vast rewards for information on the light aircraft that had arrived in Morocco five days before. Towards the end of the day he had his first snippet of information to hand. He had cultivated sources to watch over the movements of Boko Haram in Nigeria and one of these sources called him on his satellite phone.

"It is said that a Boko Haram unit was in Niger to capture some kids from a school there. They saw a small infidel plane fly over and were able to shoot it down. One of the men on the flank tried to capture the pilot but was shot dead. The unit got to the plane and saw one male infidel and one female infidel, but those infidels shot at them and then jumped into the plane and flew off. My source is true."

Kenneth thanked him and decided to transfer the reward for the information, as he had promised. He assumed that this incident could only have involved the furtive aircraft as if it had been a normal flight, news of the incident would have been reported and would have been picked up by news reporters. The fact that the occupants were one male, and one female could not be a coincidence either.

'So, last seen in Niger four days ago. Where next?' he wondered.

His next information came from an entirely unexpected source and did not cost him one cent. Of the many varied contacts that SWB had spread across sub-Saharan Africa, one was a standard security guard set-up at the construction site of the new Azambi Project in the DRC. His guards posted on that site kept routine logs of all vehicles entering and exiting the site. The guard on duty at the time of our flyers' visit there had been exceptionally diligent, and had noted their aircraft register number in his logbook.

Quite obviously Kenneth had made his entire staff aware that one of their new commissions was to find an aircraft, and when the superintendent inspected the guard's logbook that day, he reported the logging of the aircraft to his head office. This information finally filtered through to Kenneth at the very end of the day. 'This could be a coincidence,' he thought, as he could not verify if it was, in fact, the aircraft he sought, as he had no knowledge of the register number. He then simply called Alan Vosloo, the resident engineer on site with whom he dealt regarding the guarding requirements and asked him about his visitors who had arrived by air.

"Yes, we did have unexpected visitors. Really nice people who had been put off course by the massive thunderstorm we had in the area two days ago. They spent two nights with us and left at first light this morning."

"Did you perhaps get your visitors' names?" asked Kenneth.

"Yes of course. The gentleman was Sopwith Jones, a very unusual name, hey? And his wife, Alison; a retired air force pilot."

"Thank you, Alan. I am really just following up on the competence of my guards by making sure they are completing their logbooks accurately."

'Well, that was simple.' He now knew where his fugitives were that morning. He also knew that the information Alan had given him did not tie in perfectly with his briefing from Masondo. There was supposed to be a 'Jones' and a 'Murray', but he chuckled to himself that Jones was pretending that Murray was his wife so that he could sleep with her without embarrassment. He had a feeling he was going to make some very easy money out of Minister Masondo.

Chapter Six

The First Sea Lord had spent a good part of the day in his office pondering where next his Lieutenant and her companion had decided to fly to southwards from Azambi. While discussing this with Ron Hubbard, they both agreed on a probable theory, which was premised around the fact that the pair had landed at a construction site airstrip. It was safe to deduce, therefore, that they had most likely favoured this destination over any possible commercial airfields, which might have led to them being identified. Their only other option was to have put down in the bush, but there they would have had no contact with the outside world, and the reality that they could not possibly have just carried on hiding themselves away indefinitely.

Conceivably their next destination might also be another construction site. Thus, excited by this prospect, the First Sea Lord had Martha search online for large construction projects on the African sub-continent which were no further distant than two thousand kilometres south of Azambi.

A short while later she handed over a short list of construction sites, and their approximate locations, confessing: "This is the best I can do, sir." The First Sea Lord and Rear Admiral Hubbard studied the list, then drew a two-thousand-kilometre arc south of Azambi on a map of Africa, discarding the locations of any construction sites that fell outside the arc. This left only two probable sites. One was the construction of a road in Zambia, which Martha's research informed them, was being undertaken by a Chinese company. The other was the development of an offshore natural gas field, and its facilitating infrastructure, on the coast of northern Mozambique. Martha had established that the major in investor in this multi-billion-pound project was the French company, Total, but there were supporting role-players from all over the world also involved in the construction.

"This is not even worth flipping a coin for," said the First Sea Lord. "My common sense tells me straight away that that the gas site is where they could be headed, rather than the road construction. It is a far bigger site with multinationals involved, where they may think they can easily blend in. Let's find the place."

They took the information that Martha had supplied, and soon found the site on Google Earth. They noted that the closest airstrip was not far from a hotel, just north of the town of Palma, and close to the actual construction site, then recorded the geographical co-ordinates of the airstrip.

The First Sea Lord said to Ron, "Please get these co-ordinates to Joint Forces Command and tell them we have information that the fugitive aircraft may be there from late this afternoon. Ask them to have a look at the strip for us by using the NovaSAR. If they want the source of the information, tell them that it is confidential; there is no need to let them know it is just our hunch, is there?"

Rear Admiral Ron Hubbard returned to his office and had a call put through to Joint Forces Command, to whom he passed on their 'intelligence', including the required co-ordinates, as to where the plane they were looking for may be located. He was assured that NovaSAR would be tasked to photograph the airstrip near Palma.

Kenneth Le Grange had also been considering where the aircraft may have been flown to during the day. He had not come up with anything as definitive as the educated guess thought out by the First Sea Lord and Ron Hubbard. He had no clear idea at all, in fact, about Sopwith and Ali's possible whereabouts, but did however, have all SWB personnel contacted who were busy guarding job sites, reminding them to be on alert for the aeroplane being sought.

The aircraft register number was now known, and passed on to all the sites. Included in the company's contracts was the big new Total gas extraction job on the Fungi Peninsula in northern Mozambique. Kenneth put through a personal phone call to his manager there, one Phil Brown.

"Phil, you know about the aircraft we have the alert on. Well we now have a register number," Kenneth said, passing on the details.

"As a precaution, just for this afternoon, and until last light, place one of your most reliable guards at the airstrip, duly armed with a radio. The runway is not lit, so nothing will come in after dark. But if nothing lands this afternoon, don't worry about the added surveillance any further; it's only for this afternoon."

Phil acknowledged Kenneth's instructions, and immediately had one of his guards, Juma Tembe, transported to the airstrip for the afternoon, with instructions to radio him direct, should the aircraft that they were looking for land there.

Sopwith and Ali were experiencing great weather on their flight southwards. Having passed over Uganda, crossed the equator, and then the border into Tanzania over Lake Victoria, south of the famed Entebbe Airport, they were stunned by the scenery. To their west were the last virgin jungles on the continent, home to the few remaining Great Apes on the planet still living in their natural habitat. Lake Victoria, the largest lake in Africa, seemed clear and unpolluted, and as they made landfall, Mount Kilimanjaro stood proudly in the east. It looked majestic, looming higher than they were flying, with just a smidgen of snow on its peak, rising to five thousand eight hundred metres above sea level. More importantly from their point of view, its summit was four thousand nine hundred metres above ground level.

They then flew over the Serengeti Plains and saw vast numbers of wildebeest at the extreme southern limit of their annual migration, common for that time of the year. They then saw Lake Tanganyika to their west, straddling the border of the DRC and Tanzania. This lake is the longest fresh-water lake in the world; stunning in its beauty, with water so blue it was difficult absorb that such colour exists in nature.

Not much further to the south, Lake Malawi bore up on them from the west, and they knew they were getting close to their destination. Lake Malawi, renowned for its vast variety of fish species, was also stunningly beautiful; as blue as any Caribbean idyll; mostly crystal clear to its bed in the shallower waters, and with its islands appearing to float on the surface.

Immediately after crossing the border into Mozambique, and almost regretfully tearing their attention away from the beauty beneath them, they sought out the airstrip that marked their destination. It was not long before they spotted the dirt strip, circled it, and found it to be seemingly deserted. To the north-east of the strip was the huge construction site, and beyond was the vastness of the Indian Ocean. To the south they could see what looked like a hotel, with the town a little further beyond, which their Satnav informed them, was the town of Palma.

Ali, taking her turn at the controls, brought the 172 Solar to the ground as smoothly as always, and they taxied to an unpaved parking apron. Ali shut down the motor and Sopwith set about driving his stakes into the ground to secure the aircraft. While he was busy with this, he became aware that he had company.

Standing up he saw a smartly dressed young man in long khaki trousers and a white shirt which bore, on each shoulder, the insignia of a shield-shaped emblem with the letters 'SWB' in white on a black background. Beneath a wide-brimmed bush hat, he saw the shiny white teeth of a huge grin on the dark-skinned man's shaded face.

"Hello sir, how are you? I am also fine. I am Juma Tembe. My boss at SWB is here to meet you very soon. I radio for him. He comes now. You got any Coca-Cola?" All uttered in a rapid stop-start breathless staccato.

"No coke son, but some very special water," Sopwith said, realising that the man may have been standing in the heat for some time without anything to drink. He fetched some sachets of the survival pack water from the plane and handed two to Juma saying: "This is special water all the way from England. Very good for you; drink up!"

Juma looked at the sachet suspiciously, but when Sopwith bit the corner off his own and drank it down, Juma followed, his smile reappearing.

"Yes sir, very good! Very fresh."

When Juma had radioed his boss, Phil Brown, with the news that the aircraft had landed, Phil contacted Kenneth Le Grange immediately.

"Sir, my guard tells me it is definitely the plane, with a man and a woman the only occupants. How do you want me to handle this?"

"Phil don't spook them. They should in no way be a danger to you but be on your toes. Get them back to the company house on the pretext of being hospitable, but once there, and you have them secured inside, tell them that we have been contracted to take them to Pretoria. I will have our company plane at the strip first thing tomorrow to pick them up. Oh…sorry about landing this on you with your limited manpower, but you will have to post a guard on their aeroplane to secure it please."

Ali was now standing beside Sopwith, when they heard a vehicle driving down the access road to the parking apron, and then watched while a double-cab Toyota pick-up drew up alongside them. Two men climbed out, both wearing khaki trousers and white shirts sporting 'SWB' badges. Both were armed; the driver had a pistol of some type holstered on his hip, and the passenger with a small automatic rifle slung over his shoulder.

The driver came forward and said, "Phil Brown, manager SWB Palma; pleased to meet you," and stuck out his hand.

Sopwith did likewise and said, "Sopwith Jones, and my wife Alison. How can we help you?"

"Rather it is we helping you, Mr Jones," said Brown, "We keep watch over all aircraft arrivals here. As a safety measure we collect the pilots and passengers, other than those who are expected by the contractors. SWB is a private security company employed by the contractors to guard the construction site. However, of late our duties have become more than that. There is an ever-increasing terrorist threat in the area. A group known as Al-Shabaab, with allegiance to the Islamic State, is operating in the area, and becoming shockingly cruel in their intimidation of locals to join them. More than that, they are determined to stop any tourism in the area. The Mozambique Government has so far been wholly ineffectual in doing anything about it."

Other than his tale about keeping watch for all arrivals, the information Brown had given them about Al-Shabaab was totally true, and in fact, a much-sanitised version of what was taking place in the area.

"That is news to us," Sopwith said, glancing at Ali's distressed look, "but thank you. If you can drop us off at a hotel, we'll appreciate it?"

"There is no need for that. We have a lovely house on the outskirts of Palma; you will be welcome to stay with us. I believe you'll be more secure that way."

"That's very generous of you, thank you. Let us get our bags."

When Phil Brown told them there would only be a need for their clothing bags, as he would keep a guard posted on their aircraft, Sopwith started worrying about this overzealous protection. However, they collected their bags, locked the plane, and joined Phil and his companion in the pick-up. They both still had their pistols tucked into their waistbands, but the AK47 had been locked in the aircraft.

They arrived at a large, newly built brick and tile house and were shown inside. Sopwith noticed that the front door was locked behind them. Phil indicated two adjacent bedrooms but Ali, twirling her ring finger to show off her copper-thread wedding band, reminded him that they were married and would be sharing one room, which they then entered, dropping their bags on the floor. Pointing to their en suite bathroom, Phil suggested they were welcome to freshen up, and then join them for drinks followed by dinner.

"I don't feel at all comfortable with this, darling," said Sopwith. "Look at these bars on the window; it's as if we are being kept as prisoners. But we'll just have to go along with it for the time being and see what pans out."

They showered and changed into their last set of clean clothing, then joined Phil in the living room where they were offered cold Laurentino beers to drink. Sopwith noticed that every window he could see was covered with heavy bars to make sure no one ever got in or out of the house unless they happened to have an angle-grinder handy.

Once seated with beers in hand, Phil started speaking, "We have been employed by the South African Government to take you to Pretoria."

Sopwith started to stand, simultaneously reaching for his Browning, but a calming hand from Ali brought him back to his seat.

"And why should that be? We're both British citizens, and I am an officer in the Royal Navy Fleet Air Arm."

"I have no idea at all. I'm only following instructions from the owner of SWB, who'll be sending the company aircraft to collect you tomorrow morning. We'll have a permanent guard watching your aeroplane while you are away."

Sopwith said nothing; his mind racing as he wondered how on earth Minister Masondo had managed to track them. That matter was, of course, now totally irrelevant, and decisions needed to be made on how to handle their current predicament. Ali had certainly been correct in stopping him from drawing his weapon, as they had no chance of fighting their way out of the house. There were simply too many armed people around, and most importantly, he was not just going to start shooting civilian security personnel out of hand.

A dinner of maize meal, vegetables and some sort of meat stew was served, and although not the greatest tasting meal of his life, it filled Sopwith with healthy food. The two of them retired to their bedroom after dinner and sitting on the bed against pillows at the head of the bed, they discussed their options.

"I imagine that only a light aircraft will be sent to collect us. We are less than two thousand kilometres from Pretoria, and I can't see them owning any huge plane to send escorts with a pilot. So my guess is that there will only be a pilot, or maybe two, sent to collect us, so we may be able to get out of this scrape tomorrow. There is certainly nothing we can do while trapped in this house," said Sopwith, and with that they made love, fuelled by nervous energy, in anticipation of what the new day would bring.

That night, a different IT specialist manned the controls of the NovaSAR satellite which took clear pictures, even in the dark of the night, of the 172 Solar parked at the airstrip. These were sent via email to the First Sea Lord's inbox. When he reached his desk the next morning, he was gratified to discover that his guess as to where Sopwith and Alison had gone was proven correct. He called Ron Hubbard into his office, and showing him the pictures said, "Ron, please get hold of our intelligence community at MI6 to see what they can tell us about this area of Mozambique. What we would like to know, firstly, is what sort of government presence there is at that location, such as police or army, or any other Intel that may be useful. Secondly, establish from Joint Forces Command how long they can maintain surveillance of the area using NovaSAR."

Rear Admiral Ron Hubbard made his request to Intelligence via email and posed the question to Joint Forces Command.

Kenneth Le Grange contacted Barnabas Masondo first thing that same morning by the same means, informing the Minister that Sopwith Jones would be in Pretoria later in the day. Masondo was extremely happy to learn of SWB's success, thanking Le Grange; expansively promising him a 'big bonus'.

Phil Brown and his sidekick took Sopwith and Ali to the airstrip after they had eaten a large breakfast of bacon, egg, sausages, and baked beans. On arrival at the airstrip Sopwith wanted to collect a few things from his 172, but Phil told him clearly that nothing more was to be removed from it and that it would be well-guarded. Sopwith, was totally displeased about this, but managed to hold his tongue.

They had not been at the airstrip for more than fifteen minutes before a shiny Beechcraft G36 Bonanza landed from the south and taxied to the apron. After the noisy Teledyne Continental engine shut down, a single pilot opened the cockpit door, stepped onto the wing, then onto the ground, and came walking towards them.

"Hello everybody, I am your pilot today. Mike is the name; who are my pax?"

Phil Brown introduced himself, and then Sopwith and Ali as 'Mr and Mrs Jones'.

"So, it must be you, Mrs Jones who is the pilot. You must sit up front with me and give me a break, if you like?" he smiled at Ali.

"That'll be great, but please call me Ali, and my husband is Sopwith," and they all shook hands in a very friendly, civilised manner, considering the very unusual circumstances.

As they walked towards the Bonanza, Juma Tembe, back on day shift guarding the 172 Solar, came up to them to say goodbye, and added, with a huge toothy smile, "Don't worry, I will look after your aeroplane good for you."

They packed their bags into the small baggage hold and boarded the Bonanza. Mike did the pre-flight checks, explaining the checks to Ali as he went through them, and then, after checking everyone was belted in, started taxiing to his take-off position. He performed his last checks, opened the throttle, and took off from the strip.

The occupants of the Bonanza were unaware that they were being watched as they prepared to take off. Ghani Ibraimo, a trusted member of the local Al-Shabaab jihadist group, had been tasked to watch the airstrip. His instruction had come from the local leader Asim Khatib, known fearfully as AK, as AK himself had heard of a SWB guard being posted there. The previous day Ghani had observed the arrival of the small aeroplane with the infidel couple aboard and had informed Asim, who was curious about the goings on, asking to be kept fully informed.

When Ghani rang his leader on his cell phone to report that the infidels had now flown off in another aircraft, he was told to stay put, and keep watch to see what happened next. Ghani was a very patient man, well-respected for his abilities for lengthy spells of concealment in observation posts.

"Are you not calling-in your take off to any ATC?" Ali asked innocently, but eager to know what was within radio range.

"No, there's nothing within range here. Our first flight information region (FIR) will be Blantyre in Malawi, and we'll let them know where we are in about two hours. We'll be flying at an altitude of three thousand metres, at airspeed of just over three hundred kilometres per hour."

Sopwith, listening carefully, noted the time on his watch and started his planning, as he knew that whatever he was about to do must be done before Mike reported into Blantyre.

As soon as the Bonanza levelled out at their cruise altitude, and Mike had throttled the motor back to cruise speed, Sopwith made his move. He quietly withdrew his 9mm Browning from his waistband, and then leaning forward, waved it briefly in front of Mike's face. Before Mike could react in any way, Sopwith placed the barrel of the weapon on the back of Mike's neck.

"Mike, I am terribly sorry to have to do this to you, but we have just hi-jacked your Bonanza."

"What the fuck man?" exclaimed Mike.

"I'll explain everything. But first, relinquish control to Ali. After you have switched your radio off, do not touch another control again while we are with you. Do you understand?" asked Sopwith.

Glaring ahead angrily, Mike did not reply at all, and kept his hands on the controls.

"Mike, please be aware that I have no intention or desire to harm you in any way, but to maintain our freedom I have already shot one man on this journey so far, and if I have to, I'll do so again. If you have not released the controls by the time, I have counted to five, I'll kill you. One…two…three…" On the count of three Mike took his hands off the controls, then leant forward to turn the radio off.

"Good man, Mike! Ali, bring us around and head back to the airstrip while Mike and I have a chat."

"A pleasure, captain," Ali said, with a mock salute. Taking control of the Bonanza she started a gentle one-hundred-and-eighty-degree turn.

"Mike, please let me bring you up to speed with what is really going on here," said Sopwith, and he explained the false charges that the government had trumped-up against him.

"No doubt your company doesn't know the truth of the matter, so you're really innocent, and considering that you'll be returning a serving British officer to safety, maybe the Queen will give you a medal or something," he quipped, to try and lighten things up a bit. "Oh, and I would never have shot you man, but would probably have had to hit you on the head if you had not complied!"

Mike seemed to relax a little after Sopwith's explanation, while Ali brought the Bonanza in for yet another perfect touch down, and they taxied back to the apron. They stopped, and upon disembarking collected their bags while Sopwith loosely-trained his 9mm on Mike to ensure he did not have a change of heart. Sopwith explained what he wanted Mike to do.

Ghani Ibraimo observed the Bonanza returning to the airstrip and the gun-toting infidel apparently ordering the pilot around, so he phoned AK and tried his best to explain what strange things were going on. AK told him to keep observing, and that he and another militia would join him very soon.

Sopwith had been given a notepad by Mike and started writing on it. He recorded Ben Dougmore's email address as well as telephone numbers. He then wrote as briefly, but as clearly as he could, a synopsis of where they were, and what had transpired since their arrival. Without consulting Ali, he had decided he was going to turn himself in, as he was beginning to think he might be endangering his wife's life. He explained this in the note to Ben, saying that they would hand themselves over to Immigration at Lanseria Airport outside Johannesburg, and that Ben was to notify the British Embassy, and immediately start tackling the false charge issue. He handed the notepad back to Mike and asked him to send the note in an email to Ben, as well as confirm its receipt by phone. Sopwith was just about to reach out and shake Mike's hand when all hell broke loose.

He heard a fusillade of automatic gunfire and then saw Juma Tembe, who was standing about ten metres distant from them, perhaps waiting for another serving of pure English water, jerk twice and fall to the ground. Bits of earth spat up all around them as bullets hit the earth, and Sopwith pushed Mike so hard in the small of the back that he fell to the ground, then he himself dropped and rolled. He saw Ali doing the same out of the corner of his eye, then started firing his pistol in the direction from which the shots came. They heard the 'thwack' noises of bullets hitting the Bonanza and saw more lumps of dirt being thrown up around them. He became very aware that his pistol would have no effect over the distance he was trying to return fire, and that the bullets impacting the ground continued rain around them, but not too closely. He next saw one of their attackers come up on one knee with a rocket launcher on one shoulder, and saw it spit flame and smoke. Then with a whoosh of sound a rocket-propelled grenade struck the Bonanza which instantly turned into a fireball. They were lying on the ground far enough away not to be scorched by the intense heat. The automatic fire continued for a while as the blaze consuming the Bonanza gradually lessened. The automatic rifle fire then stopped as suddenly as it had started. A loud and clearly articulated instruction was called out.

"Infidels! Throw your little guns away now, far from yourselves. If you do not do that immediately we will kill you just as easily as the little traitor guard, we have already killed. Do it now!"

Neither Sopwith nor Ali hesitated, flinging their pistols as far away as they could.

"Put your hands flat on the tops of your heads, get up and start walking forward. Now!"

The three of them, all uninjured, did as they were told. Only after they started walking, did a group of about ten jihadists emerged from the bush at the edge of the apron, and upon reaching them, roughly grabbed them, and pulled them into the bush, leaving behind their pistols and luggage. They were manhandled into the rear of an old Toyota double-cab pick-up, and each of them was blindfolded with smelly hessian rags. They heard people climb into the front of the vehicle and others clambered onto the load body, then the Toyota engine started, and they moved forward.

Later that same morning, the First Sea Lord picked up the phone to take an incoming call from Rear Admiral Ron Hubbard, eager to hear any news from him.

"Sir, there are disturbing developments which you need to be aware of. I am in John Baker's office over at MI6; can you possibly join us here? I would not ask unless it was essential."

"No problem at all; I will be there as soon as possible. Thanks for calling me," said the First Sea Lord, who then hung up, asking Martha to call his driver to collect him at the Horse Guards' Avenue entrance. Gathering his briefcase and cell phone, he walked to the entrance and climbed into his car, telling the driver to take him to the MI6 building on Albert Embankment, Vauxhall. The drive was only about three kilometres, but to the First Sea Lord it seemed to take forever, and he had to bite his tongue to stop telling his driver to step on it.

The unique MI6 building overlooking the Thames from the Albert Embankment, had been designed using a combination of Art Deco styling, and clad in white granite, combined with turquoise glass facades in the style of the new millennium.

Upon their arrival the First Sea Lord was immediately escorted to John Baker's office. He knew only that John Baker was quite highly-ranked within the MI6, but more information than that about the man was purely on the proverbial 'need to know basis, but that did not bother him one iota; all that mattered to him was how much Baker could be of assistance with his current problem. He was greeted by Ron Hubbard and John Baker, and when seated, Ron began without any preamble.

"Join Forces Command has been most helpful with NovaSAR, and we have sequential images taken every hour and a half or so. Have a look," he said, pointing to the pictures (all time stamped) laid out on a board room table.

The first showed the 172 Solar alone on the apron, quite obviously in the dark at 0530. The next showed the 172 in the same position now in daylight and at 0720 but parked quite close by was another single-engine aircraft which he quickly recognised as a Beechcraft Bonanza. Scrutinising the photograph, he saw what looked like a security guard standing close to the 172. The following picture at 0910 showed the 172 still in the same place and the Bonanza was in the picture too, but in a different position. The security guard had moved closer to the Bonanza. The next image, one minute later, showed no change in the aircrafts' positions, but there were four people lying on the ground and upon inspecting the next, much enlarged image of these people, he could see that the security guard was lying on his back, arms splayed out and legs positioned oddly. With a shock he then saw that Lt Murray and Sopwith Jones were in prone positions with pistols in their hands as if they were firing in the direction of the bush alongside the apron. Next to them was another unknown man with his hands covering his head. The last picture on the table, taken another minute later showed a similar scene at a more oblique angle as the satellite flew on, and one other huge difference. The Beechcraft Bonanza was encompassed in a ball of flame.

Ron Hubbard continued, "It seems pretty straightforward to us. The Bonanza arrived at the airstrip, and by the next orbit of NovaSAR, it had moved position for whatever reason. It was then attacked by unknown people and blown up. Jones and Murray were firing at something and then disappeared. But we should have more answers shortly because John has established the ownership of the Bonanza through its register number. It is owned by a company called 'Security Without Borders', a private security business based in South Africa, with which John is familiar. He is awaiting a call from its owner, one Kenneth Le Grange." Just then, a phone on the boardroom table rang and John Baker answered.

"Good day Kenneth, John Baker here," the phone was on loudspeaker so everyone could hear.

"John, my favourite British spy; it's good to hear your voice. However, when I heard you wanted to speak to me, I immediately started worrying, as you only call me when you have problems," he said, chuckling.

"Kenneth, this time I believe it is you with the problem, being a burnt-out Beechcraft Bonanza at Palma airstrip in Mozambique. Want to tell me about it?"

"Hell, I knew you guys were quite good at keeping your ears to the ground, but this is remarkable. I thought it was only my staff that knew about this up until now."

"That's where you are wrong, thanks for the pat on the back anyway. But we really need your help to know exactly what is going on there. There are two

British subjects involved, with one being a commissioned officer in our forces, so we are particularly interested."

"Oh hell, John; I was contracted by a South African government minister to locate the Cessna 172 plane and its occupants and get them to Pretoria. We have a guarding contract at the Fungi Gas Development site and one of my guards spotted their arrival. I sent our Bonanza out there this morning to collect them. That's as much as I can say for the moment because the rest of the story will be more informative, direct from my manager on site, Phil Brown. I will have him phone you on this number very shortly. And by the way, although the South African minister told me that this was government business, and I was paid from a government account, I believe he is acting for his own pocket on this one. I will terminate my contract with him immediately."

"Thanks Kenneth, you are a good man."

"A pleasure, John; please contact me directly if you have any further questions, or requests for assistance. I'll have Phil phone you now."

Ron Hubbard quickly intervened before Kenneth put the phone down and said, "Kenneth, please can I ask you to double up on your guarding of the Cessna 172 aircraft at the airstrip? We cannot afford to lose that as well, and you can make the costs for our account. This is Rear Admiral Ron Hubbard from the Fleet Air Arm here."

"Certainly sir, but there will be no need to pay. I have received enough from the South Africans already."

The three members of the hierarchy of the British Navy and MI6 were still absorbing this astounding news when the phone rang and was immediately answered by John Baker.

"Baker here."

"Good day, sir; Phil Brown phoning from SWB in Palma, Mozambique. How can I help you, sir?"

"Ah, Phil; good of you to phone! Please fill us in on all of the events at Palma airstrip this morning."

"Well sir, I escorted Mr and Mrs Jones to the airstrip this morning where they were picked up by our company aeroplane."

"You mean Lt Alison Murray and Mr Sopwith Jones?"

"Mr Jones introduced themselves as Sopwith Jones and his wife Alison, sir. I saw her wedding ring, an unusual copper-coloured thing."

Hubbard and the First Sea Lord looked at each other questioningly. John Baker asked Phil to continue.

"They were introduced to our pilot, Mike, and behaved in a friendly way towards him. When they boarded the plane, Mike insisted that Mrs Jones should sit in the co-pilot's seat as he had been told that she was a pilot. The Bonanza took off and I returned to our compound in Palma to attend to my work." Phil paused, expecting to be questioned, but none were posed, so he carried on.

"About an hour and a half after they took off, maybe a little more, I heard gunfire and then a loud explosion coming from the direction the airstrip. Gunfire around here is common, what with Al-Shabaab operating in the area, but I had to investigate, so I gathered some of my staff and we drove out to the airstrip. We approached carefully on foot but soon realised the show was over. The Bonanza was by then a smouldering shell. We found one of our guards, Juma Tembe, lying dead with two bullet wounds in his torso. We also found two Browning 9mm pistols and a number of empty 9mm cartridges around, along with two kit bags and a notebook. I have kept all those items. We then scouted the bush alongside of the apron and found where the attack had been launched from, with many empty AK47 .762 cartridges and one empty plastic RPG 7 rocket case scattered about. It is obvious that the Bonanza returned to the strip after having taken off, but I do not know why."

"Have you any idea who the attackers could be?" asked John Baker.

"Yes. I am one hundred percent certain that this is the work of the Al-Shabaab jihadist group active in our area. They are the only militia in the area and use the AK47 as their weapon of choice."

"Do you think the Jones's and your pilot are still alive?"

"I am sure they are, sir. Al-Shabaab never remove the bodies of people they kill; they rather leave them lying around as an intimidation tactic. They also do not leave wounded, who they kill rather than look after."

"Would you possibly know where they are now?"

"Absolutely not, sir."

"Can you assist us to find them?"

"Only by means of trying to gather intelligence about the incident. We cannot possibly try and follow, or hunt them down, as the Al-Shabaab group is very large, well-equipped, and absolutely ruthless. We dare not try and take them on, sir."

"I understand. If you do receive any intelligence, please pass it to your boss, Kenneth, immediately. If those two Browning's are to hand, can you give me the serial numbers?"

"They are right here," and Phil Brown read both serial numbers out.

"Thanks. Please have them sent to Kenneth's office, along with the notebook and bags. Thank you very much Phil, you have been of great help. Goodbye."

Ron spoke next, explaining to the First Sea Lord that one of the reasons he had asked him to come across to MI6 was to hear John Baker's information on the jihadist group in the Palma region.

John went on to elaborate accordingly, "We have, for a while, had good intelligence about a growing number of jihadists in the Cabo Delgado province, where Palma is situated. We know that the group calls itself 'Al-Shabaab' and is allied to, and under the direct control of ISIS. Their leader is an evil Syrian by the name of Asim Khatib, known to the locals in the Palma region as 'AK'. As ridiculous as it sounds, this Asim Khatib once studied in England, at Oxford University, and created an extremist Islamist cell structure there, but when we uncovered the existence of the cell, he escaped the country before we could apprehend him.

"It seems he was sent to Mozambique to take command of the growing number of jihadists there. We understand that he is now successfully expanding the group throughout the Cabo Delgado Province at an alarming rate. His intimidation tactics are violent, with almost weekly beheadings and dismemberment of any defiant locals, to ensure his followers toe the line. There is an exodus of locals fleeing the region because of this. We have been keeping tabs on them as best we can because of the large number of British expats in the area who are working on the Total LNG plant on the Fungi Peninsula, and which we believe may well become a target of Al-Shabaab in time. So it seems your lieutenant is not in a very good place at all."

"On my God!" exclaimed the First Sea Lord. "This is damned awful. How can you help us get her out of there, John?"

"I am afraid I can do nothing other than feed you any intelligence we get. I will, of course, also inform GCHQ of pertinent key words to put into their internet monitoring system. I suggest you also liaise with Joint Forces Command about what other information their NovaSAR can collect. We simply cannot try and extract her. That will have to be some form of military mission, which you guys can organise far quicker than I could, if I had to try to request such help. I am sorry, but that is how it is."

Ron Hubbard and the First Sea Lord both thanked John Baker, and gathering up the satellite pictures, they returned to their offices in the First Sea Lord's car. During the short drive, the First Sea Lord said, "You know Ron, HMS Queen Elizabeth is still about five days away from that area, and I just do not know what the hell to do next."

"I understand, sir, but we will come up with something; we have to, and we will."

After his call to John Baker at MI6 in London, Kenneth Le Grange phoned Minister Barnabas Masondo.

"Good afternoon, Mr Minister, I have bad news for you."

"Ha! What can be bad now that you have my Mr Jones?"

"Well, that is exactly the point. I no longer have him or his lady. They, along with the pilot of one of my company aircraft, have been captured by a terrorist group in Northern Mozambique."

"So, you must fetch them back; we have a contract."

"Are you not interested in how this happened, or who these people are?"

"Not at all. I am only interested in Mr Jones, and you must fetch him to me."

"They have been captured by an Islamic jihadist force, which should worry you very much; their presence being so close to your country. However, worry or not, I must terminate our contract, per the legal escape clauses, as SWB cannot possibly challenge the jihadist group."

"I refuse. You will bring Mr Jones to me, or I will sue you, or whatever."

"Mr Minister, our contract has been terminated; please try to understand this."

"Ha! I will find someone else bigger than you. You must give me my money back immediately."

"I am afraid not, as it was a non-refundable deposit. On top of that, your department will be receiving an invoice from my accountants for twenty-one million, six hundred thousand rand, being the replacement cost of our Beechcraft Bonanza aircraft destroyed during the execution our contract with you."

"You cannot do that to me, Le Grange! This job was not above board anyway."

"I was very aware of that Mr Minister, right from the beginning, so you are going to have to be very creative. If you are not creative enough, I will have to claim the payment directly from you in your personal capacity, and I do know that you have, at the very least, that amount of money hidden away in various parts of the world. I will give you five days to come up with a solution to your problem, so please let me know. Goodbye now" and he ended the call.

Kenneth thought about Barnabas Masondo. The fellow thought he had been running in a one-horse race and would win millions for himself, but alas, he was no longer even in the race. And without fail, SWB would extricate the money from him for the destroyed Bonanza.

Chapter Seven

The pick-up into which Sopwith, Ali and Mike had been bundled travelled for only about ten minutes before stopping. They were forced out of the vehicle, and their blindfolds removed before being used to tie their wrists together behind their backs. They were in dense bush with only a track visible along which the Toyota had travelled, but Sopwith did manage to spot the position of the sun, indicating that it was late morning. The pick-up left them, together with six heavily armed men dressed in very well-worn jungle print camouflage fatigues, who then bustled them into single file, forcing them to walk along a very narrow path through the bush by jabbing rifle butts into various parts of their bodies. It was difficult for them to walk over the uneven ground with their wrists bound. Every now and then one or other of them would tumble to the ground, having tripped on a root or the unevenness of the going, only to be jabbed and yanked to their feet by the unsympathetic guards, and forced to move on. Ali was bearing the brunt of the manhandling by the guards, who grabbed her breasts at every opportunity. One guard delighted in rubbing his large erection against her back whenever he found the opportunity. Protests by Ali were met with slaps to her face, and when Sopwith tried to intervene he received a heavy clubbing to his head with a rifle butt, slicing open the skin on his forehead, before being forced to walk on, his right eye nearly blinded from the blood pouring into it from the cut.

Whenever he caught a glimpse of the sun's position Sopwith did manage to keep track of direction in which they were heading; determining that they were walking due north, and thus towards the Tanzanian border. Walking became ever more difficult the hotter it became, with sweat pouring into, and burning their eyes, as there was no way to wipe it away. After about two hours Sopwith eventually asked for some water, as they were by now terribly thirsty, but the only response he received was from one guard who just laughed out loud, indicating that he thought Sopwith's request was absurd. After another three hours the pilot, Mike, who was undoubtedly not as fit as both Sopwith and Ali, fell to the ground and lay immobile on his stomach, his face pressed into the dirt. Two guards tried to lift him back to his feet, but he was as limp and floppy as a rag doll. The march had now come to a halt as they propped Mike up against a tree, poured some water from a water bottle over his face, and when he had recovered a little, was allowed some water to drink. An appeal by the others to also have a drink was once again met with nothing but laughter. Forcing Mike back to his feet, they were all prodded into continuing the march.

Sopwith continuously sought out eye contact with Ali, hoping in some way he could convey positive looks to her to give her some strength in handling the ordeal. Mike was barely managing to walk, and often had to be held up by the two guards at his sides. The water that he had been given earlier seemed to have passed straight through him, as he appeared to have wet himself. After what Sopwith guessed were nearing four hours of walking, stumbling and a few stops, they came to a halt in a small, newly slashed clearing in the bush. They had so far not seen any sign of habitation along the way, and the hut they saw erected to the one side of the clearing certainly did not seem habitable. It was a low, round structure, built of small, vertical tree trunks planted into the ground, topped with a conical roof, untidily clad with grass. A door made of latticed branches was pulled open; the three of them pushed roughly into the hut, one after another, then the door was securely shut behind them.

The three of them lay sprawled across the earthen floor of the structure. Mike was breathing very heavily; semi-comatose. Both Sopwith and Ali were very tired and desperately thirsty, but nevertheless lucid and alive to their situation. Sopwith's cut had formed a scab, so the bleeding had at least stopped. He slid across the ground and gave Ali a very gentle kiss on her parched and chapped lips with his own dried blood-covered ones. They heard no sound from outside the hut, but assuming that there must be at least a guard posted, Sopwith whispered into Ali's ear.

"They have not taken my Leatherman; it is still on my belt under my shirt. I will guide you with directions as I feel your hands move on me. Try the impossible and pull it out of the pouch, then we will tackle getting a blade open."

She manoeuvred her back to his hip, and her bound hands started searching by feel. Following Sopwith's directions of 'up', or 'down', she located the Leatherman in its pouch. Frustratingly slowly she managed to ease it out of the pouch until she eventually had it firmly held in one hand. Then Sopwith, with

105

his back to her, located the implement in her hand, and by careful feel, found the top of the largest blade. He inserted his thumbnail in the grove of the blade, pulled, and out it came, into the extended position. They both wanted to cheer, but dared not, staying silent instead.

"I want you to cut my bonds," Sopwith whispered, "You are not going to be able to feel anything, so follow my directions precisely, and when I say 'cut', do so with all you might. The blade should be sharp, but the hessian strands are tough."

After an achingly long time, with Sopwith guiding her by the feel of the blade on his arms and wrists, he felt certain that the knife was able to slice through the hessian rag, so fearlessly told Ali to make the cut. She did as he asked, praying that she did not slice open his wrists. The hessian bond gave way, together with one small slice of skin on his wrist. Sopwith's hands were free. Taking the Leatherman from her, he cut the loose piece of hessian away from the knot on his other wrist and bound his bleeding wrist with it and knotted it in place, and then hugged and kissed her. By holding his wrists together, it still appeared that he was bound with the hessian rag.

"I am not going to remove yours," he said. "I am scared that if I take yours and Mike's off you may not be able to pretend to be still bound, so for the time being I will use my hands to help you with anything I can." Ali took this decision in her stride, understanding his logic. The only light in the hut, filtering in through the small gaps between the tree branch walls and latticed door, was starting to fade, and the first thing Sopwith did, with the help of the Leatherman, was to dig a small latrine pit furthest away from the door. He helped Ali pull down her trousers and assisted her to squat and relieve herself, and then he followed suit, after which he buried the Leatherman in the dirt close to the door. As the darkness deepened, Sopwith made Mike as comfortable as he could, and then curling up with Ali, they lay down for the night, exchanging whispered thoughts about what was happening to them and how they thought things might turn out.

There were swarms of mosquitoes around, biting them incessantly, but Sopwith did not say a word to Ali about the dangers of contracting malaria, as there was precisely nothing, they could have done about it. Doing their best to ignore the itchy bites, and their now desperate thirst, as well as Mike's occasional moaning, they spent the night dozing on and off until the first glimmers of light started penetrating the hut the next morning.

There was still no sound at all from outside the hut other than birdsong, so Sopwith pushed on the door. It was firmly held in place, but by what means, he could not see, so there was no way of getting out of the hut. As the light grew brighter so did the increase in air temperature. Their thirst became almost unbearable, and their throats so dry that it was difficult to whisper to each other anymore.

At what Sopwith guessed was late morning, the door to the hut was pulled open, fully illuminating the interior of the hut. Sopwith glanced at Ali and saw how drawn her face looked; her hair matted, and face and clothes covered with dirt; with swollen mosquito bite marks visible on her skin. His heart ached for her.

An olive-skinned man stooped through the door, entering the hut. He had a hooked nose, with long wavy black hair pulled into a small ponytail. He had evil-looking eyes which appeared as tiny lumps of coal in narrow slits, and he was dressed in blue jeans and button-down shirt, with a holstered pistol on one hip. He sank to a cross-legged position alongside the doorway, and with an evil leer showing brilliant white teeth, he said:

"Please allow me to introduce myself. Oh! How I love that opening line from Keith Richards' 'Sympathy for the Devil'. The words of that song so well reflect the foolishness of you infidels.

'I'm a man of wealth and taste,

I've been around for long, long years,

Stole million man's soul and faith', sings Richards, in his praise of the Devil.

"I do suppose that maybe I surprise you knowing songs by the Rolling Stones, but that came about during my many years at your Oxford University. I was rather a brilliant student I may add, but have no taste for your infidel's intellect, so I rather recruited a jihadist cell there. Anyway, I digress; my name is Asim Khatib, commander an East African cell of Al-Shabaab jihadists. The locals prefer to call me AK because I remind them of how my AK47 bullets tear into their flesh and bone if they dare to disobey me." Asim's words were spoken in good clear English, and in a soft voice, belying the man's evil intent.

"So now that you know who I am, I think it is only fair that you should introduce yourselves. I do have a few ground rules however, which must be obeyed to the letter. You must only ever refer to me as 'al-wala', meaning you are loyal to me. Any attempt to distort any truth will result in you losing a limb. Any blatant untruth will result in you being beheaded. So essentially, I want to hear nothing but the truth from you. Lastly, woman, you will never look directly at me, ever. Always avert your eyes from my face and if you do not, you will be beheaded."

"OK, infidel pilot, you start by telling me who you are."

Mike appeared to be semi-comatose, and just as Sopwith was wondering if he had comprehended anything that AK had said, Mike mumbled through a very dry throat, "Water, please al-wala, water."

AK grinned at this response from Mike, and snapping his fingers, called out, "Bring bottles of water."

A man came into the hut carrying three bottles each containing a litre of water, and on AK's instruction, poured some over the faces, and into the mouths of each captive until all the water was finished.

"OK, let us begin again. Introduce yourself to me, infidel."

"Al-wala, my name is Mike," he croaked, "I am employed as a pilot for SWB."

"Why did you fly to Palma?"

"To collect these people," he said, indicating Sopwith and Ali.

"Why?"

"Al-wala, I have no idea. I was only instructed to fly to Palma to collect two passengers and take them to Pretoria."

"Are you sure about this infidel; your life hangs in the balance, you understand?"

"I promise I do not know more than this al-wala."

"I'll accept this infidel. You look simple enough to me not to be such a liar. You are next, woman."

"My name is Mrs Alison Jones, al-wala, and I am travelling with my husband here," Ali answered, her eyes averted in the direction of the ground.

"You do not seem to have much respect for your limbs infidel. My information tells me you are a pilot in Her Majesty's Government?"

"Your information is out of date, al-wala; I was once a government pilot but resigned to join my husband on his travels."

"So be it. Why did SWB send an aircraft from Pretoria to fetch you?"

"I do not know, al-wala; that is my husband's business, and as you know a woman has no place in her husband's business."

"I think you are lying, but that means nothing to me now as your husband must tell me all, not so?"

"I am sure he will, al-wala."

"So then, infidel Jones, tell me all," AK turned to Sopwith, leering at him with his ghostly, expressionless eyes.

"Al-wala, it is a long tale to tell, but in simple terms I was set up by the South African Government who is trying to steal from me. I view theft as a very serious crime, as must you."

"I see, but I must hear the full story of this so called set up. It sounds intriguing."

Sopwith answered AK truthfully and in detail, leaving nothing out. He had begun to hope that the value both the South Africans and British felt for him might rub off onto this ISIS group and therefore helpful in keeping them alive.

"This is of interest to me," AK announced. "In reward for your truthfulness you shall receive some water each morning and evening. With that he stood up, and as he stooped out under the doorframe, he turned to them and said, "By the way, if you get hungry, I suggest you eat your faeces so that your abode will smell a bit better!" and the door was firmly closed behind him, and the semi darkness prevailed once more.

The remainder of the day passed in a thirsty hot blur for the captives, but true to his word, AK did send them water in the late afternoon. Sopwith very carefully watched the man who brought the water. He wore an AK47 slung over his back, freeing his hands to carry the water bottles. He stooped into the hut but was not wary of the captives, believing that they were all firmly bound, and came up to them and started sharing out the water. Once his watering duty was complete, he gathered up the empty bottles and turned his back on them, stooping to exit, then closing the door behind him. An idea was beginning to form in Sopwith's mind.

That day, in England, the First Sea Lord had met with the Prime Minister at 10 Downing Street and informed him and his staff of the likelihood that one of their serving officers had, likely, been captured by a jihadist group in Mozambique, along with the civilian, Mr Jones. The PM assured him that he had authority to utilise all military resources available to him but made it clear that no rescue mission into Mozambique could proceed, if it came to that, without his prior approval of any proposed plans.

Satisfied with the PM's support, he returned to his offices and met again with his staff.

"Joint Forces Command is being most co-operative, and NovaSAR will continue to monitor the area around the airstrip, and construction site on the Fungi Peninsula, for an indefinite period," reported Rear Admiral Ron Hubbard.

"GCHQ is on high alert, through MI6, and are very carefully monitoring our captives' names, jihadist cell names, geographical references and so on, so there is little else we can do at this stage."

Geoff Briggs, the Director of the Carrier Strike Force, reported that HMS Queen Elizabeth was less than four days' sailing before reaching the vicinity of the Fungi Peninsula, and the Royal Marine units aboard were maintaining a constant state of readiness pending any possible deployment.

"Thank you for your input gentlemen; it appears to be a waiting game at the moment," the First Sea Lord said, bringing the meeting to an end.

Aboard R08 that day, Lieutenant George Kemp had been grilling his Royal Marine platoon hard. This included carrying full battle kit while completing multiple laps of the R08's expansive deck, live round firing practice from the stern the deck, which involved leopard-crawling exercises under live fire. With what little information he had so far, it appeared to him that a beach landing with a small fighting force would be needed to rescue two souls who had been captured by jihadists, then return them to the carrier. He was paying particular attention to which of the soldiers he had in mind to be part of the task group. He would stay aboard R08 while directing their efforts, so he needed his very best men on the ground. He had some limited knowledge of the type of militia they would be up against and had been studying the ground conditions of the general area of the Fungi Peninsula carefully. He was doing all he could do at that stage, until he had more specific information with which to work. He smiled to himself at the thought that they were going to be acting out the Royal Marines' motto of 'Per Mare, Per Terram' (By Sea, By Land), and this thought made him feel confident and ready for the challenge.

Sopwith, Ali and Mike spent another very uncomfortable night in the hut. Although the hut smelled of faeces, they had grown accustomed to it, and as they no longer had any solids to pass, the odour of urine and sweat was the now becoming dominant.

Sopwith thought that the mosquitoes were less in number, but that could just have been his imagination. Mike had totally withdrawn into himself and was not uttering word, choosing to ignore whispered questions from the others about his well-being, but Sopwith, with his free hands did his best to try and make the man as comfortable as possible on the dirt. He did the same for Ali, trying his utmost to comfort her, and after a very long night for them, the dawn broke through with penetrating slivers of light between the branches. Not long after dawn the same man brought them water and followed the exact procedure as before; Sopwith's eyes following his every move.

Before the day had become hot, so it was probably still early in the morning, the water-bearer pulled open the hut door and instructed them to leave the hut one by one. Sopwith left first, carefully holding one wrist with his other hand to appear to be still tied up and entered the small clearing in the bush. Blinking against the bright sunlight, he saw two men in camouflage, each bearing AK47s at the ready, and one of them had a large evil-looking panga hanging from his belt. A little further away AK stood, toying with what looked like a large cell phone, which Sopwith took to be a satellite phone. When Ali and then Mike exited the hut Sopwith saw how utterly bedraggled they looked; dirty and insect-bitten, with grim expressions on their faces. They were made to stand together facing AK and then ordered to drop to their knees.

"Good morning infidels, you are to become famous today, I believe. I will be making a short video of you to show your moron masters our power," AK said, waving the sat phone at them. "I will be filming you as a group to show how pathetic you look, and then I will ask you individually what you think your masters should do to help you out of your current situation. Infidel woman you may look at me and my phone while I am filming you, without fear of losing your head," he said, chuckling quietly to himself. He picked up the phone and started videoing them, panning across the group, and then taking close-ups of each one.

"Infidel woman, tell your government of your situation and what you want them to do about it," he said, zooming in on Ali.

She responded, "I am in good health and am receiving water but would like some food. We have not been told why we are being held so I cannot say what can be done about it."

AK stopped the camera and smiled at Ali, "You think you are clever, infidel, but alas, not clever enough. Infidel pilot, your turn next," he said, zooming his camera in on Mike.

Having built himself into a nervous state, Mike wailed, "Al-wala, I will join your team; I will do anything for you. Tell me what to do and I will obey your every command. I will be on your side, not theirs, I promise!" he begged, looking at AK imploringly.

"You foolish infidel, that is totally untrue; you will never be able to accomplish that! Bend your head in shame," replied AK, who nodded at the militiaman carrying the panga, and then started filming again.

The man unhitched the panga, and taking a step to Mike's side, took a mighty swing at Mike's bent neck. The blade flashed past Ali's eyesight and with a wet thump sliced into Mike's neck. An instant later his severed head hit the dirt with a thud, blood spewing from shredded blood vessels. His body remained upright on its knees momentarily as blood gushed from the arteries, partly spraying Ali with warm blood, and then it fell forward into a heap on the ground.

Ali shrieked in disbelief at what she had just witnessed and began to retch violently. She continued to wail aloud, after which more retching followed, producing only bile from her empty stomach.

Sopwith had to use all his willpower to keep his hands together behind his back and not reach out to comfort her or try to kill AK. Ali slowly quietened down, but her whole body was trembling uncontrollably. AK stopped filming.

"I told you infidels that an untruth will result in death, and now you know I do not play around. Now infidel Jones, speak!" and he started filming Sopwith.

"I am healthy and would like to have this situation resolved quickly," was all he could manage in a shaking, hoarse voice.

"Get back into the hut now; go away!" AK gestured in the direction of the hut. Sopwith and Ali rose to their feet and staggered back into the hut. The door was secured behind them.

Ali fell to the ground weeping. Sopwith crouched down alongside her, caressing her head with one hand, while with the other he scooped up sand and used it to try and wipe Mike's blood off her.

"We have to get away from here!" she moaned in a hoarse shaking whisper, "We will not be allowed to live after what we have just seen!"

"I will get us out of here, I promise," Sopwith responded, as clearly and bravely as he could.

AK had walked off to his pick-up parked in the bush close by. With great satisfaction and pride at his efforts, he sat and reviewed the video he had taken. The scene of the beheading was especially pleasant for him, as he had captured it all in fine detail, and he watched it several times, with a smug look of sheer happiness lighting up his dark face. He then began to video the wall of bush surrounding him and started to speak.

"This is proof that we hold two British subjects' hostage. The South African pilot told an untruth and you saw the result of that. The same fate will meet the others if you do not abide by my order. My order is that you will immediately instruct the infidel company stealing our gas to cease their operations and remove all their people from our Fungi Peninsula. Any other reaction by you or your representatives, such as trying to find us, will result in the beheading of the two hostages without hesitation. Unless the world press reports within five days that the infidel foreigners plan to leave our land, our hostages will be beheaded, and you will receive excellent footage of the show."

AK ended the video, then, with great satisfaction reviewed the entire recording once again. He followed this up by addressing an email to the British Home Office general enquiry site and attaching to it the video that he had taken headed: 'From Mr and Mrs Jones', then clicked 'Send'. He smiled broadly to himself in anticipation of the reaction to his handiwork.

What he did not realise was that the new satellite telephone he was using had GPS encryption.

In GCHQ at Cheltenham, and only a very short while after AK had pressed the 'send' icon to dispatch his email, silent alarms alerted a duty operator, who immediately viewed AK's email. As it consisted only of a header with no other text, he went straight to the attached video and was revolted and sickened by it. As shocked as he was, he immediately followed a vital protocol to try and stop people from viewing the file. He picked up a colour-coded phone which was linked directly to the Home Office Permanent Secretary's office and after only a few rings the Permanent Secretary himself answered.

"Good day, sir. Duty officer GCHQ here. On instruction from MI6, we have intercepted an email headed: 'From Mr and Mrs Jones' and addressed to the Home Office general enquiry site. It is highly confidential and not to be viewed by anyone, including yourself, sir. Please instruct your staff to delete the email forthwith, and permanently remove it from the deleted items storage. This is terribly important, sir; an explanation will be forthcoming from a senior officer. If possible, please will you facilitate this personally, sir; such action will be highly commended and hugely appreciated"

The Permanent Secretary understood that he had little option but to follow GCHQ's orders. He immediately walked into his secretary's office and asked her to access the Home Office general enquiry email account. When she did, he noted, to his relief that the mail headed: 'From Mr and Mrs Jones' was in the inbox, but, as yet, unopened. He leaned over his secretary's shoulder, selected the mail, and pressed 'Delete' and then then scrolled to the deleted items, selected it once again, and deleted it permanently. He smiled at the amazed look on her face, telling her it was an instruction from GCHQ, and she should just carry on with her work.

Back in his office he was very pleased to report back to GCHQ that the mail in question had been properly deleted and received a grateful 'Thank you' in return. He also wondered if the mail that he had just deleted had anything to do with the missing Sopwith Jones.

Meanwhile, at GCHQ, the duty officer's next step was to inform John Baker at MI6 about the contents of the email, as it was, they who had issued the surveillance order. When John received the call, he was just as shocked as the duty officer had been to hear the news; however, there were other important things in his mind.

"Is there any IP address, or other means to trace the mail?" John asked.

"Even better, sir; it was obviously sent from a very new type of satellite phone with GPS encryption, so we can locate where it was sent from to the millimetre. We are working on that right now and will revert to you once we have established the co-ordinates."

"That is tremendous news! Please send me a copy of the video by secure courier as soon as convenient. Make only one other copy for records and then get rid of the whole damned thing once you have the position from which it was sent to hand."

John Baker then telephoned the First Sea Lord to bring him up to date.

"I have not seen the video yet, but GCHQ tell me that Lt Murray and Mr Jones look in reasonable health apart from being very dishevelled, dirty and a bit emaciated. I am sure that within an hour or two we should have the location from where the video was sent. Do you have any contingency plans?"

"Oh yes," said the First Sea Lord, "We have HMS Queen Elizabeth heading to the area with Royal Marines aboard to react. Once you inform us of the co-ordinates, we will be able to plan an extraction as soon as they are in range of wherever our target is. I will ask JFC if NovaSAR can do a little extra scanning of the general area to see if they can pick up anything else."

The First Sea Lord updated Ron Hubbard on the situation and tasked him to try and get some more detail out of JFC.

The civilian operator of NovaSAR just happened to be the same man who had spotted Sopwith's plane on the ground the first time NovaSAR had been tasked to look for it, so when the new request for more acute surveillance came in, he took the matter to heart because of his prior interest.

He established that the 172 Solar was still parked in the same place on the apron of the Palma airstrip where it had last been pictured, and probably because there was habitation to the south of the strip, he concentrated his efforts in the area to the north. He carefully studied orbit after orbit of the satellite's images transmitted to him, until something odd did stick out. In the dense bush just south of the Tanzanian border there was a very small clearing in the bush with what looked like a small hut to one side of it. But what intriguing him was the sighting of what appeared to be a body lying in the clearing. Concentrating on the clearing, he increased the definition of the pictures to their maximum, and on the pass of the following orbit he received several clear pictures. A small hut, apparently very shoddily erected, stood in the clearing, and there was a headless corpse lying in the clearing, with the head lying close by. The operator immediately sent copies of his pictures to Ron Hubbard with exact co-ordinates of the hut's position.

On receipt of this information, Ron promptly updated the First Sea Lord, then ensured it was forwarded, as a top priority, to Lt George Kemp in charge of the Marine contingent on R08.

George Kemp had thus far been informed of the video showing the two hostages, and the beheading of a third. No sooner had he downloaded the information and printed a picture of the hut with a corpse lying in front of it, than he received another message, this time from MI6, detailing the co-ordinates of the position from which the incriminating email had been sent by satellite phone. Comparing the information from the picture with these, he saw that only about one hundred metres separated the two points. He had a target; now he could act. First, he placed a satellite call to the First Sea Lord.

"Lt George Kemp, Royal Marines, aboard R08, sir. Do I have your authority to send rescue teams to the location in Mozambique which has been passed on to me?"

"You most definitely do!" replied the First Sea Lord, completely disregarding the PM's instruction to first get approval from 10 Downing Street.

There was no time to waste on such formalities and he was stubborn enough to take the brunt of any consequences of his ignoring the order.

"What are your plans, Lieutenant Kemp?"

"Sir, we dare not use helicopters to go ashore, mainly because we do not want to alert the enemy, so it must be a seaborne assault, departing the HMS Queen Elizabeth well before first light tomorrow morning. We will still be a considerable distance from our present position at sea to the shoreline, where we will secure a beachhead closest to our target, so I will be using our two Chinook helicopters to each transport a semi-rigid boat to within 5 km: just out of sight from our intended landfall. Once in the water the boats will be boarded by my men from the Chinooks and they will motor to the beach, landing before first light. We will then approach the target area as stealthily as possible, and then tackle whatever comes our way to ensure we recover the hostages in one piece."

"Sounds good enough to me, Lieutenant. I insist, however, that there must be no indiscriminate shooting during any contact with the jihadists; you may only shoot in self-defence. Is that understood?"

"Very good, sir."

"Good luck, son, and please keep me well-appraised of the situation as it unfolds."

George Kemp then called his Colour Sergeant, Steve Roberts, and instructed him to select his best sergeant and sixteen other men to take part in the mission. Steve was a very tough Yorkshireman, possessed of a service record studded with incidents of bravery and commendation, so George was extremely happy to place him in charge of the troops on the ground.

Once Steve had recited the names of the men he had chosen, and George had approved the list, he instructed Steve to call his men to an O-group. When they had all been gathered, Lt Kemp detailed his orders.

"Gentlemen, we have a mission. I will be in overall command, remaining on R08. You will be ferried by Chinook, together with two semi-rigids, some two-hundred-and-seventy-five kilometres westwards towards the Mozambique coast, and be dropped off at sea five kilometres from the shoreline. I estimate that your landfall should be at 04h00, one hour before sunrise. You will then carry out an eight-kilometre forced march through low coastal scrubland, later becoming thick undergrowth closer to the target, which is the hut in a bush clearing, as pictured," explained George, as he pointed at the large computer screen with images of the hut from three different angles.

"We can only reasonably assume that you will not meet resistance en route, but should you come across armed combatants, you may only fire reactively. There will be no indiscriminate firing at all. We can also only presume that the hostages you are tasked to rescue are being held in the pictured hut. The two hostages are one Lt Murray of our Fleet Air Arm, and a civilian by the name of Jones. Please have a good look at their pictures and memorise them."

George pointed at the monitor onto which he had opened a picture of each hostage. These pictures had been sent to him by MI6 and were stills taken from the video of the hostages that had been sent and pictured both in their dreadful, dishevelled and dirty-looking state.

"As you will see they are extremely dirty, so will not be simply picked out as 'white Europeans.' They are totally unaware of our mission, so make sure you identify yourselves properly on encountering them. They appear to be very weak from the lack of sustenance. The decapitated body will regrettably have to be left for others to recover. Once you have the hostages in safe hands, retreat to the boats and return to R08, which will by then be much closer to the beachhead.

Colour Sergeant Steve Roberts will be in command on the ground along with his own boat and platoon, which will be called 'Alpha'. Sergeant Gill you will be in command of the second boat and platoon, 'Bravo'. Sergeants, ensure your men are properly kitted, and get your boats onto the flight deck, in their cradles, ready for the 02h00 lift-off. Are there any questions?" he concluded.

"Is there any intel regarding the jihadists we might come up against?" asked Steve Roberts.

"Sorry Steve, I left that out. MI6 Intel reports there are many jihadists spread throughout the area, but certainly according to our satellite pictures, there is no significant concentration of them situated around the target area. You can expect them to be armed with AK47s in the main; maybe an LMG or two. We know that they used RPGs recently. Treat them as if they are properly and efficiently trained. There is no doubt you will get the better of them, as we are the best trained in the world, 'Per Mare, Per Terram'"

"'Per Mare, Per Terram'!" the troops all called out in unison. The square block of muscle that made up C/Sgt Steve Roberts burst into life, calling out, "Move along lads; let's get this show on the road!"

Sopwith had firmly made up his mind that he would tackle the man who brought them water when he arrived in the late afternoon. He had no other option at all, and if he did not try to do something, they were going to die, as Ali had so correctly observed. He retrieved his Leatherman from its shallow grave near the door and covered it in dirt immediately to the right side of where he was normally seated when they were watered.

He shared his plan with Ali in a very soft whisper, and then sliced through her hessian bond, reminding her to pretend that she was still bound when the man entered the hut. They waited nervously for his arrival, but by the time the hut was in complete darkness they realised, to their dismay, that there would be no water delivery, so they settled down to try and sleep. At least Ali could be more comfortable with her wrists now unbound.

The First Sea Lord sat alone in his darkened office, with just one reading light lit on his desk. He was in deep thought, having realised that he had really become far too directly involved in the Murray and Jones matter. He was, after all, the most senior officer in the Royal Navy. At his age it was almost a figurehead position. He just did not need to be involved in micro-managing issues like these. His mind wandered to his meeting with the lawyer Ben Dougmore; a man to whom he had taken an instant liking and hoped to meet again one day. He smiled to himself when he realised that meeting had, in fact, been the starting point of all of this, when he had been totally taken in by the injustices done to Sopwith Jones. He also liked the sound of the chap's name too and smiled even more broadly at that thought. He could, at that point, have handed the matter over to one of his support staff and let them handle it, but no, he had wanted to stay involved, and remained so.

Then, of course, the matter of rubber-stamping the order of Lt Murray being relieved of her flying duties. He hadn't even looked at the orders when he had signed them relieving her of her PFW posting aboard R08. He still felt embarrassed by how she had been treated simply as a number, dictated to by cash flow. 'No,' he thought to himself, 'that was not the way that staff should be treated', and he was sure within himself, now, that was why he had stuck to this business like a leech. He was doing all he could in his power to ensure that neither she, nor her now apparent husband, might come to any further harm. To hell with any consequences of his actions, and if it meant the end to his illustrious career, so be it, if he saw to it that his dear Lt Murray came back in one piece.

There was another man in the building also deep in thought, but he was brooding, not reflecting. Former Lt Cdr Anthony Baxter had been court-martialled for the damage he had caused but had not been discharged from the Navy. He had lost his rank and now served in the Logistics Support Office as a

Seaman. He had become a very bitter man, and was beginning to focus his bitterness on Sopwith Jones, whom he believed was the root cause of his terrible fall from grace in the Navy. He was still in the office after hours as he was busy trying to ferret out information as to what had eventually become of the Jones fellow and Lt Murray. Because of his low rank he had very little direct access to much confidential information, so he had started spending every evening pretending to be doing extra work, but was, in fact, trawling through his computer trying to find information about Sopwith.

Chapter Eight

Aboard R08 that night, Colour Sergeant Steve Roberts kept his men busy preparing for their mission. He carried out spot checks of the equipment to be carried by each man, which included night vision goggles, hand-held GPS devices, VHF communication headsets with microphones, along with their standard assault rifles, stun grenades, fragmentation grenades and spare ammunition.

Each troop of nine Marines would include a man specifically trained as a medic, so Steve checked their medical equipment packs to ensure that they were complete. They all had to have lifejackets for their initial boat trip to the shore, one day's emergency rations, and drinking water. Steve, and Bravo leader Sgt Gill, each had a satellite phone, if it became necessary to communicate with Lt George Kemp aboard R08. Once personnel kit had been readied, the two semi-rigid boats were thoroughly inspected for soundness and fuel supply. The three hundred horsepower Mercury outboard motors were started and run up to check on performance.

At 01h00 the boats on their cradles were brought to the flight deck by lift, then positioned in readiness for attachment to the lifting cables of the Chinook helicopters. Final checks were made on the co-ordinates of the waypoints on the GPS devices, which included the marking of the Rovuma River border with Tanzania. The beachhead, in a shallow bay to the immediate north of Fungi Peninsula, was pinned, along with the village of Qurinde to the north that had to be avoided, the Palma airstrip and, of course, their prime focus, the target hut. At 01h45, Alpha and Bravo platoon each boarded a Chinook helicopter, which took off and hovered while the carrier crew latched the lifting cables to the boats, and at precisely 02h00 both machines lifted into the air with the semi-rigid boats hanging beneath them and headed in the direction of the Mozambican Fungi Peninsula.

The Boeing CH47 Chinook is a double rotor helicopter used for heavy lifting and the carrying of troops. It first entered service in 1962 and is still produced, but with improvements. It has 18 metre diameter composite rotors and is powered by two large jet engines. Capable of flying at 310 km/h it remains one of the fastest helicopters in the world.

While carrying the boats, however, they only flew at 170 km/h and in just over an hour-and-a-half, having covered two hundred and seventy-five kilometres, they slowed to a stop and, hovering carefully, lowered the boats onto the sea. The nine Marines from each helicopter rappelled down ropes into the boats amidst a cloud of sea spray lifted by the downdraught from the rotors. Once they were all aboard, the lifting cable latches were released, and the Chinooks flew off. The boats' Mercury motors were started, and they headed at full speed on a dead flat sea surface to cover the five kilometres to the beach. It was a very dark night, with only stars slightly illuminating the sky, but the coxswain of each boat followed their GPS instruments unerringly until both craft nosed-up onto on a smooth, gently sloping sandy beach.

Following the order, 'Go, go!' heard in their headsets, the marines swiftly shed their lifejackets and disembarked, after fitting their night vision goggles, then raced up the beach to the low tree line, leaving two of their number to guard the boats whilst they were away. In two separate columns they moved through the coastal scrub, fifteen minutes ahead of their 04h00 target time.

They moved as fast as they could, with each of them totally alert to what was ahead and on their flanks. They made good time until they reached the thickening bush. Up until that point they had seen no sign of any other life around them at all. Once they reached the dense bush, they were slowed drastically by the difficulty of working their way through the undergrowth as quietly as possible, and were grateful for the fifteen-minute head start that they had had on their planned time line. The two columns moved forward slowly, and parallel to each other, with Alpha ahead of Bravo.

With the first rays of morning light at their backs beginning to reveal their presence, they still had about a kilometre to go to reach the clearing. Steve Roberts broadcast quietly to both platoons: "Very quietly now lads, we have come this far undetected; let's keep this up, likewise, all the way there."

By the time they were only two hundred metres short of their target it was broad daylight. Despite no longer having to use their night vision goggles, they nevertheless slowed even more, moving carefully from one tree to the next.

Alpha was tasked to enter the clearing first, with Bravo hanging back slightly to act as rear guard.

Steve Roberts was on the verge of stepping into the clearing when there was a single rifle shot close by. He called, "Single pull AK ahead in clearing. Get down!" Both platoons dropped to the ground, at the ready.

Ten minutes earlier Sopwith and Ali had been wide awake, when they were surprised by the door to the hut being dragged open, and the water carrier stooping in through the doorway, much earlier than he had ever done previously. Neither of them had slept at all during the night. Ali was still in a severe state of shock over the beheading which had taken place right next to her. Sopwith had done all he could to calm her by petting her, whispering words of comfort, and even kissing her with as much saliva as he could from his mouth, to try and relieve her dry throat, injured by her retching and crying. When the water carrier entered the hut Sopwith whispered, "Wrists," to Ali reminding her to keep her wrists together, and they sat, trying to show eagerness to receive their water. The jihadist had a litre bottle in each hand, with his rifle slung across his back as usual. He set down one bottle, and using both hands, started pouring water onto Ali's face.

Sopwith reached out, located his Leatherman, and powered by adrenalin, leapt up and grabbed the man around his chest with his left hand, while at the same time pulling the Leatherman's blade into the front of the man's neck with his right hand. The jihadist released the water bottle and reached back to try and dislodge Sopwith who was using every bit of strength he could muster. Already he had the blade sawing deeply into the man's neck, when he heard a sucking noise as the windpipe was severed. Simultaneously blood started pumping out of the cut, drenching him. He struggled to maintain his grip on the knife, which was now also coated in blood, but he did not stop, while fear and anger drove him on. As the jihadist's resistance weakened, he had almost completely cut through the neck, and when the jihadist became completely limp, he lowered him to the ground, removing his knife.

Ali was shedding silent tears as Sopwith wiped his Leatherman on the dead jihadist's clothes, then folded the blade and returned it to its pouch. He then awkwardly removed the AK47 from the body, moved the fire selector to single shot, and whispered to Ali.

"I'm sorry you had to see that too my darling, but it's over now. Please stay right behind me and follow my every move. We have no idea what we're going to find when we get out of here, but if there are any shots fired, hit the dirt immediately. Promise me that. Say it, please."

"I promise," she replied in a wavering whisper, with tears still streaming down her cheeks.

Holding the rifle at the ready, Sopwith peered into the clearing. Averting his eyes from Mike's now decomposing corpse and fly-covered head, and seeing no one, he ventured out of the hut, with Ali immediately behind him. After taking two steps, checking first to his right and then to his left, he saw Asim Khatib walking towards him from the outer edge of the clearing. Khatib spotted him a moment later and reached for his pistol. Sopwith calmly placed the rifle to his shoulder, and taking aim at Khatib's chest, squeezed off a single round, dropping him to the ground before he had time to draw the pistol. The jihadist, who had inflicted the mortal blow to Mike, was several paces behind Khatib, with his panga at his hip and rifle slung over his back. He immediately dropped into the undergrowth. Sopwith could not see the man and was busy trying to figure out his next move when a burst of automatic fire came from close by. He heard Ali cry out loudly, and a split second later felt the right-hand side of his chest exploding in pain. He fell heavily onto the ground. The next sound he heard was extremely confusing to him. A man shouted out in a broad Yorkshire accent from behind him:

"Royal Marines! Murray, Jones; stay down! Down, I repeat; we'll handle it from here!" And then he heard gunfire.

Steve Roberts had stayed prone for a few seconds after the first shot that had been heard. He had then crawled to the edge of the clearing where, after seeing the corpse on the ground, spotted someone who had to be the hostage named Jones, with Lt Murray immediately behind him. Jones had an AK47 in hand and another person lay prostrate at the opposite edge of the clearing. Just then he heard the short burst of automatic fire and saw both hostages fall to the ground. He called out to them to stay down and ordered Bravo platoon to head to the right of their position. He had an idea of where in the undergrowth the gunfire had come from, so returning to a prone position just out of the clearing, he fired a burst of gunfire into the general area. This was met immediately by a volley of return fire which went high over his head but showed him exactly where the shots had come from. Using his headset mike, he commanded all the men to hold their positions and then using hand signals, he indicated to the marine closest to him to move his position 45° around the clearing away from him. While the

Marine was moving, he fired single shots into the enemy's firing position, hoping to keep their heads down. When his man had moved into position, and using hand signals for instruction, and then a fingered countdown, Steve and his man burst into the clearing and put down a heavy barrage of gunfire into the enemy position. The jihadist in the undergrowth did not get to fire one round in return, so confused was he by the sudden two-pronged attack on him. He died very quickly of his multiple bullet wounds.

Steve was puzzled by the lack of response to their attack, and further surprised by the fact that there was only a single fighter evident. He then gave instructions by radio for Bravo platoon to secure the clearing and ordered both medics to the hut to attend to the hostages if needs be, and then rushed across the clearing to Murray and Jones, both of whom were still on the ground.

"Lt Murray…Sergeant Roberts of the Royal Marines. Are you alright?"

"I'm actually Mrs Alison Jones, but Lt Murray will do for the moment. I have been shot in my left leg," she replied, grimacing with pain.

"Mr Jones….and you?"

"The right side of my chest seems to have taken a hit," Sopwith replied.

"I'll call for a helicopter casevac immediately," Sgt Roberts told him.

"NO!" Sopwith tried to shout out, but the word came out like a whisper. "I have to get my aeroplane; it's not far from here, and I cannot leave without it. I'll fly us to a hospital."

Just then the medics arrived and took charge of a patient each. It was quickly established that Ali had received a bullet wound to her left thigh, but that no critical damage had been caused. The bullet had passed through the muscle without impacting bone, but damage had been done to some major blood vessels, and she was bleeding very badly. After injecting her with morphine, the medic disinfected the entry and exit wounds and bandaged her leg to slow the bleeding.

Sopwith's ribcage and inner arm were found to have been struck by a passing bullet, but it had luckily moved between those two body parts, doing only minimal damage. He was not bleeding too badly from the wounds, and the medic determined that, at worst, two of his ribs had been cracked. He had an open wound on his inner arm, but no damage at all to his lungs. He was disinfected, bandaged, and given a shot of morphine as well. Both Ali and Sopwith had saline drips inserted into their arms and were given an electrolyte solution to drink.

As Steve Roberts readied his satellite phone to call Lt Kemp aboard R08, he heard Sopwith say in a tone of disgust, "I shot that man lying over there. He's a

Syrian by the name of Asim Khatib who told us he was the commander of the local Al-Shabaab jihadist cell here." Then as an afterthought, and with loathing he added, "The bastard liked to refer to himself as AK, after the weapon."

Steve acknowledged what Sopwith had said, then made the call to his lieutenant.

"We have the two hostages, sir, who have both suffered non-critical bullet wounds. There is one body of a man who Jones states he shot in self-defence, and reports that he was the local commander of the jihadist force here. Jones also had to kill a jihadist in self-defence prior to that. We came under fire and dispatched a further militiaman. So far there is no indication of any more fighters in the area. The beheaded corpse has been left in the clearing. Lt Murray seems disoriented as she refers to herself as Alison Jones, and Mr Jones is insistent that he wants to fly himself from here to a hospital. It's your call, please sir."

Lt Kemp knew about the Cessna parked at Palma airstrip and was aware of the rescue of Jones over the Southern Ocean and that Sopwith hand landed his plane on R08, so his insistence on flying them out seemed like a logical move, but Kemp believed this should rather be to the aircraft carrier than to a local hospital.

"Steve, I support Mr Jones' idea in principle. Other than that, he should fly to the carrier, so make him aware that we are close by. However, the final decision as to whether he does fly himself out must be in your hands, based upon whether it is safe to do so, and that he is in good enough physical shape to cope to fly his aircraft. Please send me pictures of the slain commander."

Steve took pictures of Asim Khatib's body, sent them to his lieutenant, and then approaching Sopwith, said, "Mr Jones, we arrived here by way of HMS Queen Elizabeth which is sailing towards this area, and whose position is some two hundred kilometres distant. My commanding officer agrees, in principle, that you to fly your plane out of here, but only to the aircraft carrier, so would you be happy with that?"

Sopwith's eyes lit up in surprise that R08 was playing a part in his life again, and replied enthusiastically, "That'll be a perfect solution for us. Yes, of course I'll fly to her."

"I have two provisos before I agree that your flight will be possible. The first is that my medic confirms you are up to the task, and the second, that we can safely get you to Palma airstrip, as well as it being secure enough there for you to take to the air. OK?"

"I have no problem with that."

Lt George Kemp's report to the First Sea Lord's offices, that Murray and Jones had been in Mozambique filtered through the corridors of power. The First Sea Lord was ecstatically happy, and he sent a message of congratulation to all aboard R08. He then sent messages of appreciation to both JFC and GCHQ for their assistance in finding the hostages.

Upon receiving the news at MI6, John Baker, too, was a very happy man, over the fact that both hostages had been found, but more importantly, he was extremely pleased that the jihadist Asim Khatib had been killed. He had been easily able to positively identify the man's body shown in the pictures as being that of the elusive jihadist. John also called Kenneth Le Grange, told him what had happened, and suggested that the Marines had made the area safe enough for Le Grange's staff to recover Mike's remains.

When word reached the Prime Minister's offices, the PM asked his secretary to set up an appointment with the First Sea Lord to congratulate him.

Amongst other people to take note of what had happened was Seaman Anthony Baxter, who got his first news on the whereabouts of Sopwith Jones from the widespread euphoria that was evident round the naval establishment, causing his bitterness to reach new heights with this new-found knowledge of where Jones was.

Whilst talking to his lieutenant on board R08, Steve Roberts had no idea that he and the members of Alpha platoon were being watched from within the dense surrounding bush. The clearing was well-secured by Bravo platoon, but beyond those Marines, unsighted of each other, there were jihadists watching what was happening from behind the deep cover.

Asim Khatib had been a very clever man by hiding his makeshift prison for his hostages deep in dense bush away from any local populace but had been even cleverer still by secreting his troops over a wide surrounding area, so that they were virtually invisible from the ground or air. These troops had been alerted by the earlier gunfire to the action at the clearing and had sent scouts to find out what had taken place.

The scouts reported their findings to one of the more senior jihadists who, upon hearing of AK's demise, immediately proclaimed himself as the new leader of the group. The scouts informed him of only eight foreign soldiers attempting to free the hostages, because they had not seen any sign of Bravo platoon, in hiding, who were engaged in securing the clearing. Based on this information, the self-appointed leader decided to attack the foreign troops. He issued a command to the twenty jihadists now under his control, that they should, as swiftly as possible, start moving into position to mount the attack from the surrounding bush.

However, when the attack came, it was not the jihadists attacking the Marines, but vice versa, as they had literally crawled onto Bravo platoon's positions.

The moment the firing started, Steve ordered Alpha troop, and the two freed hostages to go to ground in the clearing, but soon realised there was no fire coming their way, then relaxed somewhat when Sgt Gill reported that his platoon had surprised incoming attackers. One of the jihadists managed to fire off an RPG before he was shot and killed; the grenade exploding harmlessly against the side of the hut and blowing most of the structure to the ground. Bravo platoon, under Gill's command, made short work of the intense firefight. Within ten minutes he reported to Steve that they had routed their attackers, with a resultant body count of eighteen. There was no sign of any further jihadists, and no injuries at all to any of his own men. Because of the quick and efficient way the Marines had dealt with their adversaries, Steve felt certain that there would be no further attacks, even if there happened to be more jihadists skulking in the bush.

The medic who had re-examined Sopwith gave cautious approval for Steve to allow him to fly. Sopwith then informed Steve that Asim Khatib would probably have had a vehicle nearby which they could make use of to travel the twelve kilometres to the airstrip. After a short search, the old Toyota double-cab pick-up was found parked in the bush on a very vague track, with its ignition key still in place. Steve instructed Bravo to remain in their positions, while he and four of his men from Alpha platoon climbed aboard the Toyota. He placed Lt Murray and Mr Jones between two Marines on the back seat, one Marine in the front passenger seat, and one on the load body while he got into the driver's seat. Starting the vehicle, he followed the track and his GPS device, and after some slow-going through the bush until they gained a gravel road closer to the airstrip, they arrived at their destination half-an-hour later without incident. The four Marines immediately set up a secure perimeter around the Cessna while Steve helped Lt Murray to the plane. Sopwith, with his body aching all over, completed a thorough inspection of his aircraft, and was relieved to find nothing untoward.

"Sarge, look what I've found!" came a shout from the bush to the side of the apron. There stood one of the Marines, holding the jihadist, Ghani Ibraimo, off the ground by his neck with one hand, and in his other, clutched an AK47, together with his own weapon. Ghani had been instructed by Asim Khatib to maintain his surveillance of the airstrip and so he had obeyed.

"What must I do with this little sewer rat sarge?"

Steve looked at the small, emaciated fellow dangling in the air, and with a half-smile on his face said sarcastically, "Throw him away; you might get the plague. No, seriously; remove the mag from his weapon and confiscate any other offensive items on his person, then render them permanently unusable. Destroy his cell phone, if he has one, and then give him a bloody great kick in the pants and tell him to bugger off and not come back any time soon. Please don't kill him, is all I ask."

Steve, on being told by Sopwith that the key to the doors of the aircraft were long lost, smashed the door window and carefully removed all the remaining glass, and opened the door from within. He then manoeuvred Ali into the cockpit and belted her in. Ali was barely conscious by this stage and Steve gave her a gentle pat and said, "Hang in there, Lieutenant; you'll be home in no time."

Sopwith, putting on a brave face, shook Steve's hand and thanked him sincerely for saving him and Ali, confiding in him that it meant so much to them as they had only recently got married. Steve finally understood the 'Mrs Alison Jones' comment from Ali.

"Mr Jones, fly on a heading of 027 from here," instructed Steve, after consulting his GPS, "and I will let R08 ATC know the minute you take off. They'll get something into the air to escort you in. Fly safe, sir, and I'll see you aboard later."

Sopwith awkwardly hauled himself into the cockpit, and in doing so, struck his forehead on the door frame, opening the wound that he had received from the rifle butt. Blood started pouring into his eyes. In addition, the right side of his body was now in searing pain as the morphine slowly wore off. Keeping his face averted from Steve, who was now standing back awaiting take-off, Sopwith went through his pre-start checks with difficulty, then started the motor, which effortlessly burst into purring life. He released the brakes and started taxiing onto the runway, the vision in his right eye totally blurred. He tried wiping the blood away with the back on his hand, which was wholly ineffective, but could not find anything else with which to wipe the blood away. Ali, who was completely unconscious by that time, with her head hanging to her side, could be of no help at all to him.

Sopwith turned the actuator to full power and heading along the runway he struggled to keep a straight course, but lifted off the ground without skidding off it.

Steve looked concerned at the way the plane weaved along the runway before it took off but having no further control over matters; he got hold of R08 ATC on his sat phone and reported the time of Sopwith's departure from Palma airstrip. He suggested that they dispatch an escort aircraft immediately, as it seemed that the incoming plane was being flown erratically. R08 ATC promptly ordered a Merlin MK4 helicopter into the air to escort Sopwith in. With less than two hundred kilometres to travel, the two aircraft would meet in under an hour.

Sopwith gained altitude while trying without success to clear his vision. His right eye was completed gummed-up with coagulated blood, and his vision from the left one was blurred, but he could just make out his instruments. Even though everything seemed so complicated to him at that stage, compounded by the wind rushing noisily through the glassless window frame, he managed to get the 172 Solar onto the correct heading and levelled out at two thousand metres above sea level.

He was now in terrible pain that was leading to nausea. In addition, he started hallucinating, not sure where he was or where he was going.

A voice in his headset revived him slightly when he heard, "Solar this is Mike Four from R08. Do you read?"

"Mike Four, got you. Where are you?" Sopwith mumbled.

"Solar, we have you visual in the distance. What is your status aboard?"

"One pax unconscious. Me, I am not so good. Bleeding…ah…yes, bleeding, and head not working…I can't think."

"Solar, just keep calm. Maintain your current heading which will take you straight in to your landing."

"OK!" Sopwith said, with a groan.

The pilot of the Merlin called R08 ATC and told them that Sopwith appeared to be losing control due to his injuries, and in order to reduce stress on him, he asked that the carrier be brought in line with Sopwith's current heading so that he could come straight into a landing without any further directional changes. This suggestion was readily accepted; commands were issued to bring the huge ship to bear.

The two aircraft gradually closed the gap to R08, and when the Merlin pilot thought it was time for Sopwith to start descending, he instructed him do so, but although acknowledging the helicopter's transmission, Sopwith continued his flight without change.

"Solar, you need to descend. Lose altitude now, urgently!" barked Mike Four.

This command shocked Sopwith, who immediately pushed the nose of the 172 into a steep dive.

"Hell no! Solar, level out please!" shouted Mike Four.

This command hit home to Sopwith, and he pulled his plane into almost straight and level flight. They were at a point where Sopwith needed to urgently start his controlled descent into the glide path necessary to approach the carrier flight deck, but he was not reacting at all, so Mike Four tried instructing him once more.

"Solar, you need to start your descent to land. Do you have the threshold visual?"

"There are no ships," Sopwith replied.

"Descend now!" the shocked voice of Mike Four rang in Sopwith's ears, and he pushed the nose down once more.

"Pull up!" Mike Four screamed, and Sopwith jerked his plane's nose up.

"Descend!" Mike Four repeated, and when Sopwith pushed the nose of the 172 down again, he was shocked to see the carrier's flight deck immediately ahead of him. He froze and flew straight onto the deck at an acute angle, and at about one hundred and twenty kilometres per hour.

The crew aboard R08 had been working frenetically to prepare for the emergency that was clearly going to unfold. The deck had been entirely cleared, and a catch net had been hydraulically erected three quarters of the way along it.

The Cessna 172 Solar slammed hard into the deck, collapsing all three of its undercarriage struts. Sopwith fainted, and the aircraft, with its propeller bent to a stop, skidded along the deck in a remarkably straight line and into the catch net, which absorbed the impact through its accumulators, bringing the wayward plane to a swift, controlled, and secure stop.

Within seconds emergency personnel gathered around the little aeroplane to recover the injured occupants, and in case of fire. Both Sopwith and Ali were lifted out of the cockpit and rushed to the ship's hospital, then the 172 Solar, after no sign of fire breaking out (which had been most unlikely as it carried no combustible fuel) was manoeuvred to a lift and lowered into a hangar on deck two. The safety net was lowered and the clearing of the trail of debris was undertaken on foot by the deck crew, to pick up any foreign matter left from the accident on the flight deck.

Staff Sergeant Steve Roberts and his marines, with R08 that much closer now, had powered up to the carrier in their semi-rigid boats after an uneventful withdrawal from Mozambique, leaving no one other than the surviving jihadists any wiser to their presence.

By the time the First Sea Lord arrived at 10 Downing Street for his appointment, the Prime Minister had been fully briefed on all the details of what had actually occurred in Mozambique, and when he was shown into the PM's office he was left alone with the PM, a most unusual occurrence.

After he was asked to sit down, the PM spoke.

"Well done, Arthur!" The First Sea Lord was shocked. He was an Admiral, and his name was Arthur Lightfoot, but no one had ever used the rank of Admiral, or used his given names, from the day he had taken office; only ever being referred to as the 'First Sea Lord' or 'Sir'.

"Thank you, Mr Prime Minister."

"The Royal Marines did sterling work as usual and must surely be put forward for commendations."

"I do hope so, Mr Prime Minister."

"You did, of course, grossly exceed your authority, Arthur. What in the world made you invade a sovereign nation without consulting this office, or at the very least talking to me about it first?"

"To save lives."

"Ah, I see, and I accept your concern for the hostages' lives, but you were under explicit orders to obtain my permission before you acted."

"There was no time, Mr Prime Minister. Had I held the mission back to first consult with you, in that time anything could have happened to the hostages."

"That's bollocks and you know it!" the PM smiled, "You were just not prepared to take the chance that I might not have authorised the operation. There is no doubt, from what I have been told, that you had become directly involved in the whole affair for personal reasons, and that is not acceptable. I'm afraid I have to ask you for your resignation, Arthur."

"You shall have it, sir; the minute I return to my office."

"Rear Admiral Ron Hubbard will be promoted to Admiral forthwith and will be your replacement. Do you perhaps have any comment on that decision?"

"That would have been my choice too, Mr Prime Minister."

The PM stood up and walked around his desk, where Arthur stood up alongside of him.

The PM stuck his hand out, saying, "I'm sorry it had to come to this Arthur. You've been the best head of our great navy for many years, and I really appreciate everything you have done, including this last mission. All of the best in your retirement," he said, shaking Arthur's hand in farewell.

Arthur Lightfoot left 10 Downing Street with a spring in his step and was all smiles upon entering his own office for his last time as the First Sea Lord, with only a few things to do before he left it permanently.

He first tasked Martha with finding a telephone number for Ben Dougmore and then asked her to get Ben on the line.

When the call came through, Arthur answered, "Hello Ben, this is Arthur Lightfoot here. You'll better remember me as the First Sea Lord you met when you were last in London."

"Oh yes, sir. To what do I owe the privilege?"

"Firstly, please drop the 'sir' bit. I'm retired now, so please call me Arthur. I picked up the phone to invite you to England for a short spring holiday. Are you up for that?"

"Well, this is certainly a surprise, but I could never say 'No' considering who is extending the invitation, and I'm certainly not overworked now. To tell the truth, another trip to your homeland is a wonderful prospect for me."

"That's settled then. All will be explained in due course. I do not have exact dates but prepare for a seven-day vacation beginning in ten to fourteen days' time. As soon as I have dates firmed up, and I have booked the tickets, I will let you know. Let me jot down your email address."

"That sounds wonderful," Ben replied, and recited his email address along with his cell phone number.

Arthur then tasked Martha with getting hold of Lt Cdr Godlonton-Shaw at RNAS Yeovilton.

"Lieutenant Commander, First Sea Lord here."

"Good day, sir; how may I help you?"

"You can be the second to know, after our dear Prime Minister, that I will be resigning as First Sea Lord today. You can also have the privilege to receive the very last order I issue before I leave my post," Arthur said, with a chuckle in his voice.

"I'm sure you're aware that Lt Murray and Sopwith Jones are aboard R08, cruising back to Portsmouth. My orders are that you must please, once again, host the two of them in the same manner as before. I am not sure of the duration of their stay but will make that your decision. They have been through a lot and need a place in England to catch their breath, so to speak."

"I'm terribly sorry to hear of your imminent retirement sir. I'll gladly host the couple as if they were on honeymoon, sir. I've not yet sent out a report of my new-found information of today's date. It came to my ears, and I've now had it confirmed, that our base chaplain married the two of them the day before they left us, so I can give them married quarters." Arthur was delighted to hear that the rumours about Alison calling herself Mrs Jones were founded on fact.

"I have already ordered that Sopwith's aircraft will be brought to your station by Chinook. It is a little damaged, I believe, but nothing that your technicians, by having a little 'practice,' can't fix under Sopwith's watchful eye."

"It's only with pleasure, sir. All the best for your retirement, sir."

"Thank you, Godlonton-Shaw. Good luck."

Arthur's second-last phone call was to the Permanent Secretary of the Home Office. He told the man of his retirement plan, and then informed him that he had not yet received Sopwith's new British Passport as per his earlier request, so asked him to expedite the matter, as he wanted to present it to Sopwith upon his impending arrival in England.

Finally, he then called R08's commanding officer by satellite phone to inform him of his retirement, along with a last request. He explained how he had organised for Sopwith and Ali to be hosted at RNAS Yeovilton and asked if Sopwith's plane could be airlifted by Chinook helicopter from Portsmouth to the air station. The Rear Admiral, expressing his sadness about the retirement news, and assured him that he would have the plane delivered.

Lastly, he called Martha into his office.

"Martha, please may I dictate a letter for you to type up for me?"

"No problem, sir, go ahead," she said, as always armed with her notepad.

As the contents of the letter became apparent to her, Martha did not say a word but continued taking notes, with tears sliding down her cheeks. She brought the completed letter back into his office for him to sign, and once he had, she hugged and kissed him hard, saying:

"Good luck, sir; I am going to miss you terribly."

While Sopwith was slowly making his way back to England, there were two people particularly concerning themselves about his future.

As pleased as he was with the demise of Asim Khatib, John Baker at MI6, was concerned about the way in which he had died. Jihadist groups were well-known for wanting to avenge the death of fellow combatants, and John was doing his best to try and contain the information regarding who had, in fact, caused the man's death. He had already met with the Royal Marines who had assured him that details of Khatib's death would remain Top Secret. The Marines had ensured that this order reached Lt George Kemp and his men aboard R08.

John Baker had drafted a similar message to the Prime Minister's office, as well as to the Navy. Other than that, he could only cross fingers that the information never saw the light of day.

On the other hand, Seaman Anthony Baxter's concerns were in direct conflict with Baker's. Now having heard a detailed account of what had gone down in Mozambique via 'scuttle-butt', he was, for his own gain, scheming about how to use the fact that Sopwith had killed a jihadist. The more he schemed, the more bitter he became, and the more and more twisted his thoughts.

Chapter Nine

On admission to hospital aboard R08 Sopwith had been stabilised and diagnosed. He was extremely dehydrated, malnourished and in shock. His chest was X-rayed which confirmed that he had two cracked ribs beneath the open wound on his rib cage. This, along with the wound to his inner arm, were sutured and dressed. After he was placed on an intravenous drip, and had a feeding tube inserted, he was left to rest.

Ali was found to be in a similar condition, with the one major difference being that she had lost a great deal of blood due to the severe bullet wound in her thigh. The highly skilled trauma surgeon on board sutured the major blood vessels which had been severed by the bullet, then disinfected and sutured the wound closed with great care and precision, to ensure as little scarring to the limb as possible, as well as enable optimum muscle recovery. After receiving a blood transfusion, she too, was placed on a drip and feeding tube inserted, and allowed to rest.

The morning after he had crashed into R08's deck, Sopwith was discharged. He was physically weak but certainly not in too much pain, unless he coughed or laughed, but was well pleased to get out of the hospital.

The R08 had a very limited number of private cabins aboard, and few of those were furnished with double beds (these usually being reserved for visiting dignitaries) so Sopwith was delighted when he was shown to one of the cabins with a double bed. He was told that he could move freely around the ship without a chaperone, and he wondered about this surprisingly preferential treatment, even though he was probably going to be extradited back to South Africa on his return to England.

After a short rest he made his way to the shop to buy some clothes. Other than the soiled clothes in which they arrived aboard, and which had all been sent for incineration, neither Sopwith nor Ali had anything else to wear, so wearing his hospital gown and feeling very self-conscious he entered the shop. He found suitable denim jeans, socks, underwear, shirts, and a pair of running shoes. After paying for them, he returned to his cabin to get dressed. His wallet and his Leatherman had fortunately been saved, so he busied himself by vigorously scrubbing the dried blood off the Leatherman. Once dressed, he returned to the hospital to visit Ali. He found she was still fast asleep, so he made his way to the hangar to see what his aeroplane looked like. He had no recollection of actually hitting the deck but knew without any doubt that is what must have happened after his last conscious memory of the deck looming up at him. He was pleasantly surprised to see that the damage to the 172 Solar was limited. The propeller was totally written off, and the three landing gear struts, along with their wheel rims and tyres were ruined, but that was the total extent of the damage as far as he could see. Along with a new pane of plexi-glass for the cockpit door, he knew it was going to be expensive to repair but would not take too much work. He then found the Officers' Mess, had a big lunch, then went back to his cabin and slept. That evening, on visiting Ali, found her awake and gave her a gentle hug and kiss.

"How are you feeling love?"

"I have felt better in my life before this, for sure, but am really not too bad now. My leg is still very sore, but otherwise I am OK. However, they say I will be in here for another day of two. And how are you?"

"I'm fine, but please don't make me laugh; that hurts!"

"You're going to have to tell me what happened, as I remember very little from the time I was shot. It feels like a big chunk of my life has disappeared. I only know we are aboard R08 because the nurse told me!"

"Yes, I'll fill you in once I have pieced everything together myself. I've been asked to attend a debriefing tomorrow, so I'm sure that should close a few gaps. I'll visit you after that and bring you up to speed. You'll be a little stronger tomorrow too. Now it's time for you to have a good sleep," and kissing her goodnight, Sopwith left.

Sopwith went to the Officers' Mess for supper and re-acquainted himself with Lt Cdr Karl Brighill, Ali's old boss, and Commander of 809 Squadron, who happened to be having a meal there too. It was good to see him again and Karl was full of questions about what had happened since they had last left the carrier. For some reason that Sopwith could not fathom he detected that the man was a little uncomfortable in his company. After a dinner of steak, egg, and chips, probably Sopwith's favourite food, he returned to his lovely double bed and fell asleep right away, lulled by the rise and fall of the great ship steaming along in a big swell.

He reported to the Rear Admiral's quarters at 09h00 for the debriefing and was pleased to see C/Sgt Steve Roberts there too, who in turn, introduced him to his commander in the Royal Marines, Lt George Kemp. Once seated at the boardroom table, Sopwith told the gathering the entire story of why he and Ali had left England, after they had been married by the Yeovilton Base Chaplain, and then of their travels through Africa to the Fungi Peninsula.

Lt Kemp asked for a lot of detail about the Boko Haram jihadists they had encountered in Niger, which Sopwith provided as best he could. After a while there were no more questions for him, so he continued his tale from the time they had landed at the Palma airstrip, up until the time of Steve Roberts' and his men's arrival at the hut where they had been held hostage. At that juncture Sopwith had to answer many questions put to him regarding the behaviour of the jihadists, with specific reference to their treatment of Sopwith and Ali, along with their discipline, about who made decisions, and so on. Once the questions had ceased, Sopwith asked,

"Can you tell me how you found us so quickly? I really thought that we had been doing quite a good job of lying low."

"Regretfully, now I'm not at liberty to tell you more, Sopwith, mainly because there's information that even I don't yet know," replied the Rear Admiral, "but I'm sure someone will be able to inform you once you are back in England."

Sopwith's final report included the details of his flight from Palma airstrip to R08, but quickly got to a point where he admitted remembering very little of the flight, and asked if the helicopter pilot who had escorted him could fill him in. The Merlin pilot Sopwith remembered as Mike Four, introduced himself and began to speak about the details of the escort flight:

"It became evident to me and my co-pilot that you were not very fit. Initially you seemed to hear, but nevertheless ignored my instructions. I then tried to get your attention with direct and loud orders, which then seemed to backfire, as you totally over-reacted to them! When you were not doing anything about entering your glide approach to land, and when I ordered you to lose altitude, you pushed your plane's nose into a steep dive. Hell, it was frightening, sir! You managed to porpoise your way closer to the flight deck on my commands, thankfully remaining on the correct heading, and then when I asked if you had the threshold visual, and you told me that you couldn't even see a ship, I nearly panicked. After my final command for you to lose altitude, you just went straight into the deck and I assumed you had lost consciousness. All I can say, sir, that in the state you were in, you did very well. Well done!"

Sopwith thanked the pilot for his assistance, and then with the debriefing officially over, the Rear Admiral asked how Ali was. Sopwith brought him up to speed, whereupon the RA asked that as soon as Ali felt strong enough, he would like to host a small gathering at the Officers' Club. He also told Sopwith he was aware that The First Sea Lord had decided for them to be accommodated once again at RNAS Yeovilton, as well as for his 172 Solar to be lifted to the air station by Chinook helicopter for repairs. Sopwith was really taken aback by this news; totally mystified about why he was being so well cared for. Once the meeting broke up and they were walking away, Sopwith spoke to Steve Roberts:

"Steve, if you have time to come down to the hangar with me, I have a present for you."

"Certainly!" and they made their way together into the vast hangar and to where the 172 Solar was being stored. Here, Sopwith opened the cockpit door and scrabbled around behind the seats, coming out with an AK47.

"There you go…here's a souvenir of this mission; one AK47 relieved from the Boko Haram jihadists."

"Oh, great! That'll be a superb trophy on our regimental pub wall; thank you! I am not allowed to have it on board though, so may I please ask you to leave it hidden in your plane, and then I can collect it from you in England?"

"Of course; deal done!" and they shook hands, with Sopwith telling him that they would be staying at RNAS Yeovilton for a while, from whence the weapon could be collected.

Sopwith then went to visit Ali, who welcomed him with her lovely trademark smile. He was pleased to see was looking much healthier than she had the day before and. He told her about the debriefing, and that he had not yet discovered how they had been found so quickly. He then rehashed what had happened after she had been shot and described the ghastly flight with his plane ending up in the catch net with broken undercarriage struts and propeller. Ali let out a peal of laughter, saying:

"You see what happens when I leave the flying to you! Now you know why I married you; to avoid such disasters, so you had better keep me in good flying order from now on. Oh, my darling; it must have been such an awful experience for you?"

"Not at all. I was so far out of it that I was not aware of what was going on, as well as passing out completely before we hit the deck. But we both came out unscathed and I'll do everything in my power to keep you in good flying order, once you've regained your abilities in the bedroom," Sopwith retorted with a big smile.

On the following morning, the fourth since they had arrived, Ali was allowed out of the hospital, dressed in her hospital gown. Using crutches, she and Sopwith made their way to the shop where she managed to buy some T-shirts and underpants. There were no bra's available nor any trousers that she could get over her damaged leg, so having told Sopwith to follow her, they headed for the quartermaster's stores and after some sweet talking, managed to squirrel a baggy pair of fatigues out of them. When Sopwith showed her to their cabin she was astounded at the presence of the double bed, never having had a clue there were any aboard.

Over the next six days, before their arrival in Portsmouth, Ali recovered exceedingly well. They slept a lot, made love a lot, (very gently, in deference to their injuries), ate very well, and did as much other exercise outside their cabin as they could. Sopwith did more walking, while Ali concentrated her efforts on more gym time; their abilities to perform the relevant exercises being, likewise, dictated by their injuries. Sopwith, as well as the many amongst the ship's company, were delighted by the spectacle of Ali's bra' less breasts; her nipples showing prominently through the thin material of her T-shirts. She berated him every time she caught him staring in public. With time, however, she lost self-consciousness about her appearance, no longer caring what anyone thought, enjoying instead, the freedom from a restrictive bra.

They had been invited to a gathering at the Officer's Club, which had been adorned with a banner announcing: 'Welcome Home Lt Murray', which brought a lump to her throat. She stepped up to centre stage as soon as she had taken a sip of her shandy.

"Thank you so much everyone, for this welcome and for the help you have been to me and Sopwith; we truly appreciate it. However, I am not coming 'home' and I am no longer Lt Murray. I have submitted the resignation of my commission, which, I think is still being processed, and am now Mrs Alison Jones; married to this wonderful man here," she said looking at Sopwith. There were several calls for her to reconsider, for her to be happy, not to have too many babies, and all sorts of witty comments; some tinged with a measure of sadness. All these served to liven-up things in the Club, until Lt Cdr Karl Brighill called for quiet.

"Sopwith, please join me," he requested, asking him to stand alongside.

"You were only recently awarded a certificate for your perfect first carrier landing on R08, and made an honorary member of 809 Squadron, so it's an honour for me, now, to be able to present you with yet another award: the very first of its type. I hereby award you the inaugural 'Worst Landing on R08' Award, with video evidence to prove it. However, your honorary squadron membership remains intact," he pronounced, and to the sounds of much cheering and laughter from those gathered in the Club, handed over a gilded certificate, together with a USB device.

"I bet not many of you could have done any better with your eyes closed like mine were," Sopwith laughed, "but thank you so much, Karl, for the wonderful memento. Huge thanks, too, to each one of you for all the help that you have given me and Ali. Like her, I will always appreciate everything that you have done." Sopwith ended his remarks to calls of: 'Down…down!' so he readily obliged by knocking back his pint of Old Speckled Hen.

Sopwith and Ali got chatting to Karl, who eventually admitted he had been aware that Ali was being taken off F-35s when she last left R08. Ali gave him a playful but hard punch to his biceps. He vowed, however, that he had absolutely no idea she was going to be posted to a logistics office, having presumed she would have been posted to flying duties elsewhere.

"Just as we were about to depart, we both sensed you were embarrassed about something," Ali said to Karl, who really looked very sheepish.

"I am so sorry, but I had been ordered to keep the matter confidential."

Sopwith asked Karl if he could use his PC, then went online to Cessna and ordered a new propeller, door plexi-glass, undercarriage struts and wheels. He was pleased to see that he would be getting upgraded struts along with a new type of oleo for the nose-wheel. He paid online for the eye-watering purchase price and delivery charges to Yeovilton.

By the time they were due to dock in Portsmouth, Sopwith's flesh wounds had healed nicely, and his ribs were hardly sore anymore. Ali was able to manage with only one support crutch, and was walking well, with her wound all but completely healed.

In R08's hangar below the flight deck Sopwith watched the engineers mount the Cessna 172 Solar on a purpose-made cradle, and then swathe the whole aircraft in a type of bubble-wrap for transport. They told him that the covering was as much to protect the aircraft from windblown debris from the Chinook's rotors as it was to disguise it so that 'plane spotters' did not get their knickers in a knot about what the Chinook was conveying.

After they had docked, they were told that RNAS Yeovilton had sent a car to collect them for the one-hundred-and-sixty-kilometre journey via Southampton and Salisbury, but first they watched as Sopwith's aeroplane was brought up from the hangar and the cradle hooked up to a hovering Chinook, which slowly gained height and then picked up speed, heading in the direction of Yeovilton.

Having said their farewells to as many people as possible on R08, and carrying with them their very few remaining possessions, they left the great ship, bound for the next chapter in their lives.

When Arthur Lightfoot had finally left his office for the very last time without any regrets, he caught a taxi straight to his home in Richmond, where he had lived happily for many years. On walking into his home and placing his briefcase in his study, Iris, his wife saw him.

"When are you going to work today, Arthur?" she enquired.

"I've just come home from work, Iris," he replied.

"Oh," she said, "I'll have Mrs Page get dinner ready."

"No Iris, I've come home much earlier than usual; it's not dinner time. I think it's time for your nap now."

"Oh yes, that's a good idea," and she walked off.

He thought sadly what a shame it that Iris was seemed to be getting quite bad. Her Alzheimer's disease was getting no better, but she seemed comfortable and happy enough. Arthur sought out their long-time housekeeper, Mrs Page, and told her that he had retired, but that it would be best to keep the information from Iris. He explained that he would be spending much time in his study, along with infrequent trips away from the house, and that Mrs Page should carry on with her duties in the same way as she had been.

He went into his office and made a call to the Navy Harbour Control in Portsmouth and asked what the due docking date was for incoming R08. Once he had that detail, he booked a Business Class return flight on British Airways for Ben Dougmore, and afterwards forwarded the details to him. The flight was booked for the day after R08 was due to dock. He then booked Ben into the 'Petersham Hotel', overlooking the Thames River, and situated close to his own home. The Petersham was an old Victorian home that had been converted into a five-star luxury hotel. Arthur felt certain that Ben would really enjoy his stay there. He next booked accommodation and a meal at a restaurant in Yeovil. He had been to Yeovil several times, and although he normally stayed at the air station, he had eaten out a lot in Yeovil, so knew his way around there. He settled on 'The Little Barwick House', situated just out of Yeovil and known as a restaurant with rooms, where he had enjoyed excellent meals before. It was one of Somerset's best long-standing restaurants with a small number of excellent rooms, and where the whole place could be hired exclusively; perfect for the evening Arthur had in mind. Luckily 'The Little Barwick House' was available for the night on which he wanted it, so he booked and paid. Lastly, he phoned Godlonton-Shaw at Yeovilton and asked him to let Sopwith and Ali know that they had been invited for the night out, and he would collect them on the evening of their arrival at Yeovilton. He also asked Godlonton-Shaw not to reveal who was taking them out.

Having achieved what he set out to do, and as it was about time for a sundowner, he set about waking Iris up. She was so happy to see him that it seemed to her that he had been away for a long time, but the moment was spoiled by her asking him if he was on his way to work.

"No Iris, I've come to fetch you for a sundowner. Doesn't that sound good?"

"Oh yes, very good indeed! I'll have mine with honey you know; those hazel nuts are not to my taste anymore." Arthur chuckled to himself, realising that his retirement could not have come soon enough, as he was going to have his work cut looking after Iris.

Sopwith and Ali enjoyed their drive from Portsmouth through part of Hampshire, and once past Southampton, found that Wiltshire was in all its spring glory. The chalk grasslands of Salisbury Plain were littered with wildflower blossoms. When by-passing the city of Salisbury, they had a wonderful view of the magnificent spire of the Cathedral. Their driver volunteered to take them on the short detour to view Stonehenge, before they had to turn west towards Yeovilton, which turned out to be worth the extra effort. The massive, and apparently precariously balanced blocks of rock left them in wonderment as to how they had been erected, (apparently even before the Egyptian pyramids) and for what purpose, essentially making them appreciate how little Humanity really knew about their very early history. After leaving there, and pushing on into Somerset, they stopped for a traditional English Pub lunch. The wildflowers continued to colour the fields, with yellow daffodils being especially prominent.

They arrived at RNAS Yeovilton in the early afternoon, and after being issued identity badges at the security gate, they were taken to Lt Cdr Godlonton-Shaw's office. He welcomed them like old friends, and walking with them escorted them to their accommodation, with Ali still having to use her one crutch to gamely keep up. En route Sopwith asked whether he could first see his plane, so Godlonton-Shaw eagerly detoured to the hangar where it was being housed. Once inside Sopwith was delighted to see two engineers busy stripping off the shroud. To one side were the new spares which had already arrived from Cessna.

"Wow! I'm surprised that you already have got chaps working on her, and delighted to see that the spares have arrived," said Sopwith.

"We were hoping to be a little further along before you arrived," replied the commander, delighted to hear Sopwith's praise.

"I'll be joining them tomorrow to give them a hand."

They were then taken to a small brick 'married quarters' bungalow (normally reserved for those officers of Commander rank) which Godlonton-Shaw generously announced as being at their disposal for the duration of their stay, however long that might be. Inside they found their clothing bags which had been left behind at Palma airstrip and forwarded by Kenneth Le Grange via John Baker's office.

"You two are being taken out for the night tomorrow, so it would be wise to launder your glad rags," the commander told them.

"Who's taking us out?" asked Sopwith.

"'Wait and see' is the name," replied a smiling Godlonton-Shaw.

Ali did unpack their bags and filled the cottage washing machine to capacity, then started the cycle. Also in the bags were two very well-sealed packages, and upon tearing them open she found her issue 9mm Browning, as well as the weapon that they had 'borrowed' from Yeovilton armoury. She showed these to Sopwith, realising with great relief, she would no longer have to explain the circumstances of how she had lost weapons on her final exit from the Fleet Air Arm. As under-dressed as they felt, they were both hungry, so walked to the Officers' Mess. There they met up a few of the staff they had come to know, and enjoyed a basic, but wholesome meal.

In bed later they mused about who the mystery host was for their 'night out' the next day might be, and then settled down to sleep after a long day.

Arthur had arranged with Uber to transport Ben from Heathrow to the Petersham Hotel upon his arrival the following morning, and when he checked into the grand old building, he was handed a handwritten note from Arthur informing him that he would personally collect him from the hotel at 15h00 for a night out in Somerset, and that he should bring an overnight bag with him.

Ben had a magnificent breakfast of kippers, followed by scrambled eggs with toast, and a cup of his favourite fine English tea. He went to his palatial room, showered, and settled onto the huge bed for a sleep, not having had much opportunity to catch any 'shut eye' on the overnight flight.

After a light late lunch, Ben was ready when Arthur arrived to collect him. They greeted each other in delight to be meeting again. Ben got into Arthur's early model Range Rover, and they set off on the one-hundred-and-eighty-kilometre drive to Yeovil. One of Ben's first questions to Arthur was to enquire after Sopwith's whereabouts, to which Arthur vaguely stated that he had been located and was well. In response Ben commented, "I'd certainly love to meet that man again!"

"Oh I'm sure you will one day," answered Arthur slyly.

Over the previous number of years Arthur had not had to drive himself much, so set about the task somewhat erratically, often making mistakes in the innumerable roundabouts on the roads, but despite the honking horns of anger directed at his bad driving, Ben was totally unaffected and carried on casual conversation with Arthur throughout the journey.

They compared notes about their respective lives and swapped amusing anecdotes. Travelling on the A303, they stopped for a pork pie and a beer at the John Russell Fox Pub in High Street, Andover, Arthur's favourite half-way stops to Yeovilton on his travels there, and then with the help of their continuous chatter, the three-hour journey was over surprisingly quickly, finding themselves in Little Barwick House shortly after 17h00. On arrival they were shown to their respective rooms by the owner and arranged to next meet up at Reception at 18h00. Arthur said nothing about that being the time he expected Sopwith and Ali to arrive there as well.

That day Sopwith had little chance to help the engineers working on the 172 Solar as Ali had convinced him they both had to shop for some decent clothes. Catching a taxi into Yeovil, Sopwith was a patient as he could be while Ali shopped, but all too soon realised why men prefer not to shop with their wives when they are buying clothes. Ali paraded innumerable items of clothing for his opinion, and most often, as soon as he announced that he liked what she was wearing, she discarded it and tried on something else. He had a complete sense of humour failure when he saw her buying new bra's and insisted on a pub lunch break at the 'Rose and Crown' to calm down, after which they went their separate ways to finish their shopping.

He shopped quickly for some new trousers, shirts, and a pair of shoes, and had watched a full game of football on TV in the Rose and Crown while he waited for Ali to finish. The whole expedition was worth it because Ali, not really a keen shopper, had had her dose of retail therapy for a while and was extremely happy that she had found some clothes she really liked; no longer having her uniforms as daily dress.

When they returned to the air station Sopwith had time to pop into the hangar where the 172 was being worked on and found that the engineers had finished removing the shroud, jacked the fuselage up off the cradle, and had started removing the broken undercarriage struts. Returning to the bungalow, he showered and got ready for the taxi that was due to collect them at 17h30. Ali looked ravishing in a not-too-modest black dress; something she rarely wore.

Upon collecting them at the security gate, the taxi driver explained that he had been instructed to take them to a small restaurant and guest house some twenty kilometres away. Twenty minutes later they arrived at the beautiful old building, which was Little Barwick House, set in lush gardens and surrounded by perfectly-mown lawns and horse paddocks. While taking their bags out of the boot of the taxi they were greeted by a very friendly brown Weimaraner dog, and then as they walked up to Reception they stopped in their tracks in surprise when they simultaneously caught sight of Arthur and Ben standing there.

Ben came forward, clearly as surprised and shocked as they were, and gave Sopwith a bear hug.

"Oh, my word Sopwith, what a delightful surprise this is. It's just too wonderful for words!"

Arthur had come forward too, and giving Ali a gentle hug, said, "Welcome Alison."

"Hello, sir, this is indeed a surprise. What on earth are you doing here?"

"There is no need to use the word 'sir' anymore, Alison. My name is Arthur, and now having retired from the Navy, I have time to take you out for dinner."

"Stranger things have rarely happened to me...uh...that is except for a flight through Africa! Well...uh...Arthur, it's very good to meet you again."

After greeting Arthur, Sopwith, now wholly intrigued by this wonderful hospitality, on what he assumed might be the eve of his extradition to South Africa, introduced Ali to Ben who complimented her on her beauty and added, "Sopwith I knew you were far too handsome to stay single for long!"

Arthur explained that the guest house and restaurant were theirs for the evening, then showed the two of them to their superb garden-facing room and asked them to join him for a drink as soon as they were ready. Having settled-in to their room, they walked to the small pub to join Arthur and Ben. Arthur explained, while toasting their reunion, he had decided to arrange the gathering, as he had important things on his mind that he wanted to share with them, after they had finished their starters in the restaurant.

Over starters Sopwith answered all the questions put to him by Ben about their adventures, leaving out only the bloodiest details from his replies. The main course choice on the menu comprised: Fillet of Ruby Beef, Rump of Local Lamb, Pan-Fried Fillet of Cornish Red Mullet or Saddle of Wild Roe Deer. After they had all expressed their preferred choice, and Arthur had asked the waitron to have their meal served in half-an-hour, he began to speak:

"Alison and Sopwith, I have asked you here today to offer you, my apologies. Ben here is involved, too, and needs to hear what I have to say. Firstly Sopwith, here is your British Passport,"

Arthur said, handing over the brand-new document. "You are finally a British subject, congratulations! The South Africans' request for your extradition was never seriously considered, and we simply exposed the trumped-up charges against you."

'Well, that certainly answers my questions,' thought a very happy Sopwith.

"My apologies encompass a number of transgressions on my part, and I offer them with honesty and sincerity.

"Firstly, to Alison, for the way I allowed you to be mistreated by my junior officers. I simply rubber-stamped their decisions without taking any of the facts of your situation into account, as you so forthrightly pointed out to me in my office, and which I failed to make clear, that you should never have been transferred to London.

"Secondly, to you, Sopwith, for allowing the ridiculous rumour to reach your ears, of a probable extradition to South Africa.

"Thirdly to you both, for not finding you quicker than we did. Upon reflection, I could have forced several actions to help us find you, like using America's satellite surveillance system, but I did not. During these events I found myself changing, from the bombastic commander dictated to by the government and money, to understanding that people are not just numbers to buy with gold, but individual human beings with souls, and for whom I was ultimately responsible. I was humbled; am still humbled, by the mistakes I have made and how well you have handled them. I am so sorry, and hope that you can bring yourselves to accept this apology. In the same breath I wish to thank you for helping me become a humbler person than I was before." Arthur sat back with downcast eyes and took a sip from his glass of wine.

Sopwith spoke first. "Arthur, I think you are being much too hard on yourself, but in any event, your apology is wholly accepted by me."

Alison got up from her chair and gave Arthur a big hug and a kiss on the cheek.

"I agree with Sopwith, Arthur. Please do not lose any sleep over the matter, and of course your apology is accepted!"

"Alison, I stopped your letter of resignation from going any further than the 'Personnel' In-tray on my secretary's desk. Are you sure you do not want to reconsider your decision?"

"Thank you for that, Arthur, but my answer is an immediate 'No'. I'm now Sopwith's wife and will be working with him, both in and out of bed, on whatever he does in his capacity as Chief Test Pilot, so please let the letter take its proper course," Ali replied, the wine already having an effect on her.

Their main course dishes were served, accompanied by more wine. They all were immensely impressed with the food, and readily agreed that the restaurant certainly lived up to its reputation. As the wine flowed, the more relaxed the mood became, with both Sopwith and Ali regaling the two men about their 'quickie' wedding at Yeovilton, Ali's deception of ATC there, and with further details of their flight through Africa, describing the scenery and the events of the trip in more detail.

Arthur eventually also opened with full details about what their search for Sopwith and Ali had entailed, along with details of Kenneth Le Grange of SWB being tasked by Minister Masondo to find them. Lubricated by the wine, he also admitted to disobeying the Prime Minister; an action which had ultimately led to his 'retirement'. Ben was enthralled by all the tales, repeatedly expressing his gratitude to Arthur for having been invited along for the occasion.

"Ben, you had to be here, as you're the one who actually started this all by having the cheek to sit in my office and suggest the Royal Navy should send an aircraft carrier to collect a civilian and his aeroplane from South Africa. Getting in to see me certainly took some perseverance, along with a whole lot of nerve. Well done, but don't forget this whole sequence of events was started by you, and you alone!"

"Yes, Bravo to you Ben," Sopwith added, clapping his hands. "I know I wouldn't be here today if it had not been for you. You're my champion, even though you are the oldest lawyer in Port Alfred."

The four of them, none of whom were usually big drinkers at any time, continued to enjoy their wine and light banter, eventually ending off the evening some fine whiskey, which saw them all making for their bedrooms on slightly wobbly courses; Ali finding that she could handle her crutch only with great difficulty.

The next morning, they re-gathered for a hearty breakfast, which quickly cured their hangovers. Thereafter the owner called a taxi to take Sopwith and Ali back to Yeovilton.

Arthur informed them that Ben would be his guest in London for the week, and that they would be doing 'retirement' things together, such as 'whatever they wanted, whenever they wanted'. Farewells were exchanged when the taxi arrived, with promises being made to stay in contact, followed by Sopwith and Ali leaving Little Barwick House a very happy couple.

After arriving back at the air station, Sopwith and Ali inspected the progress of the repair work to the Solar and then went to their quarters where Sopwith had to make an important call as he had made up his mind on a particular issue. He had given himself over to much thought about the recent events in his life, mostly to do with the help that the British Government had afforded him. He was also being affected by the knowledge that he had killed three human beings, which made him feel less of a 'civilian' than a soldier.

Based mainly on these two feelings Sopwith had decided to partner with the British Government in his quest to become an aircraft manufacturer, so needed to inform Priti Patel of his decision. When he got through to her and told her of his decision she was absolutely delighted and told him that she would set up a business meeting in London as soon as possible.

Seaman Anthony Baxter was aware that Sopwith and his wife had arrived in England and were based at RNAS Yeovilton, so he decided that it was time to put his plan into action. Using the excuse that he had to attend to some personal business, he left his office and, remaining in uniform, walked to the Embankment London Underground Station. Boarding a Circle Line train he headed west, exiting the Underground at Gloucester Road Station. From there he walked for ten minutes until he found the Embassy of Iraq at 21 Queen's Gate, South Kensington. He walked straight in, after being checked over by a security guard, and was directed to an enquiry desk. There he informed a young man that he needed to see someone in authority because he had information to pass on to the Embassy. This was acknowledged, and he was asked to take a seat in the reception area and wait to be seen. In very short order he was summoned by a short, portly and very unfriendly-looking man, and shown into an interview room.

The man sat down behind a desk and offered Baxter a seat, but just stared at him.

"I have valuable information for you," began Baxter.

The embassy official just looked at him and raised one eyebrow.

"I know who killed Asim Khatib as well as where that person is at the moment."

"I do not know who you are talking about, or what you are referring to. Is there anything else you wish to tell me?" replied the man.

Baxter was definitely not expecting such a cold reception, and felt rather perplexed, but boldly said, somewhat uncharacteristically, "If you say so. Here's my card with my contact details, should you wish to ask me more about the matter." He placed the card with his name and cell phone number on the desk in front of him, stood up and left the office and Embassy.

Baxter had decided to go to the Embassy in uniform in the hopes that he would be taken seriously by the officials there, but the naval uniform allowed watchers to identify him far more quickly than would have been the case if he had been in civilian clothing.

He was totally unaware that MI5 maintain a permanent camera watch over every person who enters and exits the Embassy of Iraq. A camera which has the facility, if deemed necessary, to identify those persons entering the building through a facial recognition computer programme. The uniform immediately caused Baxter's entry and exit of the building to be flagged, the operator responding, quickly identified him in his daily report as Seaman Anthony Baxter from Navy HQ. Along with that report being sent to his own superiors at MI5, it was also disseminated to MI6 for them to check anything that may be of interest to their office.

Chapter Ten

Peggy Smith worked as an intelligence analyst at MI6; a rather chubby lady who, to her own knowledge, was often referred to as 'Piggy' behind her back. She was totally unfazed by this as she lived, ate, drank, and slept her work. Her abilities in analysing intelligence reports were remarkable, so whenever she reported on something to John Baker, she immediately had his undivided attention, as she did now on this particular morning.

"John, a navy Seaman, one Anthony Baxter, was yesterday spotted by MI5's surveillance of the Iraqi Embassy, entering the building, and then exiting a short while later. I picked it up from their daily feed to us, and I would not have bothered informing you about this at this time; MI5 could quite easily have handled the follow-up to find out what the man was doing there. However, on this morning's immigration summary from Heathrow, I picked up the arrival there of one Fatin Saeed."

"The jihadist hitman?" asked a surprised John Baker.

"Yes, his entry photograph was picked up by facial recognition before he even went through immigration. His arrival form states some cock and bull story that he's on a ten-day visit to attend a friend's birthday. Now this may sound far-fetched, so please give me your honest opinion about my theory: Our Navy, all by itself, controls a mission to Africa from Navy HQ here, where a jihadist leader is killed by an infidel civilian. A Seaman from said Navy HQ visits the Iraqi Embassy soon after said infidel arrives back in England, and a day later a known jihadist hitman enters England to attend a birthday party. I think not, I think he has arrived to take revenge."

John Baker thought it through, but only for a short while.

"Peggy, I do believe you have once again hit the nail on the head with this one. The fearful prospect of a hit on Sopwith Jones has been in my mind ever since he did away with Khatib. Well done and add a beer to the ones I already owe you! Have we not yet got anything definite on Fatin Saeed so that we can bring him in for questioning?"

"Nothing that I am aware of. All we do know with absolute certainty is that he does act as a hitman for the jihadists."

"OK. I am going to tell MI5 that we will take the Baxter issue over from them because of its international connections, so let's not waste any time. Your priority is to please follow up with Navy HQ about this Baxter fellow. We need to know everything about him, including cell phone numbers and personal banking details. I am going to call Trevor in from his training in Europe to find and follow this Fatin bastard. Please also make a call to Mr & Mrs Jones at Yeovilton and ask them to report any planned movements away from the air station to us, and don't be shy about telling them that there may be a threat to his life, but don't give them any other detail."

"I'm onto it!" said Peggy with glee, for she loved it when there was some action, especially as a spin-off from her own analysis.

John spoke to his counterpart at MI5 who was rather pleased to have part of his workload relieved from him. John then got hold of Trevor Mommsen, one of his agents currently doing a training exercise somewhere in Europe. John did not even know exactly were.

"Trev, get yourself back to London ASAP for some real work please."

"What's it about?"

"I'll send you a message with basic detail that you can read up on during your journey back here, but when I said 'ASAP' I meant it. I want you back now!"

Peggy managed to get one of their drivers to take her to Navy HQ right away, and by being as persistent as possible, managed to bulldoze her way into securing a meeting with the recently appointed new First Sea Lord, Admiral Ron Hubbard.

"Thank you for seeing me, sir. I'm Peggy Smith from MI6, sir. I wouldn't normally have been so persistent in getting in to see you, sir, but we believe this issue could be as important a matter as life or death. An employee in this building was seen, in uniform, visiting the Iraqi Embassy. Might there be any legitimate reason for a visit of this nature?"

"Absolutely not! Do you know who this man is?"

"Yes, sir; Seaman Anthony Baxter. Are you aware of whom this man is?"

"Oh, I know exactly who you're referring to ma'am," replied the First Sea Lord, now ashen-faced.

"You look quite shocked, sir. Any particular reason for that?"

"Seaman Baxter was a Lieutenant Commander until recently. He was court-martialled and lost his rank for spreading false information. He did, however, remain employed here as a Seaman."

"What was the false information, sir?"

"He told a fellow officer that a civilian we are working with was wanted by the South African authorities for criminal activity."

"That civilian being Mr Sopwith Jones, sir?"

"Indeed!"

"Do you have any idea how this Baxter chap has taken his loss of rank?"

"I've been informed that he is disgruntled. Exactly how badly disgruntled I do not know, but it appears he is performing his duties correctly."

"Sir, please may I ask you to authorise the release of his personal bank account details, residential address and cell phone number to us? We'll have to put this man under surveillance, as we believe he may have passed on some sensitive information to the Iraqis."

"Naval secrets? Strategy? He has absolutely no knowledge of that sort of information."

"Not at all, sir. We think he may've tried to get word to ISIS jihadists about the whereabouts of Mr Jones, for obvious reasons."

"Oh my goodness! If he has done that, I'll lock him up straight away!"

"No sir; please don't do anything of the sort or say a word to anyone else about this. Let us handle it, sir; this is our area of expertise."

"Of course, ma'am, so shall it be!" said the First Sea Lord, then called Martha into his office.

"Martha please show Ms Smith here to Personnel. I'll phone them immediately. By the time you get there they should have the information you need ready for you, Ms Smith."

Peggy returned to her office immediately after collecting Baxter's personal information and reported to John Baker.

"There's definitely bad blood between Baxter and Jones. I chatted to a few staff while I was at Navy HQ, and the First Sea Lord's secretary, Martha, knows everything. It appears to some people that Baxter's decided that Jones is to blame for the misfortune of losing his rank. I suggest that we put an ear to his cell phone immediately. If we're actually on the right track I'm sure that's how any contact will made by Fatin Saeed."

"I'll have that authorised and get the Comms desk onto it. Thank you so much Peggy. You may monitor Baxter's bank account as a sideshow if you like?"

"Great stuff, sir! I love being part of the action, even if it's only a very small part. Thank you." Peggy returned to her own office and made the call to the Joneses at Yeovilton.

"Mr Jones, this is Peggy Smith from MI6 in London here."

"Good day, Peggy, how may I help you? And please call me Sopwith."

"Sopwith, we've obtained intelligence that suggests that your life might be in danger. I'm not in a position to tell you more than that, other than to say that you and your wife need to take our warning seriously. Please don't leave RNAS Yeovilton without informing us, so that we can advise you how to handle things, dependent upon circumstances prevailing at the time."

"I must say this is somewhat of a shock but thank you for the information. We'll be very grateful if you can continue to keep us in the loop as things progress, so at least we'll know what on earth's going on."

"I assure you that our office will keep you as well-informed as is possible. Thank you and goodbye for now."

With the call ended, Sopwith, still slightly bewildered, passed on to Ali the news he had just received. They speculated for a while about who or what could be causing the perceived threat but could not come up with anything that made any sense to either of them, so merely resigned themselves to accepting the warning as a fact that they most certainly needed to heed.

Late in the afternoon Trevor Mommsen arrived at John Baker's office to be briefed.

"Trev, the address on Fatin Saeed's arrivals form will almost certainly be false, but for the record just check on it anyway. Here's a file of every bit of information we have on this character. Study it thoroughly, as according to our intelligence, he really is an evil and ruthless bastard. We have MI5's co-operation, so they have him flagged on facial recognition throughout their London surveillance system. My money's on the fact that he's probably going to call Baxter and set up a meeting, so you'll be able to take it from there, but in the meantime try and find him in any event."

"OK. I'll get on top of things right away. I've heard of the bastard Saeed before and would love to nail him. It's time to get another one of these extremists out of the way."

Trev's home was a small garden flat where he spent very little time because his work was mostly out of the country. On his way there Trev visited the address given on Saeed's arrival form only to find it an abandoned building, as per John Baker's prediction.

Once he had put on the kettle to make himself a brew, he pored over the file on Fatin Saeed, who had originally come to MI6's attention when they had received information he had killed two prominent members of the Islamic clergy in Iraq (reportedly at the behest of extremist jihadists) where he had walked into a mosque while his victims were leading afternoon prayers, shot them both in their heads, and walked out.

The next report on him was from the CIA whose information was a sketchy, but very likely instance of further Saeed action. He had illegally entered America from Canada by road, and in Dearborn, Michigan, he had slaughtered all the senior members of a mosque there by single shots to their heads, leaving a message that their deaths had been ordered by jihadists. He had escaped from America by unknown means.

The file reports continued with other incidents of Islamists being killed by the man, and then his first action against an infidel occurred in France, where, following a police raid on a jihadist cell, he later allegedly killed a policeman who had caused the death of a jihadist during the action.

Five further infidel killings were attributed to him in various countries, all apparently in retribution for the death of a jihadist, but in each case, there was not enough evidence for him to be arrested. Each of the five deaths had resulted from a single gunshot to the heads of his alleged victims.

Trev was starting to have a very bad feeling about this grossly evil man; realising that he was in for some serious work to try and stop him from continuing his killing spree.

MI6's communication section was geared to listen in to any call made to, or received by, Anthony Baxter's cell phone, so when the first incoming call to his phone happened at just after 21h00 that evening, it was immediately detected and recorded, along with the initialisation of the triangulation process to track where the call had originated.

"Baxter," Anthony answered his phone, even though the screen displayed an unknown number.

"You have information for me?" stated a foreign-sounding voice.

"Who are you?" asked Baxter.

"That is of no concern to you, infidel! You have information I want. If you don't give it, I'll take it from you anyway, and then kill you. Is that, OK?"

This was going as badly as had his meeting in the embassy thought Baxter, but he answered, "First I want money for the information."

"You want money? How much money?"

"Just one million pounds sterling."

"Ha! You infidels and your money god! You shall have it when I get my information tomorrow. Where can we meet?"

"At the Ace Café on the North Circular Road at 10h00," answered Baxter. He had at least thought through the possibility that someone may want to meet with him discreetly, so had chosen the Ace Café, as it was well away from anywhere, he, or any of his acquaintances would normally go, and to top it off was a biker café, where theoretically, as far as he was concerned, would be the perfect place to conduct a little thuggery.

"I will be there," said the voice on his phone.

"How will I know you?" asked Baxter.

"Don't worry about small things, infidel. I will know you!" he growled menacingly, ending the call.

The call had been too short for the tracking process to be completed, but the tape was sent through to John Baker's office immediately. Baker, not unusually, was still in his office when the tape arrived by email. He listened to it and then promptly phoned Trevor to brief him.

"Trev, we have the bastard in our sights already. He is meeting Anthony Baxter at 10h00 tomorrow at the old Ace Café on the North Circular Road, so be there and follow him like shit sticking to a blanket from there on. Agent Norman Taylor is coming to the end of his R and R; use him as back-up. We need to know what Saeed is up to, as well as make sure he does not kill anyone, so please keep me posted."

Trev immediately made a call to Norman Taylor and told him they should meet at the MI6 building at 05h00 the next morning. Norman was delighted, saying, "Glad to get out of the house; my missus is driving me scatty."

After a few hours' sleep Trev made his way into the city, and upon arriving at MI6 just before 05h00, he found Norman already there, waiting for him. They drew body armour, communication sets with throat microphones and earpieces, binoculars and a pool car each. They would be armed with only their standard issue Glock 17 pistols. After complying with various protocols involving logging where they would be operating, and informing the duty officer of their mission, Trev gave Norman full colour photographs of both Anthony Baxter and Fatin Saeed, explaining that they would refine their plans once in situ.

They drove out of Central London to the Ace Café rendezvous in heavy traffic. They arrived there just before 09h00 and parked in the smaller parking area at the corner of Beresford Avenue and the North Circular; an area usually used for service deliveries. They walked casually around the building and found it was already open, but with no customers yet present, and one of their staff busy placing chairs and tables outside the front of the café to take advantage of the beautiful sunny day it was turning out to be.

After inspecting the whole area in and around the café, Trev decided that his car would be parked, backed up, into the service area to enable him to follow Saeed either along North Circular or Beresford, dependent upon which direction he left the café. He told Taylor to park his car at the other end of the building, also backed up, to enable him to move along North Circular in a south-westerly direction if need be. It was decided, too, that Trev would sit at an outside table just before 10h00 while Taylor would remain within the café drinking coffee and, if necessary, could then adjust their positions when Saeed arrived, dependent upon where he met with Baxter.

As the clock on the small campanile of the café ticked away, a few customers started drifting in, by motorbike, car and on foot which made it a little easier for the two agents to remain 'undercover'.

A few minutes before 10h00 Baxter arrived on foot, dressed in civilian clothes, looked around and then selected one of the outside tables, four away from where Trev was seated, busily engaged in drinking coffee and reading the newspaper. Baxter took a seat, facing North Circular Road, and when a waiter approached, made motions indicating he was waiting for someone else to join him. At 10h05, a BMW R1200GS motorbike roared into the parking lot and stopped right next to the table at which Baxter sat. Setting the side-stand down first, the rider dismounted, took off his full-face helmet and backpack, placing them both on Baxter's table and sat down opposite him. It was Fatin Saeed. His motorbike bore no number plate.

"Norman, that is definitely Saeed," said Trev into his throat mike. "Take your time but pay your bill and move to your car. I don't think this meeting is going to take long and the bastard has very cleverly arrived by bike which means he will get going very quickly when he leaves." Norman instantly acknowledged: "Roger that."

Anthony Baxter had phoned his immediate superior at work earlier that morning to tell him that he was not feeling well, so would not be going in to work that day, and then took the Underground to Ace Café. Arriving at Stonebridge Park Station on the Bakerloo Line, he took the few minutes needed to walk the rest of the way along North Circular Road to Ace Café, and on arrival, had chosen an outside table and sat down. He told the waiter who came to serve him that he was waiting for a friend, then looked around him, noticing only one other customer sitting outside, who completely ignored him, then sat patiently for the arrival of his contact. Within a couple of minutes, a large motorbike roared up to his table and stopped. A man wearing a full-face helmet, with a darkened visor, dismounted, removed his helmet then backpack, and placed both on the table, then sat down and stared at him.

"Good morning, Mr...." offered Baxter.

"What is the man's name?" asked the olive-skinned, grim-looking man in the same abrupt manner that he had heard on his cell phone the night before.

"Where is my money?" asked Baxter bravely, but with a slight tremor in his voice. The man pushed the backpack slightly forward on the table, opening the top flap. Baxter peered into it and saw an untidy jumble of many fifty-pound notes. With that Saeed closed the flap and pushed the bag towards Baxter, saying, "Keep it infidel."

"His name is Sopwith Jones!" said Baxter excitedly, pulling the backpack towards himself, feeling a nice heft to it.

"Where is he?"

"He is living at Royal Navy Air Station Yeovilton, near the town of Yeovil in Somerset. Here is a picture of him," said Baxter, sliding a small but current photograph of Sopwith to the man.

"Is he in the Air Force?"

"No, he's a civilian working with the British Government. He lives there with his wife who works for him as his pilot. He's invented a solar-powered aeroplane that our government is interested in."

"How long will he be at this Yeovilton base?"

"I'm not sure about that, but I think it'll be for quite a while still."

"Why are you selling this man out?"

"Because he destroyed my career and caused me great trouble and stress at work, as well as being a criminal by killing people."

"Which people did he kill?" Saeed asked, wanting to make sure he was not being fed false information.

"One of your men, Asim Khatib, as well as one of the guards there."

"Where is there?"

"At Fungi Peninsula in Mozambique," Baxter answered, looking at the man expectantly, anticipating the next question.

Fatin Saeed stood up, fitted the helmet onto his head, mounted his BMW, started its motor, kicked back the side-stand, and then in a flash, took a large pistol from his jacket pocket, held the silenced muzzle close to Baxter's temple and fired a single shot into his brain, causing Baxter's body to slump forward onto the table. With that he motored away at full throttle, turning south-west onto North Circular Road without giving any consideration at all to the flow of vehicles passing by. He did not encounter any other traffic impeding his way, as he simply swerved around any obstacle, as he motored off at full speed along the road.

Trevor had seen Baxter's inspection of the interior of the backpack and the clipped two-way conversation, but had heard none of what had been said. He was getting himself ready to get up to go to his car, realising that the meeting was coming to an end, just as Saeed stood up from the table to mount and start the motorbike. He then saw Saeed pulling out his pistol.

"Jesus Christ!" screamed Trev into his mike when he saw Saeed take the shot at Baxter's head. "Go Norman, go!" he screamed, while simultaneously pulling his Glock from its holster under his jacket. He managed to fire one round at the fleeing biker on his powerful machine, but the shot was very wide of the mark. He could fire no more shots because there was too much traffic around, and the bike was already out of effective handgun range. He saw Norman's car screech out of the parking area and onto North Circular Road, but held very little hope that he would, in fact, be able to catch their quarry. He briefly considered calling for a helicopter, but quickly realised that it would have been a total waste of time.

Trev walked to where Baxter lay crumpled across the table and held his forefingers against his neck. There was no pulse at all; the man was dead. He looked into the backpack, shifted the fifty-pound notes to one side and saw only crumpled newspaper, and then, after feeling around, found two bricks at the bottom of the bag. Saeed had obviously paid Baxter off with a false bag of money for some information, but Trev had no clue as to what that information might be.

He phoned John Baker and made his report of the botched encounter with Saeed, including the fact that Saeed's motorbike had no number plate so that they could not even try the ANPR system to track him down. All they had to go on at this point was facial recognition as the system was already alerted to Saeed's face.

Baker was not happy and let Trev know in very colourful language, telling him to stay on the scene and await the arrival of the Metropolitan Police whom he still had to call, which Trev did immediately after ending his call to Baker.

He noticed a few very ashen-faced staff staring out from within the café, so he approached them to tell them that the drama was over, and at the same time asked if they had any CCTV coverage of the area where the shooting had taken place. Ace Café had several CCTV cameras covering strategic points of the building, but not one that covered the crime scene at all. Trevor was digesting the fact that Saeed's 'modus operandi' of not leaving any evidence against him was uncanny, but at least on this occasion Trev was an eyewitness to the murder, and as he thought about that, he felt a cold shiver pass through his body.

When the Metro Police arrived, Trev gave them a statement and left them to handle the rest of the gory business. At about the same time Norman Taylor returned to the scene in the pool car with his tail between his legs, reporting that he had lost Saeed on the BMW within the first minute of taking up the chase. He had roamed streets for a while after he had lost him but had eventually given up in defeat.

Fatin Saeed had been well-informed and had put some research into his meeting with the late Anthony Baxter, whose photograph he had been given by an Iraqi agent to recognise him. When he had reconnoitred the Ace Café proposed as a meeting place by Baxter, he was quite delighted. Situated on North Circular Road, which is part of the first ring road around Central London, the café's site was perfect. It had been used as a venue for street café racing in earlier years, and even more so as a place for car thieves to gather because of the easy getaway routes from the building.

He had to presume that the British Intelligence community may have found out about his forthcoming meeting with Baxter, as he was aware they were very good at what they did. He therefore chose a motorbike, as no other type of road vehicle would be able to catch him in London's notoriously congested traffic. Saeed had been informed about the ANPR system so had immediately removed the number plate from the BMW motorbike he had stolen in Central London earlier in the day.

After he had killed Baxter, and then been shot at, which confirmed he had been watched, he rode away from the café like the expert motorcycle rider he was, unworried about a helicopter pursuit because he was not intending to stay on the motorbike for long at all. He had, in fact, turned left into Abbey Road shortly after leaving Ace Café (without even being seen by Norman Taylor) and then turned right into Twyford Abbey Road, where he parked the bike, abandoning it by the roadside, along with the helmet. From there he walked a short way into the 'Abbey Point B & B', a small hotel catering for long-distance truck drivers.

Going into their public toilet he set about working on avoiding the facial recognition system. From his deep jacket pockets he took out a false beard which he applied to his face with spirit gum. He inserted a pair of blue contact lenses to his dark eyes, and lastly, combed his long hair back from his forehead, then fitted a fake bald scalp and tight-fitting head cap, instantly ensuring he was no longer remotely recognisable as Fatin Saeed. Exiting the toilet as a different man, Saeed phoned for a taxi from the reception area, and when it arrived gave the driver the address of a block of flats in Wimbledon where he would hole up.

He had decided to stay in the predominantly Eurocentric suburb of Wimbledon, rather than seek out his own kind. Once safely in his flat he phoned the connection to his paymasters and told them what he next needed. His request would take some time to service, but he was used to often wiling away hours, and even days, in the waiting game of his profession, so he ordered his food online, enabling him to not have to leave the flat at all.

He spent much time planning, researching, and thinking about his next moves, along with the end game, which would result in the eventual death of Sopwith Jones. This specific thought excited him a great deal.

Sopwith had overseen the completion of repairs to the 172 Solar to a point where all that remained was to obtain and replace the rear cabin seats that he had left behind in Port Alfred and which had, upon Sopwith's enquiry, disappeared from the hangar, according to Major Rob Pretorius. He had scouted for second-hand ones in the UK but eventually resorted to ordering new ones from Cessna. As they had to be purpose-made, Sopwith was not expecting them to arrive any time soon. He had, however, in the meantime stripped out the water tank, and unpacked all unnecessary equipment he had previously installed for his long flights. He left the trophy AK47 under the front seats, as Steve Roberts from the Royal Marines had not yet arrived to collect it. Both the IFF and GPS transponders had been re-connected as per his instructions.

He and Ali took it for its maiden test flight since the accident on R08. While enjoying flying the quiet, easy-to-handle little aircraft they were relieved at being unable to detect any possible problems lingering after the 'unconventional' landing on the carrier's flight deck.

Sopwith, after checking that the name 'Sopwith Aviation' was no longer in use, registered a new business in England named 'Sopwith Electric Aviation Company'. He had initially considered 'Sopwith Solar Aviation' – but the acronym SSA reminded him too much of his time involved with the State Security Agency in South Africa.

With Cessna's permission he also registered the name *'Cessna 172 – Sopwith Solar*. In obtaining their consent Sopwith had spent a lot of time communicating with them, and it soon became apparent they were very pleased that he had chosen a Cessna for his developments and made it clear that when the time was right, Cessna would like to build the *Sopwith Solar* variant of their 172.

Sopwith then applied to the UK Civil Aviation Authority for registration of his experimental aircraft with a view to having it certified for public use. Finally, he tracked down the air station's sign-writer; one of the staff who was also an enthusiastic calligraphy artist and commissioned him to affix the new name *'Cessna 172 – Sopwith Solar'* on the engine cowling, also using him to touch-up the Gripen's bullet damage repair, and the patched holes in the rear fuselage caused by the ground-fire of the insurgents in Niger.

Sopwith was hoping to hear soon from Priti Patel with news regarding moving forward in business and wanted to have nothing left to tidy up before he set out in that direction.

It was a further disappointment when he received a follow-up call from MI6. John Baker, although not ever having met Sopwith Jones, did feel very responsible for Jones's safety, particularly as he was the first to have considered the possibility that Jones might become a target for retribution. Not only that, but his concern was increased now his men had allowed the assassin who was after Jones to escape. He had carefully and thoroughly reviewed their actions, but realised, short of having had a complete SWAT team in place at Ace Café, no one could have done any better than Trevor Mommsen and Norman Taylor had done on the day. He obtained Sopwith's cell phone number from Peggy Smith and called Sopwith himself as he had decided to be brutally honest with the man.

"Hello, Sopwith here."

"Mr Jones, John Baker from MI6 here. You recently received a call from our Peggy Smith, and I am phoning to elaborate on what she has already told you."

"Hello, John, yes, I would like hear more about what is actually going on."

"During your return journey to England from Mozambique I considered the possibility that the Al-Shabaab jihadists might want to take revenge for the death of their leader Khatib, but there was very little I could do about my fears other than trying to keep a lid on the information. We did, however, recently establish that a jihadist hitman had entered our country and we had him followed. He met with a serviceman from Navy HQ who sold him information which we presume were details as to your current whereabouts. We cannot confirm this, as the hitman killed his informant."

"Oh my word; this is not good news!"

"Definitely not good news, but I'd rather you are aware of the situation than us keeping it from you. The hitman has gone to ground, and we have no idea what his next move is going to be, but we must assume that you'll become his target at some stage, so let's not make it easy for him. You're in a very secure and controlled environment, but certainly not secure enough to prevent, say, a long-range sniper attack on you. I'd, therefore, like you and your wife to please stay indoors, with your curtains or blinds closed, until we find and eliminate this possible threat. I'd not ask this unless I perceived the threat to be very real and should be taken absolutely seriously."

"Thanks for being so honest about all this, John. We'll definitely take your advice but should only wish to ask that someone from your office keeps us as up to date as possible."

"I'll make sure that happens and am so pleased with your quick grasp of the situation. We'll be in touch. Good luck!" finished John Baker, ending the call; a very worried man, but who could do no more about the Jones's security than he had just detailed to Sopwith. Baker then called in Peggy Smith to update her. Before he could start, Peggy was already talking.

"There has been no movement in Baxter's bank account John; what next?"

"There is no movement, nor will there be, because Baxter was paid off, not via his bank account, but with a fake bag full of money. He is now stone dead; killed by Fatin Saeed in front of Trevor Mommsen!"

"Oh, what a mess!" she said, and John filled her in with full details of the 'mess'.

Peggy, full of self-confidence, assured John, upon leaving for her own domain, where she listened in, watched and picked up minute pieces of information to stitch into something tangible and useful: "John, Saeed has to surface sooner rather than later and I will find him, I promise you that. I will not let this insane killer evade us!"

Elsewhere in London, Arthur Lightfoot and Ben Dougmore were, respectively, enjoying their retirement and holiday. They were today fishing in the Thames off the manicured lawns of the Petersham Hotel, but catching fish was not on their programme. They were enjoying the simplicity of their activities on the glorious Spring Day, relishing just chatting with one another, drinking a beer together while they made short work of the Hotel's packed picnic lunch. Arthur had invited Ben to his home for dinner that evening, so once they had enjoyed their 'fishing expedition' to its fullest, they boarded Arthur's old Range Rover and headed for his home.

Iris welcomed her husband home, and on being introduced to Ben, retorted, "It is a pleasure to meet you again, Charles!" while escorting them to a patio at the rear of the house for sundowners.

"Have you heard how Sopwith is getting on lately?" Ben asked Arthur.

"No, but I am sure both he and Allison are fine. I have heard that he has accepted a partnership with the British Government for the development of his solar-powered aircraft."

"I will send them an email when I get back to Port Alfred. By the way, what does Iris think of the idea of both of you holidaying with me in Port Alfred?"

"I had honestly forgotten to tell her. Iris dear, we are going on holiday to Ben's house on the Indian Ocean coast of South Africa. What do you think of that?"

"Oh Arthur, that is wonderful news! You know how much I love the Americas. And I am very sure you must have a lovely home there, Paul; thank you for the invitation. Now I think it is time for our breakfast," Iris prattled away, both men hiding grins of understanding.

Despite every effort by MI6, particularly by Peggy Smith, who had hardly slept during her endeavours to find some information on his whereabouts, Fatin Saeed had remained undetected.

A few days after his shooting of Baxter he received a message from his paymasters. Acting on the instructions they had given him over the pre-paid cell phone he was using, he donned his full disguise then called a taxi. Buses and trains were by far the cheapest form of travel in and around London, but as money was of no concern to him, Saeed felt safer in a taxi than on public transport. He gave the driver the address in Dagenham, South London, which had been passed to him, eventually, after the tedious journey through the busy streets of London, arriving at the correct address, which appeared to be an established coachworks type of business. He dismissed the taxi after paying the driver, then entered the building and asked for Bill.

The premises were huge with mainly buses of various sizes being built, rebuilt, modified, or painted. In amongst them he saw the odd panel van. Bill arrived, acknowledged Saeed with a nod of his head and walked to the rear of the building with Saeed following. They exited through a door, and crossed a courtyard, bringing them to a much smaller building which they then entered. This was a much smaller workshop, clearly designed for body and coachwork as well, but it held only one panel van. Bill nodded towards it, indicating that Saeed should inspect it, which he did by walking around the vehicle. The panel van's appearance had been very professionally modified to accurately replicate a DHL Courier delivery vehicle, showing the exact corporate signage as displayed on the genuine vehicles. Saeed was pleased and only asked one question: "Number plates?"

"They are copies of an existing vehicle in the actual DHL London delivery fleet," replied Bill.

With a nod Saeed got into the driver's seat of the panel van, started it while Bill opened the double access doors of the workshop, then drove out into the

London traffic, instantly coming under camera surveillance, and which almost constantly monitored his progress from there onwards.

Saeed was as professionally competent at driving a panel van as he had been riding the motorbike, but even so, although he found the traffic conditions a great challenge, he however wound his way back to the Wimbledon area, carefully obeying every rule of the road and every road sign so as not to attract the attention of the traffic police. En route, not far from his flat complex, he stopped as close as he could to a dry-cleaning business and, upon entering, asked for Sam. A man came from the back of the shop carrying a suit bag, handed it to Saeed, nodded, then turned around and went about his business without any further acknowledgement of Saeed, who walked out, returning to the van.

One of the reasons the flat complex in Wimbledon had been selected, was that it had several lock-up garages available for rent. Saeed had access to one of these, which he used to securely lock the panel van away upon his arrival there. He took the suit bag with him up to his flat where he opened it to reveal a DHL delivery employee uniform consisting of long slacks, a linen jacket, white shirt, tie, and a cap. He tried on all the items of clothing to check the fit, finding them all perfect. With this stage of his preparations complete, he settled down to make his final plans.

The following morning, despite Saeed's careful planning; he had already caused a small blip on MI5's intelligence screens. This important information made its way onto Peggy Smith's computer screen. The ANPR system did not yet normally screen for cloned number plates, but MI5 had the ability to do so with computer-generated algorithms. Consequently, a daily report of cloned plates in Greater London was sent to Peggy. One cloned plate for a DHL delivery panel van stuck out for her simply because it was very unusual. One vehicle bearing this plate had been tracked from Dagenham to Wimbledon, and then disappeared from the system again, while the other, which had to be fitted to the original vehicle, was constantly in transit throughout London, and then moving back and forth to the DHL central distribution warehouse. Very few cloned number plates were fitted to exactly similar vehicles, as these clearly were, and cloned number plates were only ever fitted to try and evade the law for some reason. Peggy's gut feeling told her that she had to watch out for the cloned DHL vehicle, so she put in a special request to the Police ANPR unit to be alerted, should it appear in the system from the Wimbledon area once more. Peggy continued watching, listening, and waiting for threads to connect, and weave into her catch net.

Sopwith and Ali, now housebound, were more irritated than nervous. They had correctly speculated that Anthony Baxter was the Navy man who had sold information but could think of nothing to help improve their situation. As they could not even go out to the Officer's Mess to eat, cooking became an important way for them to pass time, along with all the normal housekeeping duties.

Chapter Eleven

On that same day Fatin Saeed had very carefully worked through the timeline for his next actions, the most critical phase of his mission. He prepared his equipment, along with the one prop that he needed to make his plan work. As he paced around the flat in thought he talked himself through the various scenarios that were probably going to play out, until he was sure he was word perfect, and thoroughly prepared for what was about to come.

After he had once again applied his full facial disguise, he changed into the false DHL uniform he had received and packed into a carry bag the few remaining things inside the flat, which he left at about 14h00, leaving the door ajar with the key in it. Unlocking the rented garage, he loaded his bag and equipment into the DHL van, climbed into and started it, then pulled out into the street and drove off, also leaving the garage wide open.

The route to his destination, RNAS Yeovilton, was clearly imprinted on his brain. He drove conscientiously, keeping strictly to the speed limit along the entire route, and without any stops on the way.

He approached the security-gated entrance to RNAS Yeovilton at precisely 16h15, then slowed down, and stopped the van on the designated road marking to await the security guard who walked swiftly up to the van.

"Good day, sir; how I may be of assistance?" enquired the uniformed guard.

"I have a delivery to make to Mrs S Jones here; can you direct me?" replied Saeed in a remarkably good imitation of a Yorkshire accent. Acting the compliant, simple, blue-eyed courier with bald head, he peered innocently at the guard.

"May I see?" enquired the guard.

Saeed held up a labelled Mayfair box with a picture of a stainless-steel casserole pot on it.

"Seems like the missus has gone and bought herself a new pot only," replied Saeed in his disguised accent.

"OK," replied the guard, while passing over an entry log on which he had recorded the DHL van details. "Just sign here, and enter your name and contact phone number, please."

Saeed duly filled in totally false information, while once again asking for directions to the Jones's quarters.

"Once through the gate, sir, turn first right. That road will take you straight into our residential quarters, and right at the very end are the married quarters. The Joneses are in bungalow 12, right at the very end of the married quarters."

The guard left the van to open the large gate and lift the boom, saluting Saeed as he drove through. Saeed almost wet himself with glee over the thought of British military personnel saluting him.

He drove along the road as indicated, eventually arriving at a bungalow numbered 12, where he stopped and climbed out, carrying only the Mayfair pot along with a clipboard of paperwork. He was very keenly observing the location of the bungalow and its surrounds but did notice a curtain twitch within number 12 when somebody pulled it slightly aside to look at him. He knocked on the door, which was immediately opened by Sopwith Jones, who was instantly recognised by Saeed from the photograph he had been given by the late Baxter. Jones, apparently ill at ease, asked:

"May I help you?"

"Yeah boss, I have here a delivery for your missus," Saeed replied, while holding forward the Mayfair pot.

"Ali, have you ordered any pots from Mayfair?" Sopwith called out behind him. Saeed heard the muffled reply of, "No," from within the bungalow, so immediately continued:

"Says here," he said holding up his clipboard, 'Mrs S. Jones, Yeovil'. "The man at your gate showed me the way to you."

"No man, you have got this all wrong," Sopwith replied in puzzlement. "This is not Yeovil; this is Yeovilton, the Navy Air Station. Yeovil is the town down the road. You are at the entirely wrong place, so please leave now."

He re-entered the bungalow, closing the door behind him. He was definitely feeling on edge and did not need this sort of thing going on to spook him.

Saeed returned to the van, got in and turned a very wide circle in the cul-de-sac at the end of the road, all the while carefully observing the layout of buildings and fences. He drove back to the gate where he explained his mistake to the same guard who had admitted him, and they both had a good chuckle about what an idiot he had been.

At almost exactly 17h00 he then drove along the A359, through Bridgehampton, and slowly onwards through the farmlands to Yeovil. Fifteen minutes later, and after a further twelve kilometres, he reached the outskirts of the town. He then navigated through the town, first finding Princes Street, then High Street, which in turn led him onwards to Middle Street where he found the Yeovil Post Office, now deserted. He parked the DHL van outside the Post Office, taking only his bag out of it, locked it, then threw the keys through a storm water drain grating, and walked away into the smaller streets of the town which were not covered by CCTV cameras.

During the day Peggy Smith at MI6 had been alerted by the Police ANPR unit to the fact that the cloned DHL vehicle had moved from Wimbledon at about 14h00 but thereafter it could no longer be tracked as there was no way of differentiating it from the real DHL delivery van. This did not worry Peggy unduly as she really had no specific reason to try and track it, and she would receive the MI5 report on the movements of cloned number plates at the end of the day when she could find out what had become of the cloned mystery van.

Saeed slowly made his way out of Yeovil on foot, through the backstreets of the town, avoiding any route when he spotted a camera. He had all the time in the world to walk back to RNAS Yeovilton, so he made sure he remained unseen. There was still light in the sky by the time he reached the junction of the A359 and Lyde Road, and when he spotted a thick corpse of trees with dense undergrowth beneath, he made his way into it until he was sure he could not be seen from either road, then he lay down on the grass to rest until it was fully dark.

Eventually, in the darkness, he set off again, making sure, when a few cars passed by, that he lay down in the drainage ditch at the side of the road to avoid being seen by their drivers.

By 18h00 Peggy had received the cloned number plate movement report from MI5, and while working through it, discovered that DHL van with the cloned number plates had left the Wimbledon area via the A3 and then the M25, eventually branching off that motorway onto the vast six lane M3 leading to the south-west of England, at which point the report ended. The M3 was outside of the greater London area being routinely scrutinised by MI5, so she once again contacted the Police and asked for a report on the movements of the DHL van along the M3 to its eventual destination. Knowing that her request would take time, Peggy decided to call it a day and go home, comfortable in the knowledge that she would get the emailed report from the ANPR unit on her cell phone when it eventually came in.

It was well after midnight when Saeed, walking at his slow, careful pace, arrived outside the perimeter fence of RNAS Yeovilton at the spot he had selected during his fake DHL delivery, for that is all it had been; a reconnaissance of where the Jones's quarters were situated within the naval air station. Directly within the fence at that point was Married Quarters' Bungalow 12.

He lay unseen in some low decorative shrubbery while watching the security fence intensely. Although the fence had spotlights spaced along its length, these were not very bright, only vaguely lighting up the fence with a low illumination, but enough for him to observe if there were foot patrols within the fence or not. Close to 03h00, some two hours later, Saeed was sure that there were no foot patrols, so inched his way towards the fence on his stomach in a leopard crawl.

Once at the fence he removed a pair of wire-cutters from his bag and, very slowly and carefully, snipped a hole in the wire just big enough for him to crawl through.

He continued with his slow and careful leopard crawl, even once he was through the fence, until he arrived at the front door of bungalow 12. Checking his watch and seeing that it was now 04h00 he decided his timing was perfect. He removed a set of lock picks from his jacket pocket, and not making any sound whatsoever, carefully unlocked the front door.

At about the time that Saeed was crawling through the fence, Peggy Smith's cell phone alerted her to an incoming email, loud enough to wake her from deep sleep. Yawning, then stretching, she switched on her bedside light, moving to sit up on the edge of the bed. She took a drink from the glass of water on her bedside table, then picked up her phone and opened the email, which was from the ANPR unit. The author of the mail first apologised for the length of time the report had taken by explaining that several different control centres had had to be used, given the distance that the van had travelled. After reading this Peggy focused on the report.

The van had travelled along the M3 as far as the junction at North Waltham, just past Basingstoke, where it had exited the M3 and continued its journey on the A303. Peggy started getting anxious because she had a feeling in her gut that she knew exactly where the van was headed. It had last been seen at 16h03 on the A303 entering the traffic circle just north of RNAS Yeovilton. Thereafter it was only detected again at 17h25 in Princes Street, Yeovil, after which it had been parked in front of the Yeovil Post Office where it had remained since 17h29. There were two enlarged photographs attached to the mail, each from the two cameras which had picked up the driver, both showing, none too clearly, a bald man with a full beard at the wheel of the van.

Peggy sat there, staring into space, thinking hard. Surely this was just an amazing co-incidence, but quickly corrected her thoughts to the maxim that she had applied throughout her career in intelligence analysis; that there is no such thing as co-incidence.

The distance from the traffic circle to the Yeovil Post Office was not much over ten kilometres, so where had the van been in the hour and a half that it had taken to get from the circle to the Post Office?

'If there are no co-incidences,' she thought, 'there is only one place it could have gone, and that was to RNAS Yeovilton.' Her hands shaking in angst, she dialled John Baker on her cell phone. John picked up his phone on the first ring.

"Hi, Peggy, early start today, eh?" John jested.

"John, I think I have something," Peggy stated, then continued to tell John, in short breathless sentences, what she had come up with, and ended with the question: "What are we going to do?"

"Firstly, I owe you yet another beer. Very well done! Secondly, leave it up to me; I'll call you immediately if I need your help."

"OK, John, you know where I am," Peggy said, ending the call.

John Baker's mind was rapidly processing his options but decided in the first instance to call Sopwith Jones to check if he was OK, so he dialled Sopwith's number.

"Sopwith here," answered a very sleepy sounding voice, after a few rings, "How can I help you?"

"Hello Sopwith, John Baker here. Sorry to wake you, but I am just checking up on you."

"Well thanks, we are fine, but there must be a reason you are phoning at this time of the morning."

"Have you had any visitors yesterday or today?"

"Funny you should ask. Yes, yesterday afternoon. Not a visitor exactly, but a DHL delivery. He had the wrong Jones family though."

"Did you see his vehicle?"

"Yes, a panel van with the DHL livery on it."

"What did the delivery man look like?"

"Bald, bearded, clean uniform. He had very blue eyes and spoke with a Yorkshire accent."

"Did he leave anything inside or outside your house?"

"Nothing. He didn't come inside at all. Along with a clipboard he had only a box with a casserole pot in it that he was meant to deliver. He loaded both items back into the van when he left."

"Well, good to hear you're alright. If I may add one further security point for your safety, don't open your doors to anyone from now on."

"Hell, John; what's this all about?"

"I really don't properly know yet, Sopwith, but when I do, I'll fill you in. Take care."

Sopwith had not switched any lights on to take the call, so he put his phone down in the darkness, while saying to Ali, "Go back to sleep love," then turned onto his side to go to back to sleep as well.

Sopwith's cell phone had rung as Saeed quietly pushed open the front door to the bungalow. Saeed froze in the doorway and listened to Sopwith's side of the cell phone conversation. By his answers to the unheard questions put to him, it became clear to him that Sopwith was being questioned about the DHL delivery man. Saeed was in awe of the fact that British Intelligence had already tracked him down, proving to him all he had heard about their professionalism and efficiency was true.

Much as he admired their skill, Saeed was not nervous because they would have no chance of knowing what he was up to until it was too late. He heard Sopwith telling his wife to go back to sleep, so he remained where he was for a while longer. Then, carrying his bag, he crept extremely slowly and quietly across the living room and into a small passageway. From that vantage point he could hear the quiet breathing of people asleep, so was satisfied that both Joneses had fallen back into that last deep sleep in the morning before waking. He continued to move the short distance until he found the open doorway to their bedroom, then felt along the wall for the light switch. Once he had located it, he pulled a pistol out of his bag, and setting that down, readied himself with his .45 Colt M1911 pistol in his right hand; his left on the light switch.

"Rise and shine!" he called out as he switched on the light, pistol at the ready. Sopwith, as well as Ali, sat up in bed with a start, and saw the DHL delivery man in their bedroom pointing a pistol at them.

"Don't make a move or I'll shoot! As you may, or may not know, Mr and Mrs Jones, I have already shot the man called Baxter who sold you out. I am meant to keep you alive, but quite honestly, it'll be far easier for me if you make a mistake and I must kill you. So make my day; disobey me and die or listen and live!"

While Saeed had made this little speech, he gently tugged the false beard off his face and pulled the bald head cover off his hair. Lastly, he popped the contact lenses out of his eyes and let them fall onto the floor of the bedroom. Sopwith and Ali sat with the bedclothes drawn up to cover their nakedness, staring at the transformation of the man in front of them.

"Now, starting with you Mrs Jones, get out of the bed and get dressed, as we are going on a trip. Don't move a muscle, Mr Jones."

Ali slowly rose out of the bed, totally naked. Saeed took in the sight of her beautiful breasts and the neatly trimmed dark hair between her legs and felt his erection growing, which so disgusted him he shouted, "Get dressed bitch, quickly!" while menacingly waving the .45 at her. Ali found a pair of panties, drew them on, followed by her bra and then she pulled on a pair of jeans and a shirt.

She pulled a thin cardigan over her shirt, then bent down to put on her socks and a pair of running shoes. All the while Saeed had kept a firm eye on both, alternating from one to the other. Once Ali was fully dressed, he instructed her to sit on the bed, then told Sopwith to do likewise. Sopwith pulled on the clothes he had left lying on a chair when he had undressed before going to bed. He sat on the bed to put on his shoes, and at the same time tried to pick up his Leatherman which he had left on the bedside table.

"Leave it!" instructed Saeed, "Not that it would do you any good anyway. Come slowly towards me with your right hand holding your left wrist in front of you." Sopwith did so, and Saeed, having retrieved a thick cable tie from his bag, used it to tightly secure Sopwith's wrists together.

"Now!" Saeed said, noticing the light of dawn starting to creep into the room, "Mrs Jones you will lead the way to the hangar where your aircraft is parked, followed by you, Mr Jones. If either of you try to attract the attention of anyone along the way, I will kill you, and, as I said earlier, if you would like to make my day, please do so. Now go on Mrs Jones."

Ali led the way out of the bungalow and started out along the pathway that would take them to the hangar.

Having spoken with Sopwith to determine that he was alright, John Baker was still trying to guess what Saeed was up to. If it had actually been him in the DHL van after all, it certainly did not look like him, but John knew how easy and effective costume make-up disguises these days were.

The visit had all the hallmarks of a reconnaissance, but to what end John could not figure, especially in view of the killer's usual modus operandi, which was one quick shot to the head. Saeed had had plenty of easy opportunity to do that already.

John phoned Trevor Mommsen and instructed him, together with Norman Taylor, to drive post-haste, to the DHL van parked outside the Yeovil Post Office. He then phoned the local constabulary in Yeovil to tell them that the DHL van at the Post Office was probably abandoned but that they should keep away from it, as MI6 would be investigating. Furthermore, he also informed them they would be emailed a picture of the driver, whom they should be on the lookout for, as was a wanted man. He then tasked Peggy with sending an email with pictures of Saeed to Yeovil police.

In the pre-dawn glow the line of four pedestrians wove its way along a series of paths at RNAS Yeovilton, without encountering anyone, as no-one else was up and about at that early hour.

They arrived at the hangar, entered through the unlocked pedestrian door on one side, to reveal the *Sopwith-Solar* parked in the dim light.

"You are the pilot," stated Saeed looking at Ali. "I will sit in the front with you. Jones you'll sit in the back…."

"There are no seats in the back," interrupted Sopwith.

"I don't give a shit if you have to sit on a bed of thorns, but you'll sit in the back. Mrs Jones you will take off without notifying the control tower. In fact, the radio must be off, but once in the air you are to call them up and I will talk to them. Do you understand?"

"I do, but where must I fly to?"

"I will tell you later, just get us into the air. Jones, open that bloody door. Hurry now!" demanded Saeed, becoming increasingly concerned to note the rapidly-strengthening amount of light in the hangar.

Sopwith walked to the hangar doors, and awkwardly removed the latches with his bound hands, then pulled one wide open, followed by the next. He hurriedly returned to the plane and clambered into the back to sit on the floor, his back to the bulkhead, with his knees drawn up.

He heard more than saw Ali and Saeed boarding, then heard Ali going through her pre-flight checks. Saeed remained quiet until Ali had started the motor and was beginning to taxi out of the hangar.

"I really think I should talk to the tower. They may shoot us if we do not," she told him, taking the chance of trying to frighten him.

"Don't talk bullshit woman!" Saeed snarled, "Just get this toy into the air!"

Ali taxied far further than was necessary, trying to attract some attention, but the most attention she got were friendly waves from the technicians who were earliest to arrive at their workplaces. She could see two people in the control tower, and thought she spotted the reflection from a pair of binoculars trained on their little aeroplane.

She eventually lined up on the runway for take-off and drew out her checks as long as possible until Saeed demanded, "Get going, bitch!"

She released the brakes, and with the actuator wide open to provide full power to the electric motor, the *Sopwith-Solar* took to the air in no time at all. Ali switched the radio on immediately.

"Solar, this is Yeovil Tower; respond!" was emitted from the radio as soon as Ali switched it on. This was a small comfort because the tower knew at the very least who was taking to the air.

"Yeovil Tower, this is Al-Shabaab!" Saeed had grabbed the microphone from its cradle and had begun talking.

"Now listen carefully, I have two hostages aboard this aircraft. One being your precious princess pilot Alison Jones, nee Lt Murray; the other being your prince of little aeroplanes, a certain Sopwith Jones, I believe. Did you hear all of that?"

"Solar, Yeovil Tower, Roger that."

"OK. Excellent! I repeat my descriptive noun: 'Hostages'. These hostages will remain alive only if I don't see any other aircraft around this one. Keep the airspace around us clear of all other aircraft, and they'll be fine. I repeat, if we're approached in any way by any other aircraft, I'll retaliate by shooting a hostage. End of story, goodbye!" Saeed leant over and switched off the radio.

"And now, Mrs Jones, you'll fly across France to Libya, where we'll spend the night with friends. From there we'll make our way to my Al-Shabaab friends in Mozambique, where Mr Jones will face justice."

"We can't fly that far!" cried Ali.

"Yes, you can, and you will, if you want to stay alive."

"I'll have to let the tower know our flight plan. We can't just fly into French airspace without them knowing who we are."

"OK, tell them, but remind them that you do not have a death wish, so the French had better keep clear of us as well!"

Fearing that the man was serious in his intention to get to Libya, Ali first set a compass heading of 145° on their Satnav for Libya, turned the aircraft onto that heading, and then switched the radio on and called Yeovilton.

"Yeovil Tower, Solar; do you read?"

"Solar, Yeovil Tower; roger."

"Yeovil Tower this is Allison Jones. I confirm that Sopwith Jones and I are being held hostage at gunpoint and I am being forced to overfly France to Libya. There appears to be no possibility of negotiation, so we request you direct French FIR that we are left to fly unhindered along the course from here to Libya. Our IFF is on as well as our GPS so you and they will be able to track us without any problem."

"Solar, Yeovil Tower; Roger to all of that. Proceed at flight level three thousand metres. Anything else?"

"Yeovil Tower, negative. Out to you, as I suspect our radio will be switched off again," said Ali, who was quite correct in her assumption, as Saeed leant over and switched the radio off. If the fact that they had a GPS transponder had been understood by Saeed, it did not seem to trouble him in the slightest.

Word of the hostage drama spread from Yeovilton ATC like wildfire, firstly to all FIRs on the indicated route of the Cessna's flight.

The second call made by the duty air traffic controller was to Lt Cmdr Godlonton-Shaw who accepted Saeed's demand that the flight was not to be interfered with, so kept any possible chase aircraft firmly on the ground. He then phoned the First Sea Lord to pass on details of what had transpired that morning.

The First Sea Lord immediately passed the information on to John Baker at MI6 asking him to come to his office to discuss how the situation should be best handled. John, in turn, phoned Trevor Mommsen to update him, telling him that they were too late to try and apprehend Fatin Saeed, but that he should inspect the DHL van before letting the police take over. He then called Peggy into his office.

"Saeed outwitted us, Peggy. You picked him up so quickly on two occasions, but he has got the better of us. The whole DHL guise was to reconnoitre the area before taking the Joneses hostage in their aircraft. Had the ANPR system been quicker and more effective, especially insofar as tracking cloned number plates was concerned, we would have nailed him, thanks to you. I must go to a meeting at Navy HQ. Keep up the good work."

Sopwith, sitting uncomfortably on the floor of the rear passenger compartment with his wrists bound, knew exactly what he wanted to do, so was working slowly and methodically on achieving his aim. The AK47 he had taken from the Boko Haram jihadist in Niger lay before him, still under the front seats, where it had been awaiting collection by C/Sgt Steve Roberts of the Royal Marines. He clearly recalled that the weapon was still loaded with a round in the firing chamber and was certain he had applied the safety catch when he had taken it from the dead man.

He was slowly dragging the weapon forward with one foot as the *Sopwith–Solar* gained altitude to the required flight level. He eventually pushed it alongside his hip with the heel of his shoe, knowing that the difficult part of picking it up, and firing it with his bound hands, was still to come. He also had another consideration, so asked from the back:

"I can't see anything from here. Are we over the English Channel yet?"

"Why do you want to know that Jones?" asked Saeed.

"Just interested and making conversation. It's a bit lonely down here."

"Just thank your luck that you are still alive infidel. We are just passing over the English coastline now, if you're so interested in knowing something you, personally, will never again see."

That was all that Sopwith wanted to hear, so began trying to pick up the weapon. His right hand was bound beneath his left wrist, so he was able to pick the weapon up with the fingers of his right hand and tuck it under his left elbow, pointing directly into the back of the seat that Saeed was sitting in. Holding it firmly with his elbow, he felt his way around with the same fingers until he found the safety catch. Very slowly and carefully, without a sound, he managed to move it from 'safe' to 'automatic', so was able to breath out in relief. He was not going to chance a single shot, so possibly missing Saeed. He then managed to get his right index finger into the trigger guard and onto the trigger, with his left hand cupping the top of the slide cover. Holding the AK47 as firmly as he could under his elbow, he manoeuvred the barrel upwards until it was most likely aimed into the centre of the back of the seat, then he pulled the trigger.

The weapon came to life in an extremely loud stream of explosions and smoke, then jerked upwards, despite his attempt to hold it firm.

Ali screamed out loud, and in the dense smoke from the exploding rounds Sopwith saw Saeed's head flopping forward, and simultaneously the windscreen of the Cessna bursting into a million pieces, showering the interior of the cockpit with minute shards of plexi-glass.

Ali, very quickly absorbing what had happened, and with her eyes squinting into the blast of wind coming through the non-existent windscreen, she turned the power actuator down so that they lost airspeed. She groped around in a door pocket and found the pair of sunglasses she knew was there, putting them on to help improve her vision in the slowly diminishing blast of wind.

"You have saved the day, Sopwith, you superman!" she shouted out.

"Before you contact anyone, I want to get rid of this body into the Channel. Circle this spot and get as close to the sea as possible, then when I give the word, I want you to bank steeply to assist me when I push it out of the door," Sopwith directed her. Struggling with his bound wrists, as there was absolutely no way to undo them at that moment, he released the safety belt holding Saeed's lifeless body in place. To add weight to the body so that it would quickly sink into the ocean, he forced the AK47 down the back of his jacket until it was lodged firmly in place. Feeling Saeed's .45 Colt pistol in his jacket pocket, he left it there, keeping it in place by zipping up the pocket. Then, by unclipping the steel solid-state fire extinguisher, which was mounted on the side of the cockpit, he also forced that into the front of the dead man's jacket. While doing this Sopwith noticed that the man's torso was peppered with bullet holes, which although sickening to see, made him believe there was little, or no air left in the lungs to keep it afloat. He leant over the body and opened the cockpit door, which rattled against the latch in the airstream but remained unlatched.

Then, positioned behind Ali's seat, Sopwith placed a foot against the torso, and said, "Now Ali, bank as steeply as possible!"

As Ali lowered the starboard wing into an eighty-degree bank, Sopwith shoved the body with all the strength in his leg. Aided by gravity, the body fell against the door, pushed it open, and tumbled into the sea with a splash. Sopwith craned his neck so as to keep an eye on the bubbling water, but he did not see the body re-surface, as Ali righted the plane and worked at regaining altitude to the designated flight level.

The ATC staff busy monitoring the flight of *Sopwith–Solar* had hardly noticed the sudden change in course and loss of altitude before the Yeovilton Tower radio sprang into life.

"Yeovil Tower, Solar here, do you read?"

"Solar, Yeovil Tower, strength five, go ahead!" replied the excited operator.

"Yeovil Tower, our issue has been resolved and we're on our way back. Permission to come straight into land, please."

"Solar, that's wonderful news! You may come in on a direct approach to any runway of your choice. You're the only bird up there now; pun intended," replied the ATC's joyful voice.

Sopwith looked around the cockpit properly for the first time. The windscreen had a few pieces of shattered plexi-glass here and there in the frame. There were two bullet holes in the roof of the cockpit, and was largely undamaged, despite the avionics display panel having splatters of blood across it. The back of the seat in which Saeed had sat was torn to pieces with blood all over it. The airstream had quickly blown all the smoke away, but there were tiny slivers of plexi-glass scattered everywhere.

"Allison, this never happened!" said Sopwith, using her full name to emphasise the importance of what he was saying.

"We are going to deny that this ever happened. There was no jihadist aboard my plane; the evidence is gone because we do not want this to follow us around any longer. We have never heard of the man nor seen him. That is our story, and we are going to stick to it."

"You are proving to be as brilliant a strategist as you are a fighting man Sopwith, and I totally agree with your thoughts!"

Flying quite slowly, to lessen the wind into the cockpit, it took longer to return to Yeovilton than their outward journey had taken, but soon enough Ali brought the *Sopwith–Solar* back to earth in her usual style; a smooth, soft landing, then taxied directly back into their hangar whose doors still stood wide open. Lt Cdr Godlonton-Shaw stood awaiting their arrival in the hangar, and as soon as the aircraft had stopped under cover, Sopwith got out and drew the hangar doors closed, still struggling with his bound hands.

"Are you two, OK?" enquired Godlonton-Shaw.

"We are both in show room condition," replied Sopwith.

"What the hell happened up there?" the Lt Cdr asked.

"Absolutely nothing. If there was no Al-Shabaab, there can be no further problem from them, do you get my drift?" replied Sopwith.

"I think I know what you are on about," he replied, a short while later, after mulling it over.

"I do believe that the ATC voice tapes should quietly disappear, sir. That should be easy enough for you to organise. There will be no debriefing because nothing happened, and likewise no comment to any queries, because absolutely nothing unusual has happened at RNAS Yeovilton today. We can keep this hangar off limits until I clean and repair the damage to *Sopwith-Solar*."

"I fully understand now; so that is exactly how it will be. You are a clever man," smiled Godlonton-Shaw, as he made his way out of the hangar.

The entire course of events relating to the attempt on Sopwith's life was carefully expunged from all records. Seaman Anthony Baxter's murder was not ascribed to any individual, with the case docket stating that there were no suspects. Sopwith did not want the jihadists to plague him for the rest of his life, so apart from the idea of his wiping the attempt on his life under the carpet; he adjusted his planning for the future as well. Consequently, he informed Priti Patel that he would buy in to a new aircraft manufacturing business by giving the Government the rights to his intellectual property concerning solar-powered flight but would not play any active role in the business.

He negotiated with Cessna, selling them the rights to build the *Sopwith-Solar*. He then put his designs and innovations on the open market, which in a short time saw him realising a small fortune from their sales to almost every manufacturer of aircraft in the world. He was pleased that aviation's transition from the use of fossil fuel to solar power would be quickened in this way.

Most importantly, it enabled him and Ali to disappear from the media limelight to pursue various ideas of their own, well out of the mainstream, making them difficult to be found should anybody have any inclination to try.

THE END